HECTOR

OUTBACK SHIFTERS BOOK ONE

ZOE CHANT

THE OUTBACK SHIFTERS SERIES

This book is a standalone with an HEA. However, it's also the first in a series with each book focusing on a different couple. They can be read in any order, but reading the series in order is recommended for maximum enjoyment!

1. Outback Shifters: Hector
2. Outback Shifters: Callan
3. Outback Shifters: Euan
4: Outback Shifters: Trent
5: Outback Shifters: Rhys
BOOK 6 COMING SOON!

You can also grab the first three books here in one convenient collection:

Outback Shifters: Collection One

CHAPTER 1

MYRTLE ATKINS WAS USED TO NOT LOOKING HER BEST. You spent enough time hiking your way through mountainous terrain as part of your job, and you pretty quickly got over the idea of things like *looking nice* and *having neat hair* and *wearing makeup* or even *daily showers*.

Still. She was new here, and stomping into the only place in town she could get a hot meal looking like the creature from the Black Lagoon (if the creature from the Black Lagoon had kind of let itself go lately) *might* not have been the best first impression to make. She'd only been out getting the lay of the land for a few hours, but somehow, in that time, she'd managed to scrape up her legs on some boulders, have her hair frizzily tumble out of the bun she'd pulled it into, spill part of her lunch down the front of her shirt... and *now* she could feel the beginnings of a *really* nasty sunburn across her shoulders and upper back.

Goddamnit.

There was no way to deny it: her pasty Washington state complexion was *really* not cut out for burning hot Australian summers.

She paused, standing in the darkening street, trying to arrange the strap of her bag so it was touching as little of her shoulders as possible. That done, Myrtle scratched her fingers through her sweaty hair, and tried to think.

Go back to my hotel room, or just forget the humiliation and go get something to eat?

Her stomach growled, urging her to forget how much of a complete mess she looked and just go get some dinner. And honestly, she was inclined to agree with it.

What's the worst that could happen? No one asks me out on a date?

If anything, this was good. She could look like a scary frump now, but that would only make it even more impressive later when she returned looking *amazing*, like the nerdy new kid who magically transforms into the prom queen.

Not that I was ever prom queen, Myrtle thought. *Well, come to think of it, not that I even* went *to prom.*

Myrtle was just a *little* too old to be entertaining beauty queen transformation fantasies now. Like it or not, she was what she was: late twenties, unmarried (and not even boyfriended), frizzy-haired, *way* too dedicated to her job, and now, sunburned.

"Hey, check it out. It's the moth lady."

Myrtle glanced up just in time to see two girls in their late teens or early twenties looking over their shoulders and nudging each other, before they quickly looked away.

Well, add that to the list, she thought. *Moth lady.*

Word traveled fast 'round small towns like this, where, she guessed, there probably wasn't a lot to talk about. She'd grown up in a town just like it, after all – albeit in a totally different hemisphere, and with *way* less chance of being killed by the sun. And everything was a little less coated in dust.

Myrtle supposed that she'd brought *moth lady* on herself,

really – when she'd been making her booking at the one motel in town, there'd been a question on the form: *What is the reason for your visit to Good Fortune?*

Without thinking, she'd typed up the truth:

I'm a lepidopterist visiting on an academic field trip funded by the American Advancement of Science Association to study the migration patterns of the valeleaf moth, which departs from this area's caves and natural rock formations in the early summer in order to travel to cooler climes; I'm hoping that with study I can determine the reasons for certain moth species' recent decline in numbers, putting not only their own survival at risk but also the survival of creatures such as the lesser possum, which relies on the moth as a food source...

She didn't necessarily like to include the part about the cute possums since they weren't strictly her area of study, but after one too many confused or disinterested looks when she'd told people she studied moths she'd started adding it in – it seemed like the only way most people would care was if something with soft fur and big brown eyes was also being threatened. It was the way of the world – *she* thought the moths were plenty fascinating on their own, but not everyone agreed.

And so, she'd typed up quite the paragraph and already hit *Submit* before realizing they were probably just after a more standard 'Business or Pleasure' type of answer.

Well, too late now.

Now, I'm Moth Lady.

Clearly, word had gotten around. Myrtle wasn't sure she liked the fact that the motel proprietress had blabbed about her embarrassing misstep all over town before she'd even gotten here, but it wasn't like it was a HIPAA violation or something. Studying moths was what she *did.* Becoming a lepidopterist was something she'd dreamed about ever since she'd watched the moths playing in the porch lights when she was a kid. They were a lifelong fascination. Certainly, moths had played a more significant role in her life than any of her boyfriends had. All two of them.

No, she really didn't care if people wanted to call her Moth Lady. It was better than what her mom had been calling her over the past few years, which was 'the only one of my daughters who hasn't given me a grandchild yet' and 'ahh, the family brain,' which *should* have been a compliment, but the way she said it – with a small sigh and a slight *What can you do?* shake of the head – left Myrtle with no illusions that her mom would *way* rather she was putting all that brain power toward finding a suitable man with whom to procreate, as quickly and as often as possible.

All right, well, part *of that doesn't sound so bad,* Myrtle thought, her lip twitching. And, she supposed, somewhere deep down, her mom *was* proud of her: she still had all her childhood report cards up on the fridge, after all, each of them with a perfect line of A+s, except for gym class, which had a perfect line of Ds. Could she help it if a bunch of asshole sixteen-year-old boys throwing a ball at her head wasn't her idea of a good time? She was fit enough these days, though – mountain fieldwork saw to that.

No, it wasn't that her mom wasn't proud. It was just that, ever since Myrtle's eldest sister Lily had given birth for the first time ten years ago, their mom had contracted the condition recognized worldwide as 'baby mania', and she just couldn't get enough of them. Myrtle had thought having six older sisters and two younger brothers might have spared her, but no chance of that, apparently.

And so, here she was.

She'd always wanted to visit Australia anyway, and this study opportunity had fallen right in her lap, just when she'd felt her mom was about to drive her completely nuts with her daily emails about the nice boy from her church who

Myrtle just *had* to meet, since her then-boyfriend clearly wasn't going to buy the cow if he could get the milk for free.

Sorry Mom, can't make a baby, gotta go to Australia!

Not that even *that* had slowed her mom down – she'd just attached a photo she'd obviously googled of a bronzed, six-packed, thong-wearing man-god, standing on a beach holding a surfboard with the caption *100% AUSSIE BEEF* underneath him.

Bring one back for me too!! her mom had written, which Myrtle had only rolled her eyes at as she'd dragged the whole email into her trash folder.

She'd only guiltily gone and looked at the picture two or three more times – all right, *five* – before deleting him and his abs for good.

It'd taken all her self-restraint not to email her mom to explain she wasn't even going to be anywhere near a beach for the duration of her stay: she was going to the tiny one-motel, one-main road, one-restaurant town of Good Fortune, an eight-hour drive from the nearest beach, so the closest she'd get to any water or the tanned beefcakes who might be cavorting in it was when she flew over them.

And that is that.

Her stomach grumbled again, pulling her out of her thoughts of her mom back home and just exactly how far she was from any kind of beach where she might be able to cool off after her long day of exploring the vast, rocky territory outside the town of Good Fortune, following her terrain maps to the caves that the scientists and explorers who had come before her had marked.

And all I have to show for it is some scratched-up legs.

Myrtle winced a little as she crossed the only road in town, heading toward what she would have called a diner, but which she'd quickly learned she should actually be calling a pub. She'd been too exhausted to eat anything at all after she'd arrived last night, completely worn out from the what-seemed-like-100-hour bus ride from Coffs Harbour, so she couldn't say what the food was like – but all she cared about right now was that it take the edge off the gnawing hunger in her belly.

Rounding the corner, Myrtle stopped in her tracks. Parked outside the red brick facade of the Good Fortune pub was row after row of gleaming silver and black motorcycles, some of which looked bigger than her little hand-me-down hatchback back home. There were at least twenty of them, parked in lines by the side of the road – and, in some cases, even up the sidewalk.

Myrtle bit her lip. On the one hand, she'd grown up in a small town by a highway, which had also been a pitstop for riders on their way across the country, as well as home to local charters of a few clubs. Her own father had shared plenty of drinks with the guys from the club, and she knew in a lot of cases bikers were pillars of their communities, using their fearsome appearances to protect those who couldn't protect themselves.

There was no reason to believe things weren't the same here – or that the bikes outside didn't simply belong to people who loved riding, and who were on a roadtrip across the country. Sometimes those kinds could be rowdy, but it didn't mean they were bad people.

Either way, if she wanted a hot meal, then she'd have to go inside.

Thinking of the canned fruit and saltine crackers in her motel room, Myrtle shook off her misgivings, and, setting her jaw, marched across the road and in through the front door of the pub.

It was noisy inside – it was well after knock-off time on a Friday, and this was clearly the social center of the town for the farmers, workers and anyone else who wanted a drink after a long day. What she *didn't* see, however, was a bunch of tough-looking bikers – that, or the men who'd parked the motorcycles outside weren't conforming to any stereotypes about bikers that she knew about.

Whatever the case, she let out a quick sigh of relief, sidling in past two men standing by the bar drinking beer and chatting.

Looking around, Myrtle quickly realized she didn't have anything to worry about in terms of sticking out, with her dusty shorts, scraped legs and old tank top. If anything, she was beginning to feel a little *over*dressed – 'come as you are' was clearly the dress code of the day, and Myrtle for one was grateful for it. Not feeling out of place at all, she slipped into a chair by the window and picked up the laminated menu, which had exactly four things on it.

"What'll you have, love?"

Myrtle looked up to find a woman in her fifties, with platinum blonde hair, bright blue eyeshadow and bright pink lipstick, and several gold necklaces disappearing down a bust that was as impressive as it was tanned, with no visible tan lines. She was smiling at Myrtle in a way that made the corners of her eyes crinkle, and Myrtle couldn't help but take a liking to her. She looked exactly like her father's favorite waitress in his favorite steakhouse back home.

"Can I get the steak, medium rare, with the side of fries and salad?"

"No salad at the moment, love."

"Oh. Right. Just the steak and fries, then."

"Right, steak and chips. Coming up." The woman paused. "American, eh? Don't get many Yanks 'round here. Where're you from, love?"

"Oh – Washington."

The woman laughed, deep and rich. "Work for the White House, do you darl?"

Myrtle shook her head, smiling. "Ah, sorry. I meant Washington *state*. I guess we just really love naming things Washington."

"Well, fair enough, love. Hope you enjoy your stay – let's see about getting you that steak."

The woman bustled off, and Myrtle couldn't help but smile a little. She'd been asked about her accent more and more the farther away she got from Sydney, but people had generally just been curious to know what part of the US she was from, what she thought of Australia, and whether she knew to be careful of drop bears (that last one she knew to simply laugh politely at).

Looking around the pub again, she decided that perhaps small towns like this one and the one she'd grown up in weren't so different as they might first appear: sure, the guys drinking beers after work back home were more likely to be lumber workers than farmers, and her hometown was surrounded by deep, dark green Douglas firs and gray, snow-topped mountains rather than the plains of dried grass and short scrub, red dust and even redder crags of rock that stuck up from the landscape at random here, but at this moment, they didn't seem so different.

It was a harsh environment out here – as her sunburned shoulders, scraped legs and blistered feet definitely attested to – but there was a raw beauty to it too, and the sky was the most brilliant, unbroken blue she'd ever seen.

Or maybe she'd just been in Washington for too long, she thought with a sigh. As much as the jokes made her roll her eyes a bit, it really *did* rain a lot.

"Righto love, steak and chips."

A plate with a thick steak and some thick-cut potato wedges landed on the table in front of her.

"You want a beer with that?" the waitress asked, smiling down at her.

"Ah, no thank you," Myrtle said. She'd never been much of a drinker.

"You sure about that? You're missing out."

"I'm sure," she said firmly. She was going to have a very early morning tomorrow if she wanted to get out into the landscape before the sun was up – the last thing she needed was to get even slightly tipsy the night before.

"All right, love. Suit yourself."

Myrtle tucked into her steak – though she admitted, her lip twitching, that the thought *did* cross her mind to snap a photo of it with her phone and send it to her mom saying she'd found the 100% Aussie Beef she was after, but in the end she decided that would probably just encourage her, and she wouldn't stop hounding her until she'd found Hugh Jackman and given him her phone number.

Whatever the case, Myrtle decided that out of a choice between a man and this steak, she'd *definitely* choose the steak. It was rich, tender, smoky and *just* pink enough in the middle. She could definitely get used to these thick-cut fries as well – God, this was *just* what she needed after a long, hot day getting the lay of the land before she went off moth hunting tomorrow morning.

Going out before dawn meant she'd see them when they were still active after a long night of flying and feeding.

I can follow them back to their lairs and count their numbers, she thought, biting into another forkful of delicious steak. *Find out whether they're really down, like the ones in America are, and try to figure out why...*

She looked up, jerked out of her thoughts as the door of the pub suddenly swung open, and raucous male voices filled the air.

Ah. It seems the bikers have arrived.

These guys looked a lot more like she would have expected – all long gray beards, leather vests and headbands.

It seemed like bikers, just like small towns, were pretty much the same all over the world.

She'd kind of been hoping she could relish her meal, but with the increased noise level in the bar Myrtle scooped up the rest of her steak and chewed it quickly. The waitress came and put her check down on the table, and Myrtle pulled out her travel wallet, sorting through the assortment of brightly-colored bills. *That*, at least, was something she wouldn't have trouble with – the money came color-coded here.

She hadn't had a chance to get any coins yet, and, after dithering a moment or two, she put a blue ten-dollar bill down as the tip. Her grant money had covered the cost of everything else – she could afford to be a generous tipper with her own money.

Myrtle had managed to sidle her way back toward the door when she heard the waitress's voice, loud and brassy above the din, call out, "Oi, love! You forgot something!"

Forgot something?

Myrtle quickly glanced down at her possessions. Nope, she had everything – her bag, her water, her wallet…

"Here, love." The waitress appeared in front of her, the ten in her hand. "This is yours – I know you do things differently over there, but there's no tips here unless you want to throw a few bucks in the jar at the front. If anyone tries to tell you otherwise they're having a go – you send 'em here to me and old Barb'll sort them out."

Myrtle blinked. "Oh – are you sure? That steak was really good –"

"Sure as eggs, love," Barb said, winking and pressing the bill into her hand. "You go spend this on a hair brush, all right?"

Myrtle couldn't help but laugh. "All right."

She turned away, moving toward the door – only to find

her path blocked by a bulky figure. She looked up – and up – to find herself staring into the face of an older man, clearly a biker, who was looking at her with a raised eyebrow and a slight smirk on his face.

"So. American, eh?"

Myrtle nodded, looking past him and trying to signal how very uninterested she was in conversation by failing to maintain eye contact. "Yep."

"Big spenders, you Yanks. Bet you've got quite a bit to throw around."

Myrtle swallowed, still trying to edge toward the door. "Not really. And I'm just leaving."

"Are you *sure?*" The man shifted slightly so he was standing right in front of her once more. "There isn't anything I could help you with?"

"Nope," Myrtle said, shaking her head firmly. It seemed like not only bikers, but also sleazebags were the same everywhere you went. "I'm fine. Just heading outside. Okay?"

To her surprise, the mountain of a man in front of her simply cocked his head slightly, before nodding. "All right. Outside. Got it."

He moved to let her past and Myrtle gratefully slid past him, opening the door and stepping out into the heat of the night. Sweat broke out over her skin immediately – in the slightly cooler, air-conditioned atmosphere of the pub, she had *almost* forgotten just how hot it was outside.

Nothing a cool shower won't fix, she told herself determinedly as she set off down the sidewalk, heading for her motel, shifting her bag on her sunburned shoulder.

"Hey!"

Myrtle groaned as the man's voice rang out behind her. *What the hell does he want?*

Of course, she already knew the answer to that, and

clearly, her hope that he'd got the message and backed off had been a futile one.

I'll just keep walking, she decided. *He's not going to chase me down the street. Probably.*

She'd only taken a few steps down the sidewalk, however, when she heard the man's voice again, this time *much* closer.

"Hey, wait! We're leaving in the morning, so if you wanna do this, it's gotta be tonight."

What the fuck?!

Myrtle had been on the receiving end of catcalls and lewd comments before, but this was *ridiculous.* Fury momentarily overrode her good sense, and she swung around, ready to give this pig a piece of her mind.

"*Excuse* me?!"

The man simply shook his head. "You wanna see the goods or not?"

Myrtle rolled her eyes. One thing she knew about men who got their kicks by hooting at women was that they often tended to shrink when their bluff was called. Fine. If that was the way this guy wanted it, she'd play along.

Fixing him with a glare, she crossed her arms over her chest. "All right, then. Whip it out. Show me what you got."

Just as she suspected he would, the man hesitated. "Here? In the middle of the street?"

Curling her lip imperiously, Myrtle lifted her chin. "C'mon, you're so desperate to do it, then go ahead."

"Fine," he grumbled. "Have it your way. Let's just get this over with." He gave her a quick once over. "At least you listened to us and didn't come waltzing in here with your fancy suits and car. You woulda stuck out like a sore thumb."

What the hell is that supposed to mean? Myrtle had time to think, before the man plunged one beefy hand into the bulky bag he was holding, pulling out a square, black box. Grasping it carefully in both hands, he held it out to her. She stared at it.

"What's this?" she asked, too surprised to formulate any other response.

"It's what we agreed on," the man growled. "And two months earlier than scheduled, which means we get our bonus. Check it out if you don't believe me, but it's exactly what we told you about."

This is a drug deal, Myrtle suddenly realized, her mouth popping open. *And I'm an idiot.*

The goods wasn't the guy's dick at all – it was probably crystal meth or coke or some other illicit substance. And he'd mistaken her for the buyer.

Not that a whole lot of drugs could fit in that one box, Myrtle thought as she looked down at it, trying to figure out how to extract herself from this stupid – and kind of dangerous – situation.

"Take a look, if you like," the biker said, opening the box. "It's genuine. But you can tell that just by touching it, right?"

"No, I –" Myrtle started, before actually catching a glimpse of the contents of the box.

No white powder, no blue crystals, or whatever real meth actually looked like.

It was an egg.

But it wasn't like any egg Myrtle had ever seen before: it was bigger, for starters, bigger even than the ostrich or emu eggs she'd seen in museums. And it was colored differently too – a beautiful pale blue that shone with a faint luminescence in the bright orange streetlights. It was perfectly smooth, without even one single blemish or ridge on its oval surface.

It's beautiful.

Myrtle couldn't help but stare at it, her breath catching in her throat. She felt her fingers twitch with the desire to reach out and touch it – and then, without her conscious will, she was doing just that.

She gasped a little when her fingertips first brushed against it. To her surprise, the surface was quite warm, but she supposed that made sense – she knew animal smugglers had to keep the eggs of the exotic birds and lizards they trafficked warm so the baby that was growing inside them wouldn't die.

Because that was *definitely* what was going on here.

The bikers were smuggling this egg, and they'd mistaken her for the buyer.

Biting her lip, she gently picked up the egg from where it rested in its foam casing.

She knew about the horrible world of animal smuggling – tiger cubs, exotic lizards, rhino horns and rare parrots – and it made her sick.

She'd loved animals all her life, and yes, while moths might not have been all that cute or the first thing that sprang into people's minds when they thought of creatures that needed protecting, a lot of the animals that needed them as a food source *were*. With all her research on moth numbers and migration patterns, Myrtle was fighting for their future as well.

And anyone who tried to make money off smuggling poor defenseless creatures to sell them into a life of misery – well, they deserved everything they got.

"So. You know it's the genuine article," the biker said with an oily smile. "Put it down and get out the money. Just like we agreed on."

Myrtle looked up, his voice shocking her back to reality. Well, she didn't have any money. And nor did she intend to let this guy leave with his egg to go and find the person who did.

This creature wasn't theirs to buy or sell.

No way I'm letting them get away with this.
So, she ran.

Ignoring the screaming blisters on her toes and the balls of her feet, Myrtle swung around and took off down the street, clutching the egg tightly to her chest.

She heard the man yelling behind her, but his voice was incoherent; she could barely hear a thing over the pounding of her heart in her ears anyway.

Where's the police station, where's the police station, where the fuck is the police station –

She'd seen it as she went past it on the bus yesterday afternoon, so it had to be around here *somewhere.* It wasn't like there were many places it could *be* – Good Fortune only had one main street, and she was on it!

As she ran, she heard a clatter of footsteps behind her. Chancing a glance over her shoulder, Myrtle almost tripped over her own feet in shock. She'd figured the biker she'd swiped the egg from would chase after her – but she hadn't expected that somehow, in the time it'd taken her to run thirty feet, he would have assembled the rest of his gang, and now what looked like an entire army of bikers was chasing her down the street, like a solid wall of gray beards and black tank tops charging toward her.

Oh, shit.

"Go 'round the back and cut her off," she heard one of them yelling, and, without taking a moment to think, Myrtle pivoted, changing directions on a dime and shooting across the street.

Oh, shit. Shit, shit, shit, shit.

Myrtle knew she couldn't have simply left the egg and whatever was growing inside it with the biker, but now that her brain had had time to catch up with her feet, she realized what a truly stupid thing she'd done. She didn't know what Australian bikers did to people they figured were trying to rip them off, but she was willing to bet it wasn't anything nice.

If I could just find the police station – !

She let out a small cry, clutching the egg tightly to her chest as a car suddenly roared out of the night in front of her, headlights blaring, dust spooling up from beneath its tires.

Fear knifed through her gut, her throat so tight she could barely breathe.

They'd caught up with her.

Myrtle was about to turn to sprint away again – though with the rest of the gang still chasing her down from the other direction, she had no idea where she thought she was going to go – when the door of the car in front of her swung open, and a man's face, illuminated by the car's ceiling light, appeared.

"Get in."

Myrtle hesitated. One thing she knew was that you never got into a car with strangers. Not even handsome strangers like this, whose slightly curled golden-brown hair fell in waves over their forehead and into their deep brown eyes, or whose jawlines looked like they might have been sculpted from marble. And *definitely* not when their biceps clearly bulged under the rolled-up sleeves of their flannel shirts.

"Um," Myrtle said.

"Get in – I mean, if you don't want to end up as mincemeat," the man said again, gesturing to her to jump in the passenger seat. "C'mon, chop chop. We haven't got all day."

Um, Myrtle was about to say again, when a shout from behind her made up her mind for her. It wasn't really a choice, anyway: Option One was certain death at the hands of a bunch of really, *really* pissed off bikers. Option Two was *maybe* death at the hands of a total stranger in a car... but, well, *maybe* was better than *certainly*, at least where grisly death was concerned.

Taking a deep breath, she jumped in the car, slamming the door closed behind her.

"Good." The man turned away, the dashboard lights catching on his high, perfect cheekbones. Not that Myrtle was staring or anything – it was just the kind of thing you noticed.

He slammed his foot down on the gas and sent the car roaring into the night.

CHAPTER 2

Three months. Three months of work, down the drain.

That was the only thought in Hector Richardson's mind as he floored the accelerator, sending the car tearing down the dirt road.

Shit. Shit. Shit. Shit.

Well, maybe not the *only* thought.

After a moment, he flicked the car's headlights off. He didn't need them to drive at night – his griffin's powerful eagle's vision picked out every bend in the road and every potential obstacle in its path, and driving dark would make them a lot harder to track by the meathead bikies he'd left on the road behind them.

Meathead bikies who nonetheless managed to get their hands on something extremely *valuable, and meathead bikies I've been stalking for three months.*

All of which work had now been entirely ruined by the woman sitting next to him.

"What'd you think you were playing at back there?" he asked, realizing his voice sounded harsh, but not really able to care just at this moment.

The woman turned to him, eyes wide. "*Me?* I wasn't *playing* at anything. I got followed out of a pub, and the next thing I knew I was getting chased down the road by a bunch of bikers. And by the way, I *really* don't think you should be driving without your headlights on."

Oh, she's American, Hector thought. Maybe that explained a few things. Though it *didn't* explain how she'd come to be clutching an over-sized egg to her chest. Trying to steal from bikies generally wasn't a smart idea, though he'd been under the impression everyone knew that.

"What do you mean, followed out of the pub?" he asked.

He ignored the remark about the headlights. He wasn't about to explain to her why it wasn't a problem. Not when she was clearly human. Later, he could give her the cover story he usually gave to humans if he absolutely had to – that he was a cop working on a case – and leave it at that.

The woman glanced at him, eyes narrowed. "I mean just what I said. That guy followed me out of the pub demanding that I let him show me the goods. I thought he meant… well, you know."

Hector frowned. "What?"

The woman sighed, rolling her eyes. "I thought he meant his dick, obviously. Geeze. You can tell you're not a woman."

Okay, fine, I deserved that.

He glanced across at the woman again, taking her in for the first time. Blonde hair, blue-gray eyes that reminded him of the sky just before a storm for some reason. Freckles across her nose. Full lips, slightly parted. A pointed chin, and a jawline that some would probably call too square, but which he called 'attractive as hell' – he'd always liked women with strong features, who looked like they could hold their own in any situation. She'd have a nasty sunburn on those shoulders tomorrow, but at least she was dressed properly for the scrub: good sturdy hiking boots and shorts – no heels, no skirt to fly up in the wind.

Nice figure, too.

The thought popped into his head without him meaning it to, but he could hardly help but notice it: she was all soft edges and rounded curves, but it was obvious there was plenty of muscle in her thighs and calves. She clearly led an active life. She'd certainly outrun the bikies easily enough.

"All right, all right," he said. "Point taken. So he offered to show you the goods, whatever definition of 'goods' you wanna use. What happened then?"

The woman turned in her seat to look at him, blue eyes still narrowed. "Any reason I'm getting the third degree here?" She glanced back down the road behind them. "And shouldn't we be going to the cops?"

Time to roll out the cover story.

"It's fine – I'm a cop." He checked the rearview mirror. So far, no bikies.

The woman's mouth popped open a little. *"You're* a cop?"

It wasn't *technically* true, Hector knew. He wasn't a cop by the definition humans – or most shifters, actually – would use. What he *was* was an operative of a highly trained, highly specialized undercover law enforcement agency, designed entirely to take on some of the nastier criminals of the shifter world: assassins for hire, smugglers, mercenaries, and the like. The kind of people human organizations just couldn't deal with. It was a bit hard to track an assassin who could turn into a tiger at will, after all, or a spy who did their spying as an eagle. Or find a wyvern who sold its venom on the black market as an untraceable and totally deadly weapon.

Well, unless you were another shifter, and even then, it was hard to find a shifter who was *really* determined not to be found.

They were a pretty secretive organization, even by shifter standards. Even Hector didn't know which government department oversaw their operations, and wouldn't have been able to name more than ten other agents. He had direct contact with exactly half that number.

Most people wouldn't even know they existed, which was entirely the point of them. Blabbing out your business to anyone who asked was no way to run a top-secret law enforcement organization.

None of the bikies were shifters, but they'd somehow managed to get themselves involved in the shifter underworld, which was why Hector had been following them.

That's all shot to hell now though, he thought dully. *Fuck.*

At least the woman was unharmed – which had been a close-run thing. She had some scrapes on her legs, but Hector's shifter sense of smell could tell they weren't new: the blood was hours old, and he could detect the sharp scent of antiseptic from where she'd patched herself up.

Lucky we were there, his griffin piped up. *In another moment, we might have had an even worse problem on our hands.*

That, at least, was true. He might not have found out who the buyer for the bikies' egg was, and he may potentially have blown his cover completely. But the woman was safe. And that was the whole reason he'd gotten into this line of work in the first place: to protect people.

"Yeah, I'm a cop," Hector said, though for some reason, the half-truth that usually came so easily to him tasted wrong in his mouth somehow. "And this is hardly the third degree."

"What, so I should be grateful you didn't throw me over your shoulder and toss me in the trunk?" the woman demanded. "And if you're a cop, how about I see some ID?"

"I don't have ID on me. I'm not that kind of cop."

"A cop without ID," the woman repeated. "Well, that's convenient."

He could hear the rising thread of fear in her voice. He couldn't really say he blamed her. She was clearly far from home, she'd just escaped from a pack of bikies, and had jumped into the car of a man she didn't know from Adam out of pure desperation.

A man who was now apparently refusing to show her any ID, and was driving her out through the scrub without his headlights on.

All right, fine.

Now that he'd gotten his head out of his arse and stopped sulking about all the lost work and time, he could see how all this might look a bit suss.

He saw a small movement out of the corner of his eye, and turned his head in time to see the woman's fingers inching toward the car door handle.

"Wait, don't do that," he barked out. "We're in the middle of nowhere. You won't find your way back to town unless you can navigate by the stars. And you can't tell me you really want to go back there, anyway? Those bikies'll be on the lookout for you –"

"And what's my other option?" she asked, her voice tight. "Stay here with you, the 'cop' without ID?"

He could practically hear the air quotes around 'cop'.

"Hector Richardson," he said, hearing the desperate note in his own voice. "My name's Hector Richardson, and I'm working undercover. I was after those bikies. I *have* been after them for three months."

The woman said nothing. The fingers of her left hand still rested lightly on the door handle, while her right still cradled the egg protectively to her chest.

"Those guys are wildlife smugglers," she said finally. "Is that what you were tracking them for?"

Wildlife. That's one way of putting it.

"Yes." That was the easiest explanation for now. What the

woman held was no ordinary egg, which was why he'd been sent in after it, though no one even knew if the egg was real – though they'd know soon enough now. As a mythical shifter, he'd know as soon as he touched the egg whether it was real or not. But recovering a possibly fake egg had only been *half* of his mission

The other half had been finding out who wanted to buy it, and why. Which, thanks to this mess, they now definitely *wouldn't* know. Unless the woman across from him turned out to be an especially good actor.

He glanced at her.

No chance, his griffin said. *She's not lying. We could sense it if she was.*

"So if they're smuggling poor defenseless animals, shouldn't you go arrest them?"

"That's not the only thing they're smuggling," Hector said. "The cops up in the Gold Coast've been tipped off, and they're gonna pick 'em up for the six mil worth of meth they're moving."

"Oh."

That was something the human cops could definitely deal with. This egg and whoever wanted to buy it... not so much.

Hector glanced at the egg curiously, doing his best to ignore the way it nestled against the full curve of the woman's breast.

Could it really be...?

It seemed hard to believe. Pegasi were rare enough – the idea that there could still be an unhatched one anywhere in the world that no one knew about until now almost defied belief. His fingertips prickled with the desire to touch it and find out if it really was what the bikies had claimed.

Be patient, his griffin counseled him. *She already doesn't trust us. Try to snatch the egg off her now and she never will.*

It was right. The griffin, despite how irritating it could be, sometimes gave surprisingly good advice and made him think twice about the best way to approach a situation. It was only when its blood was up and the red mist of rage descended over its senses that Hector's human side needed to pull it back, and temper its wild animal instincts.

The woman hadn't said anything else, and Hector realized he couldn't just keep referring to her as 'the woman' in his head.

"What's your name?"

She glanced at him, hesitating. "Myrtle," she finally said. "Myrtle Atkins."

Myrtle.

For some reason, the name seemed to echo within him, like a bell had been struck within his chest.

"That's... a pretty name," he eventually said, still confused as to why it would have such an effect on him.

To his surprise, Myrtle let out a small, bitter laugh.

"Do you really think so? I've always hated it." She gave him a tight smile. "But when your mom seems determined to name all her kids after flowers and plants, I guess eventually you start to run out of nice ones." She shook her head. "Anyway, that's not really important, is it? What're we going to do about this?"

She held up the egg, gently cupping it in her palms. She was holding it carefully, like she was used to dealing with delicate things.

"If it doesn't stay warm, whatever's growing in here will die," she continued. "And that'd be just as bad as whatever those guys were planning to do with it. We have to get it under something warm, like a heat lamp. And fast."

Hector nodded. "I know. And I can do that. But you might have to trust me a bit."

Myrtle laughed again, but once again there wasn't a lot of humor in it. "Trust the guy who says he's a cop but won't

HECTOR

show me any ID, who's currently speeding across the outback without headlights on? Sure, why not. I don't have much other choice, do I?"

Well, she has a point there.

"I don't want you to feel like you're only doing this because you have no choice," Hector said.

"Well, I don't really. Like you said, bikers aren't really the forgiving type, and there's no way I'm giving them back this egg. So unless I really want to end up at the bottom of a lake with concrete shoes on, I guess I better stick with you." She paused. "Not that I guess there's a lake anywhere 'round here for them to dump me in."

"Trust me, they have their own way of taking care of things," Hector said grimly. "So yeah, that's about the long and the short of it. Whatever you might think of me, I can't just let you go waltzing back into town. Not until we know it's safe. Which may take a few days."

Myrtle stared at him, her eyes wide. "A few *days?* I'm not here on a vacation, though. I'm here to do research. I can't drop everything just because –"

"Just because some bikies are after you for revenge for stealing from them?" Hector asked, shaking his head. "Sorry, but whatever it is, it can wait until after I know those bikies have been picked up. They have a delivery schedule for their meth, but who knows – they may decide to hang around if they think what you have there is worth more to them."

"Now, wait just a minute," Myrtle said, the volume of her voice rising. "I thought it'd only be – I mean, like I said, I'm here for work, and I have my grant money budgeted down to the last *dime*. Once it's gone, it's gone. And I prepaid for my accommodation. I'm happy to let one night slide, but *days* –"

"Whatever you're studying, I'm sure it'll still be there when you get back," Hector said.

"But that's just the point!" Myrtle threw a hand up in the

25

air, while still cradling the egg carefully with the other. "It won't be! I'm studying moth migrations! As in, they'll migrate! Before I've had a chance to find or count them!"

"Moth migrations?" Hector asked, shooting her a confused look.

"Yes! Moth migrations! I know it may not sound very interesting or cool to you, but it's actually really important! Lots of animals – you know, the kinds of cute animals that people care about – eat the moths, and without them, they'll starve. So think about it that way, if you have to."

"No, it's fine, I know how important moths are to the ecosystem," Hector said – which he did. He knew this land. He'd grown up on a cattle station not far from here, which was why he'd been chosen for this mission. It was the perfect cover story: he was just back paying a visit to his childhood home. Even people who'd known him as a kid who had no idea what his job was now would vouch for him. And he cared about this place more than he could say. It'd been his home for twenty years, and he knew it like the back of his hand.

"You –?" Myrtle blinked at him as if surprised, but then quickly closed her mouth and looked away.

"But I'm sorry," Hector continued. "Now that you're here, it's my duty to protect you. And I can't let you go out there until I'm sure those bikies won't be a threat."

Myrtle said nothing. She sat back in her seat and stared out the window at the total darkness beyond. Hector glanced at her.

"Look, I get it," he said. "The drought's been hard these last few years. Moth numbers are down, and while that may not *seem* important to most people, it has a knock-on effect to the rest of the environment. You do important work, and I admire it. I'm not saying you can't go back just to be an arsehole. Those bikies mean serious business, and it's just not worth the risk. The moment I know it's safe for you to be out there, you can go."

Myrtle had turned to him while he spoke, her eyes still guarded, but she was looking at him now like she at least *wanted* to trust him.

"You mean it? As soon as you're sure?"

"I can't make a promise about the time frame. But yeah. As soon as possible."

Myrtle sat back again, looking out the window. "Okay."

They drove on in silence. Hector knew where he was heading, now that he was certain the bikies hadn't tailed them. And he knew they didn't have much time, if what Myrtle was holding really *was* a genuine pegasus egg.

They didn't like to get cold – not that there was a huge chance of that, what with the way Myrtle was cradling it against her, uh, chest.

Hector swallowed, pulling his eyes back to the front.

Inappropriate in the extreme.

Just because Myrtle was gorgeous and sexy and *curvy* and –

Eyes in front!

Hector cleared his throat.

"We're almost there," he said.

Myrtle turned back to him, stormy gray-blue eyes narrowed. "Almost where?"

"Where we're going to have to stay for the next few days."

It hadn't been his plan to take anyone back to his headquarters – and really, he wasn't even supposed to. But thanks to his impulsive move, he didn't have any other choice. He didn't really trust anyone else to look after Myrtle just now – and besides which, he needed to take a closer look at the egg.

"It might look a bit… shabby from the outside," he warned her as he pulled the car up. His griffin's night vision had guided him perfectly to the right place, a little off the road and far enough out of Good Fortune that he'd know it if anyone tried to sneak up on him. "That's why I said before you might have to trust me a bit."

"Oh... kay..." Myrtle said. She hesitated; then, setting her strong jaw – *Unf*, Hector thought – she opened the car door and swung her legs out.

"It's... really, really dark out," she said when she closed the car door and the overhead light went out again. "I can't see my hand in front of my face."

"Your eyes will adjust in a moment. There's plenty of starlight to see by," Hector said. Starlight he didn't need in order to see everything around him perfectly.

He could see her hesitating, looking around her, still clutching the egg protectively to her chest. Hector realized that leaving her effectively blinded was *not* likely to engender any trust, so he walked around the car to join her on the other side and extended his hand.

"Here," he said. "I'll help you."

He reached out, placing his hand gently on her shoulder, over her tank top. A warm tingling sensation immediately began throbbing in his palm, before running up his arm.

Within him, his griffin sat up, tail twitching. *What is this?*

Hector pulled his hand back, looking down at his palm. The sensation stopped.

It's nothing, he told the griffin. *Just been stuck out in the desert for three months, and Myrtle's the best-looking thing I've seen in a while. That's it.*

"Does the offer of help still stand, or am I just going to have to stumble around until we get to your house?"

"Uh – right," Hector said, swallowing hard. "This way."

Placing his hand back on her shoulder, he guided her over the dusty, rocky path to the place he'd called his home for the past several weeks.

It was nothing to look at from the outside – which was

exactly the point. It was two battered old shipping containers, abandoned here in the middle of nowhere, dented and scraped up, their paint peeling off under the harsh, unyielding sun. Anyone who happened to see them while driving by would barely take a second glance at them.

But *inside...*

Hector unlocked the heavy steel door at the rear of one of the containers. It creaked as it opened, and the light from inside flooded out.

"O-Oh..." Myrtle's eyes went wide, one hand raised to her open mouth. "I – is this – *wow.*"

CHAPTER 3

Hector watched as Myrtle stepped inside the shipping container, her eyes wide.

"My headquarters, I guess you'd call it," he said.

Seeing her surprised awe made Hector look at the place he'd lived for the past few weeks with new eyes. And feel relieved that he'd thought to tidy up a little earlier in the day. This place would probably have been a little less impressive as it had looked about six hours ago, with instant noodle cups sitting in front of the computer screens and protein bar wrappers littering the blinking server banks. Not to mention the pile of dirty clothes he'd collected from between the satellite monitors and the police scanner equipment and tossed into the hamper in his sleeping quarters.

"This is like something out of James Bond," Myrtle murmured, looking around. "Am I allowed to be here? Am I going to have to swear an oath of silence or go into a witness protection program or something?"

Hector hesitated. It was true that *technically* he was breaking a lot of rules by bringing her here.

But my first priority is always to ensure the safety of civilians, he thought. *Doesn't that override everything else?*

Not really, but that was what he'd be arguing to his handler, Callan. Who he'd now have to call and explain himself to.

He'd just have to hope Callan saw things his way.

He watched as Myrtle wandered amongst the blinking computers and equipment. She hadn't been far wrong when she said this was like something out of James Bond. Working alone out here in the middle of nowhere meant he had to be pretty self-sufficient. All this equipment allowed him to access everything he needed – whatever data, whatever information he required to complete his mission was at his fingertips here.

"How do you power all of this?" Myrtle asked, turning to him.

"Solar batteries," he said. "The hidden panels on the roof soak up rays all day, and all the excess is stored. I have a generator for emergencies of course, but as you can imagine, 'not enough sun' isn't usually a problem out here."

Myrtle only nodded. "And... this is all for the sake of catching some bikers... bikies... whatever they're called out here... with some meth? And an egg?"

"Not quite." Hector hesitated. *How do I explain this?*

It wasn't like he could just say, *Yeah, the meth was part of it, but what I'm* really *interested in is the egg of a mythical creature we all thought was extinct long ago. Which, by the way, you're holding in your hands right now. Maybe.*

Until he touched it, he wouldn't know if the egg was genuine. It didn't seem likely. No one had seen a pegasus in centuries. Amongst shifter types, they were the rarest of the rare. Even his griffin – uncommon as it was – was nothing compared to the rarity of a pegasus.

Which was what made the egg so valuable – and why,

Hector was guessing, the mere *possibility* it was genuine was enough to tempt a buyer with deep, *deep* pockets all the way out here from the United States.

Not that I managed to find out who they are.

Shaking off the gloomy thought, Hector pulled in a deep breath.

But at least I have what they were after.

"Pass me the – the egg," he said, holding out his hand. "I need to make sure it's genuine."

Myrtle glanced at him, holding the egg against herself. "We should warm it up. It's gotten cooler since I took it off that guy."

"I will in a moment," Hector said. "I just need to inspect it first."

Myrtle visibly hesitated. "But then you're going to put it under a lamp, right?"

"Yeah, for sure." In fact, he had an incubation lamp all set up on the off-chance the egg *was* for real.

Somehow, Myrtle seemed reluctant to give up the egg. She held it against her chest, her fingers wound protectively around it. She was looking at him with narrowed eyes, as if she suspected he might snatch it from her at any moment.

Finally, with what looked like a lot of effort, she held it out to him.

"Here. Take it. But be careful."

"Ta." Hector reached out for it. It really was beautiful – an iridescent blue, and perfectly smooth. He had no idea what a pegasus egg was supposed to look like, but if this was fake, someone had done a good job of it.

"Carefully," Myrtle told him again, her voice hard.

Their fingers brushed.

Zap.

"What was that?!" Myrtle snatched her hand back, still

holding the egg in one hand, staring down at her fingers, eyes wide.

"I – I don't know," Hector started to say, before his griffin reared up inside him, beak open in a mighty screech, talons raking the air, wings extended.

Mine!

Hector's breath caught in his throat. He stared down at his hand, almost expecting to see the pads of his fingers branded from the shock of electricity that had passed between them. There was nothing there of course, but he could almost still feel the aftershocks coursing over his skin.

Shit. She's my mate.

Dragging his eyes upward, he stared at her.

He'd thought she was a very attractive woman before – and she was. But now, she'd taken on an almost otherworldly gloss. Nothing about her was *different* from how it'd been five seconds ago, but at the same time, *everything* had changed. It was as if he could see her heart in her beautiful storm-colored eyes: her heart, her soul, everything that made her *her...*

"Uh, hello?"

Myrtle's voice snapped him out of the rapture he'd wandered into.

C'mon, get your head together. Concentrate. Shit.

The truth was, though, he was shaken right down to his bones.

His mate? Here?

I can't think about this right now. I have to concentrate.

He forced his mind back to the here and now. Gritting his teeth, he reached out again.

"Nope, no way," Myrtle said. "You almost dropped it! You could have killed whatever's in here – just show me where to put it, and I'll take care of it. I'm a scientist, I'm used to handling these kinds of things."

"I told you, I have to inspect it," Hector managed to get out. He was so distracted he could hardly think straight. His mate was standing right in front of him, glaring at him.

"Then you can do it while I hold it," Myrtle said. "Or once it's under the lamp."

Hector's brain was too addled to argue with her. "Okay, fine." Turning away, he uncovered the incubator he'd kept warming up while he'd been away, just in case the egg was real. It was a simple thing – just a heat lamp positioned over a soft bed of feathers and hay, the kind of nest pegasi were supposed to have built for their eggs many eons ago, before they'd disappeared. "Bring it over here."

Myrtle followed him over, carefully placing the egg down in the center of the nest. She glanced at him as he crouched in front of it.

Hector did his best to ignore it when she leaned forward to look over his shoulder. It was as if he could feel the heat of her body against his skin, warmer even than the heat lamp in front of him. But at this distance at least, there was no spark of electricity, no almost-painful jolt. The only thing out of the ordinary was a warm tingling on his skin where their fingers had touched.

Well, that, and the tightness in his pants, which Hector was sure was going to become noticeable at some time in the very near future.

He cleared his throat.

I have to focus.

Reaching out carefully, he ran his fingers gently over the shell of the egg. He waited, hoping to feel any spark of life from within.

C'mon. Are you real or not?

For a moment, he *thought* he felt something – something gentle and soft, tentatively reaching out to him.

But then, it was gone.

Whatever it was had been entirely within his imagination.

Hector sat back, disappointment knifing through his chest.

Shit. It's a fake after all.

"So what kind of egg is it?" Myrtle's voice broke into his thoughts. "I've never seen anything like it before. Is it –"

"It's a fake," Hector said, shaking his head. "It doesn't matter."

Myrtle blinked at him. "Fake?"

"Yeah. Someone's gone to a lot of trouble to do this, but it's not genuine."

Myrtle frowned, looking down at it. "I don't think so – I mean, I –" She cut herself off suddenly, biting her lip. "There still could be a living creature in there. And if that's the case, we have to take care of it."

Hector doubted that, but he wasn't sure he could explain things right now. And besides which, he had to make a report to his handler, Callan. About what a mess he'd made of this operation, and about how the egg wasn't really a pegasus egg after all. As far as anyone knew, they were still extinct.

And how we found our mate, his griffin said, tail twitching.

Yeah, maybe I'll leave that part out.

"I – I have to make a report," Hector muttered, standing. He *hoped* she couldn't see the effect her proximity had had on him.

Myrtle frowned, putting her hands on her hips. "And what about me?"

"You?" Hector blinked, confused.

"Am I just supposed to sit here on my ass waiting for you to let me go free?" She glanced at the egg. "And do you know how to take care of that?"

It's not alive, he wanted to tell her – but that would take *way* too long to explain just now.

Our mate is troubled, his griffin piped up, twitching its feathered ears. *We must comfort her. Now! Comfort her!*

Hector was so befuddled by his griffin's directive that he'd taken a step toward Myrtle before realizing what he was doing.

Comfort her how?! he demanded of it, before his griffin suddenly bombarded him with images of him taking Myrtle in his arms, sweeping her backward and kissing her deeply, her breasts pressed against his chest, her fingers clutching at his back, her breath warm against his skin –

Hector shook his head, forcing himself to take a step back.

Trust me, she won't *find that comforting,* he told the griffin. *At all.*

The griffin seemed confused. *But in times of trouble, humans need to be shown attention and affection. We both know this.*

Attention and affection is one thing, Hector told it. *Kissing her completely without warning is another!*

Myrtle was staring at him, her eyes narrowed, hands on her hips. "Well?"

"Just – just stay here," Hector said. "I'll – be back in a moment."

He turned away, heading into the second shipping container, joined to the first through a steel door. He had to get away from Myrtle before he did something stupid – or before she noticed the bulge in his pants.

He'd *never* been affected by a woman this way. Just being near her was enough to stir up his blood in a way he'd never felt before. He'd known some good-looking women in his time, but *no one* like Myrtle.

"Fine, then, I guess I'll just stay here," he heard her mutter as he closed the steel door behind him.

You are being an oaf, his griffin informed him. *With no manners whatsoever.*

Sagging against the door, trying to ignore the painful rush of blood southward, Hector was forced to agree with it.

I have to get my head on straight.

This was the last thing he'd expected to happen. Finding his mate in the middle of a mission wasn't exactly convenient. He realized in some distant part of his brain that was still functioning properly that he was breaking just about every protocol that existed by leaving her alone in his operations room, but he just couldn't bring himself to care right now.

Besides, she is our mate, his griffin rumbled. *What's ours is hers. It is only fitting that she see what we do, know everything about our lives. We have no secrets from our mate.*

That's fine, Hector told it as he stumbled over to the desk by his messy, unmade bed. *But I don't think she knows she's our mate. In fact, she doesn't even seem to like us very much.*

Taking a deep breath, Hector tried to focus as he typed in the password for his laptop. This laptop had one use only: to make secure satellite calls to his handler, Callan, in Sydney.

Hector bristled as he typed in the one-time code to make the call. He was a little annoyed at having to do it – he'd never liked the feeling that someone was looking over his shoulder – but it could be worse. At least he'd been assigned to Callan for this mission. He and Callan had known each other for years, and had come up through training together and had shared a dorm. They'd spent more than a few of their extremely rare free days and nights out on the tear together. Hector counted him not just as a colleague, but as a friend.

Now, Callan picked up immediately as per usual, his face appearing on the laptop screen.

"Hector." He squinted. "You look like shit."

"Ta for that," Hector muttered. He rubbed his eyes. *How am I supposed to look after a mostly failed mission and unexpectedly finding my mate?!*

"Things go that well, did they?" Callan asked, his voice measured. That was one of the most infuriating things about Callan, in Hector's opinion – he never seemed ruffled, never seemed angry. He was the most easy-going person Hector had ever met, which, considering Hector had grown up on a farm, was saying something.

"Yeah, everything's perfect," Hector said, shaking his head. "Just great. I didn't find out who the buyer is."

Callan cocked his head. "You all right though?"

"Oh, I'm fine." Hector waved a hand. "No dramas."

"*Some* dramas, clearly."

Hector sighed. "I didn't get the buyer, but I *did* get the egg. Bad news, though – it's a fake."

Narrowing his eyes, Callan frowned. "You sure? The information we had –"

"The information we had was the same as what the buyer had," Hector cut him off. "And *they* thought it was real, unless the reason I didn't see them around tonight was because they had second thoughts and bailed on the deal."

"It's possible."

"It's *probable.* I touched the egg. I couldn't sense anything inside it. I dunno how the Reaper Angels bikies got onto this, but they got us good. What a waste of fucking time."

Hector ran his fingers through his hair. *It wasn't a waste of time, though. It meant I found my mate. And that's worth any cost.*

"It wasn't a waste of time."

Hector glanced up, convinced for a moment that Callan had read his mind, and that he'd have to add 'telepathy' to his already maddeningly long list of skills.

"Fine, so it's not a good result." Callan shrugged. "But if, like you said, the buyer was never here in the first place, then we were never going to get them. The regular cops still get the meth haul thanks to the work we put in. That's something, right?"

Hector nodded reluctantly, not ready to let go of his sulk *just* yet.

"Anyway, that's all I had to say. Report in, mission failed. No buyer, egg's a fake. So that's it. I'm turning in. Night."

He reached for the keyboard to end the call. He couldn't sit here chit-chatting to Callan. He had to get back out to –

"Wait just a moment," Callan held up a hand. "You reckon you can fool me? I've known you for ten years, Hec. What's going on?"

Callan's words weren't so much a question as a flat directive. Hector swallowed.

No getting out of this, unless I just flat-out lie.

That… really wasn't an option. And besides, after the mess he'd made so far with Myrtle, he could probably use the help.

"No, that's not all," Hector admitted. "There *is* something else. But it's not related to the mission."

"All right," Callan said in a measured tone, though Hector could see the curiosity glimmering in his eyes.

Hector took a deep breath. "It's my mate. I found her. She got caught up in all this mess tonight – the bikies heard her accent and thought she was the buyer."

"Her accent?"

"She's American."

Callan looked puzzled. "What's a Yank doing all the way out there?"

"She's a scientist. She's out here for research."

"Ah." Callan paused. "Are you sure about this? Your head's not just being turned by a brainy beauty with a cute accent?"

Hector was insulted. "*Of course* I'm sure! How stupid d'you think I am?"

"Were you wearing your Uggs on the carpet again? You know those things can build up some wicked static electricity. Maybe if you –"

"That's not what happened," Hector cut in, trying and failing to keep the growl out of his voice. "This was *real* – I felt it. Stop taking the piss."

"I wasn't," Callan said calmly. "I just wanted to make sure *you* were sure."

"I am." Hector had never been more sure of anything before. Well, except for maybe one thing: that Myrtle absolutely despised him. "There's a problem, though. She thinks I'm a complete arsehole."

"To be fair, you do have your moments, Hec."

"Right, cheers mate, just what I needed to hear," Hector muttered.

"I'm serious. Remember when you went on the rampage because someone ate your boiled eggs?"

"Not even a slightly comparable situation," Hector growled. "And it wasn't 'someone', it was *you*. Are you gonna be helpful, or are you just gonna hang shit on me?"

"I'm not hanging shit," Callan said. "I'm trying to get you thinking clearly. You're sure, though."

It wasn't really a question.

"Completely." Hector nodded. His heart beat with total certainty. He'd never been so certain of anything before in his life, not even about joining up as an agent.

Callan sighed, running a hand over his face. "Well, I guess you better go back out there and convince her you're at least a *little* bit less of an arsehole than you first seem."

Hector felt his heart sink. How was he going to do that? He'd barely had any time to think about dating since he was a teenager – and then, there hadn't exactly been a huge number of girls around to try to impress. He'd had a few relationships while he'd been at the training academy, but those had been short-term things, and both of them had known they couldn't last once they graduated and went out into the field. As much as he'd liked the girls involved, they'd mainly been relationships of convenience.

Myrtle was human, so it was safe to say she didn't know anything about mate bonds or shifters. And it wasn't exactly the kind of thing he could spring on a girl even at the best of times. It *definitely* wasn't the kind of thing he could spring while they were in the middle of nowhere – and it was the middle of the desert scrub, and the worst kind of nowhere. If she took it badly, she didn't exactly have anywhere else to go.

And it's not like I can take her out on a date, either, Hector thought despondently. *Do all the things that might impress her the way a human would. What am I going to do? Whip her up a fine dining experience of protein bar and UHT milk?*

"Well, I guess I can only try," he muttered. It wasn't like he had a lot of choice. A shifter who'd met his mate and had to be without them was subject to a slow, painful life sentence of never feeling whole ever again.

"Well, don't look so fucking happy," Callan said sarcastically. "Gosh, finding your mate – must be awful."

"All right, all right," Hector said. "Point taken. But I just –"

Before he could get any further, there was a thunderous bang on the steel door.

What the hell?!

He turned in his seat.

"Hey! Hey, Hector! Or Officer Richardson? Whichever one it is, you better get out here! Right now!"

Myrtle?!

His griffin scented the air, tail twitching, everything on high alert – but there was no danger in the air, no nothing.

"Sounds like your lady love," Callan said, grinning. "You better go see what she wants."

And with that, he ended the call. Hector stared at the blank screen.

"Well, thanks for your help, mate," he muttered.

Go to our mate! She needs us! Go now!

Hector found himself jerked up out of his seat and running across the room before he knew what he was doing. He yanked open the steel door.

Of course, Myrtle was on the other side. And in her hands was – was –

Oh. Shit.

CHAPTER 4

MYRTLE DIDN'T KNOW WHAT TO DO WITH HERSELF AFTER Hector had left in such a rush. Left to their own devices, her thoughts kept doing things she *really* didn't want them to, like dwelling on the way Hector's thigh muscles bulged under the worn jeans he was wearing. Or thinking about how his profile had looked in the half-light of the car, his masculine jaw, perfectly straight nose and high forehead all *more* than qualifying him for someone who looked like they'd win *Cosmo*'s Hunk of the Day.

Hunk of the Century, more like, Myrtle thought. *And that accent... and the muscles... and the... the everything...*

Myrtle felt her knees go weak, and she resolutely forced her mind elsewhere. Nothing could be less appropriate right now! He was a cop who'd just rescued her from bikers... bikies... whatever... *not* someone she should be fantasizing about.

Not to mention the fact that her research might be completely ruined now, because she'd just *had* to stick her nose in and get involved in something that was none of her business.

She gulped guiltily at the thought, even as she felt sick at the idea all her time here might be wasted, and she wouldn't get to do anything to help the valeleaf moth.

Though at least *something* good had come out of this, she supposed.

Myrtle looked at the egg beneath the heat lamp. She'd saved an innocent creature from being smuggled.

She shuddered at the thought of what might have been in store for whatever was growing within the egg. *Poor baby. But you're safe now. I promise.*

In order to try and keep her mind off both Hector's distracting hotness *and* the possibility of her research being ruined, Myrtle attempted to content herself by studying the egg. She hadn't seen anything like it before. Hector had been quick to say it was a fake – but a fake *what?*

She'd held it in her hands, and back in the car she'd been almost certain she could feel something stir within it. Whatever Hector had meant by *fake*, it was definitely *alive*, that much was certain.

She turned her head this way and that, watching the light from the heat lamp reflecting off its iridescent surface. It was almost mesmerizing in its beauty – so much so that when it moved, Myrtle initially just wrote it off as a figment of her imagination.

What she *couldn't* write off, however, was the *crack!* sound as a long line suddenly appeared down the side of the egg.

Oh my God, is it... is it really...

She held her breath, waiting to see what would emerge. A bird chick? Some kind of weird Australian lizard? She certainly hoped Hector had the means to care for a tiny baby creature that – that –

The next moment, her thoughts froze.

No. What? That can't be right.

The egg shifted on its little feather bed, as the creature

within struggled to get free, its nose poking out of the hole it had created.

It let out a small whinnying sound – little more than a tiny squeak. A few more pushes, and its head broke free.

That is definitely not a bird or a lizard.

Myrtle stared.

Nope. That's definitely *a tiny horse.*

"Meeee-eh?"

The – the *tiny horse* blinked wide, silvery eyes at her, twitching its ears. It was pure white. It shook its head, and its mane shimmered under the glow of the heat lamp.

"Oh my God," Myrtle whispered. Her gut clenched. She'd heard about – and seen – some weird Australian animals. Numbats, quolls, thorny devils, bandicoots, cassowaries, echidnas, frill-necked lizards... she'd read up on them all, and the scientist in her was excited at the chance to see so many things in their natural environments. But she had *never* heard of an Australian native tiny horse.

Oh, an Australian native tiny horse with wings, she thought dizzily, as the little creature hauled itself out of its shell to *plop* down amongst the feathers of the nest. Its wings were as pure white as the rest of it, but where its body was obviously covered in hair, the wings were beautiful, sweeping, delicate feathers.

"Meee-eeh?"

The horse made another tiny sound, before blinking at Myrtle again. She stared at it. It struggled to its feet, knees wobbling, just the way a foal would, before flopping back down into the nest.

Yeah, but this is no ordinary foal!

Myrtle's mind was racing.

Okay, okay, this isn't so weird. Australia has monotremes – mammals who lay eggs. There's two of them, echidnas and platy-

puses. *Everyone knows they're born from eggs. They're the only two egg-laying mammals in the world.*

Well, make that three, apparently.

She supposed the horse *did* have wings, though... would that make it at least *part* bird?

Myrtle shook her head, trying to calm her racing mind. No, she couldn't think about this right now. Because if she thought too hard, she'd realize she knew *exactly* what this creature was.

A pegasus.

She didn't need to be an expert on mythical animals to know what she was looking at here. A winged horse? Obviously a pegasus.

Yes, obviously, she thought. *Except for how, you know, they don't exist.*

The baby pegasus blinked at her. Myrtle didn't know if horses could express *indignation,* but that was definitely what this one was expressing right now.

"Meeee-*eeeh!*"

"Okay, okay, you exist!" Myrtle murmured, as the baby opened its wings, stretching them out. The feathers were so delicate they were translucent on the tips, the rachis as thin as a needle.

Beautiful.

That was the only word in Myrtle's head as the creature wobbled to its feet once more – and this time stayed there.

All right, *adorable* and *oh my God* were on high rotation as well. The tiny pegasus flexed its wings once or twice more, took a few wobbling steps – and then launched itself into the air.

"Oh no! Baby!" Myrtle raised her hands, waiting to catch it if it fell. The baby pegasus wasn't exactly a skilled flier – which was understandable, since it'd only been born a couple of minutes ago – and it dipped and bobbed in the air, wings fluttering, legs churning, until it came to rest gently upon Myrtle's shoulder.

"Mee-eeh?"

Myrtle scarcely dared to breathe.

"Okay, baby – oh – *ouch*."

She could feel its little hooves scrabbling against the burned skin of her shoulders, and she bit her lip, trying not to swear in front of it.

"Maybe – maybe you could just –"

As gently as she could, Myrtle lifted the pegasus up, cradling it in her hands. It didn't resist at all. In fact, it seemed perfectly content to be held by her. It sat in her palms and blinked once more, long silver lashes sweeping down and then up.

"Well, well, well," Myrtle said, looking down at it. "Just where in the world did *you* come from?"

Maybe Hector will know, Myrtle thought. Quickly followed by, *Oh, shit! Hector!*

"Hector!" she called out, moving across the room. "Hector, I think you better come out here!"

The pegasus made its small whinnying sound once again, as if asking her, *Who's Hector?*

Hector's the guy who better have some damn answers for me! Myrtle thought as she moved across the room, moving the baby pegasus onto her arm like she'd used to do with her mom's cats back when they'd been kittens and she'd needed to shift them so she could vacuum.

"Hector! Or Officer Richardson? Whichever one it is, you better get out here! Right now!"

And that was when he opened the door, looked down at her, and his eyes went wide.

"I didn't touch it, I swear!" Myrtle blurted out when she saw Hector staring down at what was in her hands.

Well, that's pretty obviously untrue, Myrtle thought.

"I mean, I only touched it after... after..."

After it *hatched.*

"Oh. Shit." Hector's voice was low and shocked.

Myrtle stifled the obviously ridiculous impulse to cover the baby's ears.

"I suppose that just about sums it up," Myrtle said. "I didn't know you had *pegasi* in Australia."

Hector looked at her, and seemed to hesitate a moment. Then, he appeared to make up his mind, and shook his head. "We don't. *Nowhere* does. They've been extinct for centuries. Or so everyone thought."

Myrtle looked up at him, eyes wide.

"Extinct?" she asked, hearing her own voice as if from very far away.

Hector nodded, and she looked down at the little creature she was holding, which was now resettling in her hands, folding its legs beneath it. The pegasus gazed up at her again, its large, beautiful eyes filled with... trust?

Myrtle shook her head. She was a scientist. She knew better than to assign human emotions to animals. It didn't mean they were any less deserving of all the love, care, and affection that humans could give them, but they just didn't feel things the same way humans did.

"Well, I suppose there's at least *one* of them in the world." Myrtle bit her lip as the creature whinnied again. Desolation swept through her chest.

Are you really all alone?

Myrtle frowned.

But that can't be right. Someone *had to have laid that egg...*

"Maybe you'd better sit down," Hector said. "I think I've got some explaining to do."

"Just a little." Myrtle walked across the room, sitting down on a small metal crate that didn't *seem* to be any kind of high-tech piece of equipment. The pegasus settled on her lap, looking up at her.

I better not get too attached, she thought. But at the same time, when she went to lift the pegasus off her lap to move it back to the nest, she found her hands completely unwilling to move.

"Bear in mind I don't have all the answers myself," Hector said, sitting across from her. He leaned forward, resting his elbows on his knees, looking at the pegasus foal. It regarded him with something Myrtle thought looked like mild distaste.

Clearly, pegasi have no taste in men, she thought, her eyes roving over his body before she could stop them. Her stomach turned over, her insides feeling like they'd turned to Jell-O.

Hot fucking damn, but he was attractive. She'd never really thought she was susceptible to male beauty, but clearly, she hadn't known what she was talking about.

And then there was the fact that he was just so... *manly.* He was tall and broad and muscled, of course, with a chiseled jaw covered with a light dusting of stubble, but that wasn't it. It was something about the way he carried himself, the confidence in the way he stood. He'd handled the car – *in the pitch dark!* – with skill and competence.

And the way he was sitting now – loose-limbed but with an undeniable power just behind the apparent casualness – was making her mouth water.

Okay, stop! Myrtle shook her head. *You want answers! Not his hot, hot body!*

Though, she was forced to admit, *I probably wouldn't say no to his hot, hot body as an add-on to some answers...*

Focus goddamnit!

"You said the egg was a fake." Myrtle realized if she didn't start talking now, she was liable to start drooling. And that wouldn't do any of them any good. "Did you expect it to hatch at all?"

Hector shook his head. "No. To be honest, I'm as surprised as you are. I didn't sense anyth– well, I mean, when I looked at it, it seemed like it wasn't real."

Myrtle's eyes narrowed as she noticed his slip. *He didn't sense anything? What does that mean?*

"You probably get now why that egg is so valuable, and why I'm concerned that those bikies – and whoever was going to buy it from them – might be interested in getting it back," Hector continued. "Since it *is* real, then what you're holding there is the last living pegasus in the world, as far as anyone knows."

The pegasus shuffled on her lap, spreading and then folding its wings. It let out a small squeak.

"Then… who laid the egg?" Myrtle asked. "There has to be at least *one* other one left."

Hector shook his head. "It's possible. But not very likely. Pegasus eggs can lie dormant for decades – maybe centuries – before they hatch. It might be that this little fella was hidden in a cave for who knows how long before he was discovered. His mum and dad are probably long gone."

An orphan.

Myrtle looked down at the creature. Sadness welled up inside her.

The poor thing is all alone.

"Does anyone know how to look after a pegasus bab– uh, foal?"

"A little. I brought what I needed here just in case the egg *did* turn out to be real." He gestured to the nest. "But since no one's seen a real pegasus in centuries, it was all based on guesswork. And we don't have his mum here to feed him. There's old stories of horses raising pegasi, but they're very different animals."

"Well, yeah," Myrtle said, glancing at the broken pieces of egg under the heat lamp. "What do pegasi eat? I mean, I'm guessing we don't have any pegasus milk on hand."

Hector stood, the movement fluid and easy.

"No problem there – not in the sense that we have any pegasus milk, but in the sense that we probably don't need it."

He leaned over, opening a minifridge sitting on the floor beneath a shelf and getting out a series of small bottles.

"That's baby food," Myrtle said, confused. "*Human* baby food."

She should've been able to recognize it by now – after all, her older sisters between them had an army of babies she'd helped feed at one point or another. There'd been a time when she thought if she'd smelled pureed yams one more time, she'd throw up.

"Yep." Hector laid out the bottles on the table, taking the lids off one by one. In her lap, the pegasus stirred, its nostrils flaring as it clearly scented something that interested it. "All the records we have say that pegasi can drink horse milk, but they can handle mashed-up fruit and veg as well. Their mums used to crush apples for them to feed on."

"*Meee-ehhh!*"

The pegasus whinnied insistently, standing up on Myrtle's lap.

"You want some?" Myrtle asked it dubiously.

It looked up at her, its tiny front hooves pawing a little at her thigh.

Carefully, Myrtle lifted the pegasus from her lap, placing it on the table. Its hooves made tiny *tap tap tap* sounds as it made its way over to the bottles of food, much more steady on its legs now than it had been before.

"We got you a variety," Hector said, gesturing at the food, his eyes intent on the foal. "What'll you have?"

The pegasus hesitated, moving its head to look at him, before looking at the food once more.

"Go on," Myrtle coaxed it, her voice soft.

Her words seemed to overcome whatever misgivings the pegasus might have, and it trotted forward, going to the first bottle.

"Oh, sweet potato and peas. Not my first choice, but you may like it," Hector said.

Evidently, the pegasus did not, as it took a moment to delicately sniff at the food, before shaking its head and prancing backward.

Next up was carrots, which got much the same reaction, to Myrtle's slight surprise. Weren't horses supposed to like carrots?

Avocado too was rejected. And mixed berries.

Myrtle was just about to ask Hector if he'd heard any other legends about pegasi, when the foal came to the last bottle in the line: pureed apple.

The tiny creature gave it a skeptical sniff, nose wrinkling, before it paused for a moment – and then stuck its whole nose into the open bottle, snuffling up the puree with a ridiculous snorting sound.

"Looks like we have a winner," Hector said, sitting back. "Just as well. I was just about to get out the Vegemite."

"I guess that'd be a way to get it to eat literally anything else," Myrtle muttered.

To her surprise, Hector burst out laughing. "That's all right – more for me."

She felt a small smile tugging at her own lips. She couldn't help it – Hector's relief that the pegasus was finally eating was obvious, and his laugh was so genuine and unguarded. She'd been so intent on watching the pegasus, worried that it would reject all the food Hector had brought for it, that she hadn't noticed how tense he'd been.

But then, she supposed having charge of the last living specimen of a creature everyone had thought was extinct – or, as she'd thought until about twenty minutes ago, never extant in the first place – *was* pretty stressful.

She felt her heart speed up a little, thumping against her ribs.

"I *really* hope you've got something else to eat around here aside from Vegemite," she said, shuddering at the horrible memory of the one and only time she'd tried to eat it. It had been like swallowing a sack of salt stirred into a vat of sump oil to form some kind of horrible goo. "That's got to be against some kind of Geneva Convention, surely?"

Hector laughed again. "You keep insulting my national dish like this and it's gonna be pistols at dawn."

"Bring it on."

Hector glanced at her, his dark eyes seeming golden in the glow of the heat lamp. "Sure you can handle it?"

Myrtle swallowed.

Is he... flirting?

Surely not.

Myrtle had always been terrible at telling when people were interested in her. It so rarely happened, and the couple of boyfriends she'd had, she'd been set up with by matchmaking friends.

And neither of those ended well, she thought gloomily.

Unsure how to respond, she looked back down at the pegasus, biting her lip. There was an awkward silence, broken only by the sound of the foal snuffling up its food, its head getting deeper into the bottle the more it ate.

Hector cleared his throat.

"Well, at least he really likes apples."

"I guess I should have known," Myrtle impulsively blurted out, still feeling awkward. "I played enough Shadowrun in high school."

Hector shot her a mildly confused look. "Shadowrun?"

"It's, uh, a tabletop game. Like DnD." Myrtle felt herself flush. *For God's sake, he doesn't want to hear about your nerdy past.*

She swallowed.

Although what would you tell him about instead? Your nerdy present?

Myrtle had felt even more overlooked in high school than she had during college. All her sisters had been popular and beautiful, with boys trailing after them waiting to do their bidding. Poppy and Bryony had been homecoming queens and had later modeled, and Lily had been a track and field star. Her brother Thorn was at this moment attending college on a football scholarship.

Myrtle had distinguished herself with her academic record, but her school had been more focused on its athletics program. Looking at Hector now, Myrtle couldn't imagine him as anything other than a gym class hero – effortlessly athletic, devastatingly good-looking, the star quarterback... did Australia have quarterbacks?

"Anyway, it doesn't matter," she said quickly. "It was just... you know, a game I used to play. But the pegasus in the game ate apples."

"Seems like whoever came up with the game knew what they were talking about," Hector said, as the baby continued to eat. "Do you think we should stop him at some point?"

"Um. Probably," Myrtle said.

God, who knows? Myrtle felt totally at sea. But then, what else was she *supposed* to feel? She was taking care of a baby pegasus! And with the hottest guy she'd ever seen!

"And should we give him a name? We can't just keep calling him 'him,'" Hector said.

Myrtle hesitated. She knew the dangers of getting too attached.

But this is different, she thought. *This isn't a lab animal, or a specimen I'm helping tag and release. She's the only one of her kind left in the world, and right now, we're the only ones she has to take care of her. She needs a name.*

Myrtle shook her head. *She?*

Hector had been calling the foal a *he*, but somehow, Myrtle knew that wasn't right. She ducked her head as the pegasus switched its tail happily, taking a quick look.

Yep, definitely a girl. And you're too pretty to be a boy, anyway.

The little pegasus lifted its head to look over its shoulder at her and whinnied, as if to convey its approval. At the same time, a warm feeling washed over her. It was a comforting feeling, affectionate and sweet.

She blinked. *Did that come from the pegasus?*

"Maybe we should," she said. "Give her a name, I mean. Something mystical, like Eurydice or Odine."

"Too fancy for me," Hector said, shaking his head. "What about Bruce?"

Myrtle shook her head. "I'm pretty sure she's a girl."

Hector cocked his head, but didn't argue. "Girl Bruce, then."

"Ruby," Myrtle said firmly. "That's got some of the same letters in it. It's my final offer."

"All right, Ruby it is."

They sat in silence together, watching as the tiny pegasus – Ruby – lifted her head from the bottle for what seemed like the final time, her pink tongue darting out over her pure white muzzle, which was absolutely covered in apple puree.

"Oh boy, looks like you really made a mess of yourself there, Rubes," Hector said, laughing lightly. "Need a hand?"

Ruby – Myrtle refused to think of her as *Rubes* – shook her head, snorting delicately and sending tiny spatters of mushy apple across the tabletop.

Hector stood up, crossing the room to the tiny kitchenette tucked away to the side, so small Myrtle hadn't noticed it until he'd gotten the baby food from the minifridge. He tore off a square of paper towel and ran it quickly under the faucet.

"Come here," he said gently, reaching out with the damp towel. "Come on Rubes, that's it…"

Ruby pranced backward, shaking her head, her hooves tapping lightly on the tabletop.

"*Meee-ehh!*"

"I don't think she likes that," Myrtle said, as Ruby tossed her head, evading the towel once again.

"She'll like having crusty old apple puree stuck to her face even less," Hector said, as he gently tried to approach her for a third try. "C'mon – this is for your own good –"

But Ruby wasn't having it. She sidled away, snorting indignantly.

"Here, let me help," Myrtle said, laughing. She reached forward, corralling Ruby with her hands, not giving her anywhere to go when she tried to prance away from the towel again.

The tiny animal shot her a look with her big, luminous eyes as if to say *traitor!* and tried to go around her. Seeing she was blocked in, Ruby fluttered her wings and began to clumsily take off, but Myrtle was too quick.

"Nuh-uh, no you don't!" She scooped Ruby up gently, holding her so her legs stuck out through the gaps between her fingers, her hooves just off the table's surface.

"*Meee-eeh!*"

"It's like he said, it's for your own good," Myrtle said soothingly as Hector finally managed to wipe off some of the puree. "C'mon, Ruby, just relax…"

And to her surprise, Ruby did.

She became calm in Myrtle's hands, stilling her legs and folding her wings back by her sides. She didn't even try to move her head away when Hector ran the towel gently over her muzzle, wiping away the last of the puree.

"That's it, Rubes," Hector said softly. "There. Nice and clean. You're fit to be seen again."

Ruby blinked at him, her eyes dark and liquid.

"I think she likes you," Hector said. "I wasn't having any luck until you talked her into it."

"Maybe." Myrtle looked down at Ruby, who was now regarding them both seriously. "You don't think she... well, that she imprinted on me?"

She felt silly asking, but of course everyone knew about ducklings hatching and attaching themselves to the first thing they saw.

Hector shook his head. "I suppose we don't know. Obviously the first thing any baby should see, ideally, is its mother or father. But since we don't know if this little one even *has* a mother or father anymore..."

Hector trailed off.

Sadness welled up inside Myrtle. *She might really be all alone.*

As soon as the thought occurred to her, she felt a strange, sweeping feeling of comfort wash over her. It was as if someone had just run a warm hand over her forehead, soothing away all her doubts, all her fears...

It was only then that she noticed just how close she and Hector were standing to each other.

In the struggle to get Ruby clean, they'd unconsciously leaned into one another, their heads bent toward each other, their shoulders nearly touching.

Oh. Um.

Myrtle felt a new kind of warmth within her – one that started in her belly and curled slowly downward.

Hector's breath was warm against her cheek. He was standing so close to her that she could make out the individual flecks of gold in his deep brown eyes, the flicker of his dark eyelashes when he blinked.

All I'd need to do to kiss him is just move my head a little...

She heard Hector swallow, the sound loud in her ears. His eyes flicked down, settling on her lips.

The air between them crackled, and Myrtle felt her stomach turn over.

I –

The sound of a tiny snore jerked them both out of whatever trance they'd drifted into.

As one, they turned their heads to look down at Ruby, who had fallen asleep in Myrtle's hands, her tiny head resting against her palm, wings folded against her sides.

"Oh," Myrtle said, feeling almost as if she was waking from a dream – an *extremely* vivid dream. But she'd woken up before she'd got to the best part!

She shook her head, trying to clear it.

Did that really happen just now?

She glanced at Hector from beneath her eyelashes. He looked mildly stunned, blinking as if he too was just waking up. Though in this case, he looked like he was just waking up from a twelve-hour nap and wasn't too sure what day it was. Or maybe even what *year* it was.

"Uh, I guess we better get this one to bed," Myrtle said, her words coming out in a rush to fill the awkward silence between them. "She wore herself out eating, clearly."

"She sure did."

Myrtle laughed shakily in response. Carefully raising her arms so as not to jostle her, she carried Ruby across the room to the feathery nest beneath the heat lamp. Hector was already turning the temperature down a bit, the light dimming.

With infinite care, Myrtle placed Ruby down in the nest.

She barely stirred except to make another small snorting noise, kicking her feet a little in her sleep.

"I wonder what she's dreaming about," Myrtle said, looking down at her. Affection swelled up within her. She'd only known Ruby for a short time, but she was already more attached to her than she wanted to admit.

Apprehension suddenly filled her. As the last remaining pegasus on the planet, what would happen to Ruby now? Would she go to a lab to be studied? Would she always have to be under protection, never safe from people like the ones who'd tried to buy her egg, just so they could have boasting rights of owning the one and only remaining pegasus?

"What will happen to her now?" she asked Hector, looking up at him. "You must have had plans for what would happen to her if the egg turned out to be real after all."

Hector glanced at her. He still looked mildly dazed, and Myrtle's heartbeat sped up a little.

Maybe it wasn't a dream after all. Maybe he was on the verge of kissing me before...

"I'll be honest, Myrtle: I don't know," Hector said. "Before, when I said I was a cop... that was only half the truth. I *am* in law enforcement. But what I do... well, it's more complicated than that. And it'll take a lot of explaining."

"Well, obviously," Myrtle said, sweeping her arm out to gesture at the range of high-tech equipment that filled the room. "Either you're no regular cop, or things are pretty different around here. No cop I've ever heard of sits around in the middle of the desert monitoring... well, just what *are* you monitoring here anyway?"

"Like I said, it'd take a lot of explaining," Hector said. "But I *can* say that no one will be taking Ruby away or... dissecting her, if that's what you're worried about."

Shock coursed through Myrtle. "Was that a risk?!"

"No! No. Not at all." Hector hesitated. "It's complicated."

Myrtle rolled her eyes, aware she was being impatient, but not able to care right now.

"You keep saying that! Look – I'm a scientist. I'm *used* to hearing difficult things. And part of my study involves endangered animals, so I'm used to hearing bad news. Just *tell me*."

"All right, all right," Hector said. "No more giving you the runaround. The truth is, Myrtle, that –"

He broke off suddenly, twisting around to face the door. At the exact same moment, Ruby woke from her slumber, her head shooting up, eyes wide. A tiny, anxious whinny escaped her.

"Hector?" Myrtle asked, her breath catching in her throat. "What is it?"

Hector didn't answer her. She stared up at him. He had an expression of fierce concentration on his face, like an animal scenting the wind. She could see all the coiled, latent power in his limbs come to life.

And for a moment, she could have *sworn* she saw his eyes flash gold.

What – what the –

"Myrtle," he said, his voice low and urgent, "get down."

CHAPTER 5

He could sense it as Myrtle's breathing sped up, her heart beating wildly.

"Hector? What is it?"

"Just go into the other room and get down," he repeated, before, leaning over, he carefully scooped Ruby up in the palm of his hand, passing her to Myrtle. The foal didn't struggle, though for a moment, he thought he could feel a sense of *confusion* and *fear* bubbling up against his mind. "And make sure Ruby's safe. Hold her and don't let her go. And don't come outside until I give you the all clear."

Myrtle opened her mouth, looking for a moment like she might argue. But then she simply closed it again, nodding.

"Okay. I won't."

He watched as she bustled across the room, holding Ruby to her chest. He'd been on the verge of telling Myrtle everything – that aside from being a pegasus, Ruby had a human form that she'd be able to take on when she got a little older. The same way that he had an animal form he could take on when he needed to, along with an annoying griffin living inside his head that occasionally gave him irritating and only partially correct life advice.

One thing it was rarely wrong about, though, was when it sensed danger. And all the griffin's senses were bristling now, warning him that *something* was coming.

God, I hope I'm wrong.

But deep in his heart, he knew he wasn't.

Shit. Shit shit shit. Fuck. Shit.

Sparing a backward glance at the door Myrtle had disappeared through, Hector vaulted easily over the table and then strode over to the steel door leading outside.

We must protect our mate and the cub, his griffin screeched, rearing up inside his head, sending a burst of fury through him so strong that for a moment, all Hector could see was a mist of red.

Of course I'll protect them, he shot back as he went out into the night. *Forever. With my life, if I have to.*

He hoped it wouldn't come to that – after all, he didn't even know what kind of danger he was facing yet, only that it was *there.*

It didn't take him long, however, to figure out exactly what his griffin had sensed. The roar of motorbike engines sounded from somewhere distant, cutting through the silence of the night.

So they did track us after all, Hector thought grimly. He supposed he shouldn't be surprised. It would have been difficult, but a real pegasus egg was obviously worth the effort.

Fucking shit.

Hector cursed himself. He'd been too distracted by Myrtle's beauty, Myrtle's scent, Myrtle's *everything* to think straight. And until it'd hatched, he'd really thought the egg was a fake.

I still don't understand how I missed that, Hector thought. He *should* have been able to sense the tiny pegasus inside the egg.

And he didn't exactly understand why it'd chosen *now* of all times to hatch…

… But that wasn't important right now. Myrtle might not know yet that she was his mate, but it didn't matter. The only thing that mattered was her safety. As long as he was alive, he wouldn't let anyone touch a hair on her head.

Or Ruby's either, Hector thought as he turned his head, getting a bearing on the approaching motorbikes. He knew it wasn't smart, but he'd let the cute little gal get to him. And as of now, she didn't have anyone else in the world but him and Myrtle.

I really need to apologize to her, Hector thought as he began running. *To them both.*

Myrtle had saved Ruby. She'd protected her even though she'd been risking her own life to do it. She'd known what Hector had missed: that there was something living inside that egg, and it had needed her help.

A fierce warmth welled up inside Hector's heart.

Our mate is strong, brave, and smart, his griffin said. *And you have not yet proved yourself worthy of her.*

But I will, he promised it. *If I get out of this, I will.*

The regret that he hadn't just kissed her back in the ops room simmered in his belly. He had wanted to – *fuck,* he'd wanted to, more than he'd ever wanted anything before in his life – and she'd wanted him too as well. He thought she had, anyway. Maybe, despite her misgivings and his shitty behavior, she could feel their connection too.

No more secrets after this, Hector promised her in his mind. *No more hesitation. I'll tell you the whole truth – and then we can finish what we* almost *started.*

The roar of motorbike engines became louder, and headlights blared out of the darkness as the bikies crested a rise, their bikes tearing up the dirt road.

Hector wasn't as far from the shipping containers as he

would have liked, but at this stage there wasn't a lot he could do about it. It would have to be here.

I'll stop them. Right here. They won't get any closer to either Myrtle or Ruby.

Inside him, his griffin glowered, flexing its talons, its lion's tail flicking back and forth. He could feel that it was just *itching* for a fight.

And maybe these bikies would oblige it.

Hector lifted his arms, and bellowed.

"HEY! HEY, DICKHEADS! *HEY!*"

He supposed there was a risk they might just drive on past him – but in that case he'd simply shift and swoop down on them from above. There would be no time for niceties or not blowing his cover if there was even a chance any of them could get close to his mate.

And if they'd been trying to sell a pegasus egg in the apparently full knowledge of what it was, then they must have already known about shifters, anyway.

The leader of the gang jabbed a finger in Hector's direction, bringing his absolute monster of a bike 'round to face him.

Hector counted four of them. Far from the whole gang, then, but who knew where the others were? This was probably just a scouting party, sent out into the desert to search.

It might have been pure chance then that they came in this direction, Hector realized.

But maybe not, his griffin reminded him. *Were you really going to leave it to chance that they'd drive on by?*

Might've been wiser to wait, Hector told it as the bikies slowed, circling him, filling the air with red dust and the sound of roaring engines. *That's your problem. You never wait.*

His griffin didn't respond, but he could tell by the flick of its tail that it was caught somewhere between irritation and apology. Though the balance was tipped *way* in favor of irritation.

"Well, lookie here," the first bikie said as he cut the engine to his motorcycle, the headlights still on. He planted his feet on the ground and leaned back in the saddle, crossing his arms over his gut. "Reckon you've just made our lives a whole lot easier. Saved us the trouble of being out half the night lookin' for yer skinny arse and dragging it back with us."

Skinny?!

Hector's griffin was outraged.

He ignored it, focusing on the bikies. He could only see the two that were parked right in front of him, but nonetheless, he could sense the exact location of the two behind him as well. If either of them moved, he'd know it.

"You reckon, do you?" he asked, clenching his fists and staring the leader of the pack directly in the eyes. The man – his face a patchwork of white beard and red blood vessels – didn't flinch.

"We can do this one of two ways. We can drag you back kicking and screaming – or we can just drag you." He shrugged, as if it was all the same to him, which it probably was. "Your choice, mate."

"Boss said it was a chick who took off with the egg." One of the bikies behind Hector spoke up next.

The man in front of him smirked, cocking an eyebrow. "This guy's pretty enough to be a chick," he said. "Sure he didn't make a mistake?"

Hector rolled his eyes. "If you're asking me out, this is really not the right way to go about it."

The bikie chuckled, learning forward and resting his forearms on the handlebars of his bike.

"You're funny. But Terry's got a good point there. Where's

your little girlfriend? Was this whole thing a setup from the start? Pretty stupid plan, if you ask me. What, just a smash and grab? Did'ya think we'd just shrug our shoulders and write it off?"

They still think Myrtle's the buyer, Hector realized. *That she always intended to skip out with the egg.*

"Worth a try," he said, shaking his head. Anything he could do to misdirect them was good. He had to keep his cover intact as far as possible. Let the bikies think he was just a particularly stupid scammer who'd messed with the wrong scumbags.

"Worth what? You ending up in bits and pieces from here to Coolangatta?" The bikie laughed. "Not likely."

"We need to get back, Baz." Terry the bikie spoke up again, sounding nervous. "We found him, so let's just grab him and go back."

The lead bikie – Baz – shook his head. "Nah. Not yet. While we're dragging this guy back, his little lady's off and running. We're not going back without both of them. *And* the egg."

Hector shrugged. "You won't find her. And the egg... well, sorry to say it met with an accident. It broke. Those things are more delicate than they look."

Not even a lie, he thought. The egg really *had* gotten broken into about a hundred pieces when Ruby had burst out of it.

Baz the bikie went dangerously still. "I'm gonna hope for your sake – and for the sake of your girl – that that's a joke."

"We don't have time for this shit," Terry broke in again.

Baz nodded. "You must think I'm a fucking idiot if you think I'm gonna go for that 'whoops we dropped it!' bullshit. You're just buying time for your girlie to escape." He pointed a finger at Terry and one of the other bikies. "You two – get going. Find the girl." He paused, reaching over his shoulder. When he lowered his arm again, he was holding a sawn-off shotgun, which he leveled at Hector's chest. "We'll deal with this bullshit artist."

Hector tensed, clenching his fists. His griffin lowered its head, hackles rising. *Here we go.*

There was no way he was letting Terry and his offsider get anywhere near Myrtle and Ruby.

As a shifter, he could move faster than any ordinary human – and as a griffin, he could move faster than any ordinary human could *see.*

Ducking his head, he swung around to Baz's left, out of the line of fire of the shotgun, and out of the middle of the ring of bikes.

"What the –"

He heard the surprised shout, but he didn't stop. He came up right behind Baz, smashing his elbow into the side of his neck. It was a move that would incapacitate, not kill – he wouldn't be able to justify killing, not against a regular human. Even if Baz *had* shot him, his shifter healing meant it was unlikely to inflict a fatal wound.

And by the time Baz and his little friends here came to, Hector was planning to have Myrtle and Ruby well on their way to somewhere safe.

Baz's massive body jerked, muscles going slack as he lost consciousness, shotgun sliding from his fingers. He toppled over like a fleshy landslide, taking his monster of a bike with him.

"Fuck!"

The other bikies, thrown into confusion, were twisting around in their seats, or reaching for their own weapons. Terry jumped off his bike, snatching Baz's dropped shotgun and swinging it around, trying to track Hector's movement.

No chance.

Hector moved again as the shotgun blast went off, spraying shot over the area where he'd just been.

Hector was on him a moment later, taking him out with the same move he'd used on Baz. A quick elbow to the neck and Terry's eyes were rolling upward, before he slumped over into the dirt.

"Fuck this shit – let's get the girl and go."

"No fuckin' way – I'm going back to town. Forget this shit."

The two remaining men – sensible lads, it seemed – had realized this wasn't a fight they were going to win. They kicked their bikes to life.

True to his word, one tore off the way they'd come, throwing up a massive cloud of dust as he went. The other pulled his bike around, heading into the desert. Right toward where Myrtle and Ruby would be hiding.

Ah, shit.

Hector had to make a split-second decision. If he let the bikie heading back to Good Fortune get away, they were sure to be back in numbers.

Forget him! his griffin screeched. *Protect your mate! If there's even a chance she could get hurt, it's not a chance you can take!*

In the end, it wasn't even a choice.

Hector dashed forward, after the bike that was even now disappearing into the night toward the shipping containers, leaving a trail of dust in its wake. His inhuman speed was only meant for short bursts, however. He couldn't keep it up over long distances, and he couldn't outrun a motorbike gunning its way across the desert at full speed.

No choice, then.

He called to his griffin, allowing it to burst into the forefront of his consciousness.

It screeched as it came forward, taking over his mind, its animal instincts – the howling in its blood to protect its mate at all costs, to kill anyone who might so much as threaten her – drowning out human reason. He felt his wings spread out from his back, lifting him into the air with two powerful sweeps.

He'd done this enough times since he was a teenager for him to control the shift – the change from human into the half-lion, half-eagle hybrid that was his griffin form.

Controlling it came hard, the first few times. The griffin was a powerful creature, and it would take over his mind if he let it. Shifters who couldn't control their animal sides and bring them into harmony with their human selves could sometimes find themselves stuck in their shifted forms, their minds taken over entirely by the instincts of the beast within them. Without hard work and training, shifters could easily lose either one side of themselves or the other.

And when the creature that lived inside you was as powerful as a *griffin*... well, that took an extra layer of control.

Even now, Hector found himself struggling to assert himself. With his mate's life on the line, the griffin's instincts were in overdrive, screeching for blood. Power and strength coursed through him, and he reined it in only with difficulty.

No killing! he told his griffin as they surged through the night air, the bikie below them, his headlights clearly visible in the darkness. *Are you listening to me?!*

His griffin only growled in response, but Hector was *pretty* sure it got the message. He'd never had a problem with it losing its shit and killing anyone before, and even in life-or-death situations he'd managed to incapacitate rather than kill when in his griffin form.

But those were times when his mate hadn't been involved. Could he be sure he could hold the griffin back if Myrtle were seriously threatened?

He didn't know. The fury seething through the griffin

now was like nothing he'd ever felt from it before. It was taking all his strength just to hold it back even *this* much. He'd built a sturdy relationship with his griffin through the years, to the point where its occasional lecturing more amused him than irritated him. But in this situation, he knew he needed to keep it tightly under control.

He is there. The one who threatens our mate. He must bleed!

Hector concentrated all his efforts into controlling the griffin's wild fury as they folded their wings, swooping into a dive.

Bleed, maybe. Die, no, he told it again as they sped downward, talons extended out in front of them. *No matter how much he may deserve it.*

He couldn't be sure that the griffin was listening to him at all, but Hector still had at least some control over his body, and he forced the griffin to snatch away its claws a second before they embedded themselves in the man's flesh.

Instead, he sped up at the last moment, swooping down to land heavily a few meters in front of the man, rearing back on his lion's hind legs, spreading his wings wide and opening his beak in a mighty screech of rage.

He could see the look of terror on the man's face, illuminated by his own headlights, as he hit the brakes, coming to a screeching halt and tumbling over in the dirt, the engine of his bike stuttering and then stalling completely.

"Shit! Shit! *Shit!*"

The man's scream cut through the night as he scrabbled in the dust, trying to disentangle himself from his bike. He tried to get the bike upright to speed away, but after a couple of failed attempts he left it where it was, and ran, still screaming, into the night.

We should go after him, the griffin told him as he reared up again, screeching at the man's departing back. *Show him what happens when he tries to harm a griffin's mate!*

I think he gets it, Hector said, pulling it back only with some effort. *Look, he's gone. And he'll have some explaining to do about how he got that wet patch on his jeans, I bet.*

He'll bring others if we let him escape, his griffin argued, growling.

It had a point there – but Hector had already let one bikie go this evening, who'd raise the alarm a lot faster than the guy who could still be distantly seen moving at a run, the sound of his screams drifting back to him on the wind.

Right now, we need to focus on getting Myrtle to safety. The bikies are a problem for the police now.

The griffin, however reluctantly, was won over by the argument that Myrtle needed to be taken to a safe place.

Hector gave the man's bike one last contemptuous look, its wheels still spinning slightly as it lay on its side on the ground, before turning around to –

– To see Myrtle standing in the doorway of the shipping container, light flooding out from the room behind her, a mid-sized kitchen knife clutched in one hand, and an utterly stricken expression on her face.

Hector almost called out her name to ask her what was wrong, when he suddenly recalled that as far as Myrtle was concerned, she was looking at some kind of terrifying, bloodthirsty monster.

Myrtle! Don't be scared!

He tried to reach out to her with his mind, but, unlike other mystical shifters, griffins had no powers of telepathy that he could call on.

The only thing that happened was that his eagle's beak let out a low, worried croon.

Our mate is frightened, his griffin insisted, trying to force his legs to move. *We must go to her!*

Myrtle gasped, tripping a little as she stumbled backwards, lifting the knife. She looked terrified.

Hector froze.

He knew he needed to explain, to show her that he'd never harm her – but in the end, there was only one thing running through his mind.

Ah, fucking hell.

CHAPTER 6

Myrtle stumbled back, her fingers wound tightly around the knife she'd found in the makeshift kitchen.

The – the *whatever it was* stood a few feet away from her, half-illuminated by the headlights of the motorcycle that lay on its side in the dirt. Aside from letting out a small, soft sound at the sight of her, it hadn't moved at all, but she guessed that it was what had made the terrifying screeching sound just a few moments earlier.

She knew Hector had told her to stay where she was, but at the sound of the screech followed by a man's screams and the roar of a motorcycle engine, she'd felt she couldn't just sit around and wait. Hector might have needed her help.

Myrtle hadn't known what exactly she'd expected to see when she'd flung open the door, but it wasn't this – this *thing*.

She could hear her heart hammering in her ears as she stared. She could only see part of it in the beam of the headlights, but that was enough to know she'd never seen *anything* like it before. No one had. She could see massive wings on the creature's back, but those were *definitely* mammalian legs. And its eyes…

No, it can't be. It looks like... like...

"Hector!"

His name was out of her mouth before she could think.

Oh God, if this monster has hurt him, I'll –

Myrtle shook her head. She couldn't allow herself to complete the thought. The idea that Hector could be out there in the darkness, hurt or – or –

"Hector, can you hear me?!"

At her shout, the creature seemed to pause, its only half-visible head cocking slightly. It let out another soft sound, almost like the comforting chirp she knew some species of birds used when calling to their mates to keep track of them.

Strangely enough, she *felt* the sound as much as she heard it – felt it washing over her like a gentle wave of warm water, soothing her frayed nerves, calming her hammering heart...

She shook herself, blinking.

You don't fool me, Myrtle thought desperately, staring at the beast.

"Hector!" she called out again.

At this, the creature seemed to take a small step back, as if hesitating. It shook its huge wings – *Just how big are they?!* – and then began to... *shrink?!*

Myrtle watched, eyes wide, as the creature seemed to fold in on itself, its massive wings retracting, head pulling back. It seemed almost to shimmer as it changed its shape, turning from something that was definitely a four-legged animal into – into –

"*Hector?!*"

Myrtle gasped out his name as she realized what – or rather *who* – she was looking at, standing there in the glow of the motorcycle's headlights.

Vaguely, she felt her fingers go slack, the knife clattering to the floor beside her.

This has to be a dream, Myrtle decided as she stared, her

legs wobbling beneath her. *A really freaky dream, brought on by jetlag. Yeah, that's gotta be it. I'll wake up tomorrow and find out this whole thing has just been one really, really bizarre dream...*

She'd miss Ruby on waking up and finding out she'd dreamed her up, Myrtle supposed. But on reflection, it made complete sense for Hector to be a figment of her imagination. Men that hot just didn't exist in real life.

Ah well. I suppose I should've known.

"Myrtle!"

She hadn't realized she'd sunk to her knees until she felt strong arms around her shoulders, pulling her against a warm, solid chest.

Mmm. This is a good *dream. I may as well enjoy it.*

She looked up into Hector's face, letting her gaze linger on his golden-brown eyes, before slowly drifting down to his lips. His breath was warm on her face, and when she lifted her hand to cup his cheek, his stubble was rough beneath her palm.

That's okay, she thought. *I like a man who looks like a man.*

"Myrtle –"

Hector's voice as he said her name was low and hoarse, and she shivered, feeling heat pool in her belly.

"Myrtle, I –"

"No talking," she whispered. She knew what she was about to say was corny as hell, but fuck it, this was *her* dream. She'd do what she liked. "Just this."

She leaned up, seeking his lips with hers. Myrtle gasped as they brushed against each other, a jolt of electricity running from him into her, setting her nerves on fire.

Mmmm, she thought, pressing closer. *Definitely a* really *good dream...*

The kiss was searing – the kind of kiss she *knew* could only exist in a movie or on the pages of a romance novel. *She'd* certainly never experienced a kiss like this before in all her life. White hot liquid fire shot through her veins, filling her with desperate heat.

She could feel Hector's own answering heat, his tongue sliding against hers, his large hands drawing her even closer against him.

Myrtle gave herself up to it. She never wanted this to end. She'd be perfectly happy if she just stayed in the bubble of this little dream world her brain had created, with this endless kiss…

"Uh, Myrtle."

Hector's voice seemed to throb with heat, but talking wasn't what Myrtle wanted from him right now. But when she leaned up again, seeking his mouth, he pulled away.

Uh, what?

Myrtle opened her eyes to find Hector looking down at her, his eyes dark with desire. But he was still very definitely out of kissing range.

Oh great, now even my dream man doesn't want me anymore.

"Myrtle, I won't… I won't pretend I wouldn't love to keep doing this, but right now, I think we need to –"

"Shit," Myrtle muttered, cutting him off. "I'm not dreaming, am I."

Hector blinked. "Uh, no. Sorry?"

Oh God. How embarrassing.

Myrtle closed her eyes, willing herself to sink into the earth.

Of course, she didn't do any such thing. But when she opened her eyes again, Hector was still staring down at her with a passionate intensity that made her toes curl, his arms still around her shoulders.

But if it's not a dream, that means he really did kiss me just now, she thought vaguely. *Though it* also *means that I just saw him shapeshift from being some kind of monster.*

Well, she supposed there had to be *some* differences

between American guys and Australian guys, but this just seemed ridiculous.

"What are you?" she blurted out, as Hector moved to help her to her feet. Hector hesitated.

"I'd love to tell you everything, Myrtle, I really would. But right now, we have to move. Those bikies'll come back, and we shouldn't be here when they do."

"You mean you didn't –" Myrtle bit her lip, halting her words. She'd been about to say *eat them*, but she realized that that might not be the most tactful thing to say just now.

I'm worrying about tact with a guy who turns into a giant winged beast, she thought as Hector urged her inside. *I must have something wrong with me.*

She shook her head.

Uh, you just kissed *a guy who turns into a giant winged beast,* she reminded herself. *Is that better or worse than worrying about hurting his feelings?*

There was too much going on right now for Myrtle to figure that out. Hector was hurriedly throwing a few things into a sports bag – clothes, a few smaller electronics, pre-packaged food, bottles from the fridge – before he hurried away into the second room.

"You'll need to grab Ruby," his voice drifted out to her a moment later. "I think she likes you more than she likes me. And we'll need her to feel safe for this."

Myrtle didn't argue with him. What could she say? Everything was happening so fast she felt like she barely had time to think. She walked over to where Ruby was sleeping beneath the heat lamp, her sides rising and falling gently with her breath, her tiny head tucked beneath one feathery wing.

"Hey little one," she whispered, reaching out to stroke a finger over Ruby's silvery mane. "Hey, it's time to get up. Not sure what's going on, but your dad says we gotta move."

Your dad.

She hadn't meant to say it. The words had just rolled naturally off her tongue.

But that, just like everything else that was going on right now, wasn't something she had time to think about.

Ruby blinked her huge, liquid eyes sleepily as she woke, lifting her head and gazing at Myrtle with something close to resentment. She yawned, treating Myrtle to a full and complete view of the inside of her mouth, before shaking her head and starting to stand up.

"Meee-eeh?"

The whinny had a definite questioning sound to it, as Myrtle carefully scooped Ruby up, tucking her under her arm, her chest resting on her palm. Ruby didn't make a fuss – she simply looked up at Myrtle, eyes full of trust.

"That's right, little one – you know me," Myrtle murmured. "We just need to get going. And then you can get some more sleep, I promise."

Hector emerged from the other room, holding a laptop.

"I just need to do one or two more things," he said. "And then we're off."

"Things?" Myrtle felt stupid, but she was pretty sure she could be excused, given the circumstances.

"One, I need to send a beacon up," Hector said. "An electronic beacon. That'll let my colleagues know that something's gone wrong, and we need picking up. And then I need to set this place to self-destruct."

Myrtle caught her breath. "You mean like… to explode?"

Hector shook his head. "Nothing so dramatic, I'm afraid. I just need to flip a kill switch that'll completely wipe the hard drives of everything here totally beyond recovery. If anyone finds this place, all they'll find is a bunch of bricked computers."

"Oh. Okay." Somehow, Myrtle felt disappointed. It would

just top off the already *ridiculous* evening she'd had if, along with everything else, she were to stride off across the landscape, a tiny baby pegasus tucked under her arm and a stupidly good-looking man who just *happened* to turn into a giant winged monster by her side, while a giant fiery explosion went off behind her. As if things weren't already *Mad Max* enough around here.

To be honest, however, Myrtle wasn't sure she was cool enough to pull it off. She'd probably trip over a rock or something. So a boring kill switch was probably for the best.

She watched as Hector zipped up the sports bag, all his movements quick and efficient.

"You don't have any clothes other than what you're wearing, do you?" he asked.

"No," Myrtle said, shaking her head. All her clothes were back in the hotel in Good Fortune. Along with all her notebooks, data collecting equipment, her laptop, everything she needed to do her work…

The only things she had were her cell phone, a notepad, and a bottle of water.

But somehow, she didn't think she was going to get much work done out here after all.

"No worries – you can borrow some of mine," Hector said. "Gets colder than you'd think out here at night, especially up high."

Up high?

Myrtle opened her mouth to ask, before closing it again.

Do I really want to know?

She supposed she probably did, but just… not right now. She was still processing. Wasn't that what it was called when you felt like you needed to lie down for about a decade to think about everything you'd just seen in the past five minutes? Processing?

"Myrtle? Myrtle, are you okay?"

Myrtle shook her head, realizing she'd been staring blankly into space. Ruby shifted herself on her arm, making a low, comforting sound, and Hector stood in front of her, his hands resting lightly on her shoulders.

"Myrtle?"

She blinked.

"Hector," she finally said after a moment or two, "what the hell is going on?"

Hector hesitated. "Myrtle, I *promise* you, I'll explain everything. But right now, I'm just going to have to ask you to trust me."

Swallowing, Myrtle looked up into his eyes.

I trust you.

She wasn't sure why she did, considering everything she'd seen in the past few minutes.

"I know what you saw, Myrtle, and I know how frightening it must have been," Hector continued. "But I swear to you, I'd never hurt you. Never."

His words echoed through her, beating within her like her heart. Somehow, she knew they were the truth – the complete and total truth.

Myrtle wasn't used to relying on her emotions. Emotions had never gotten her anywhere. Every time she'd opened herself up to them, she'd only ended up getting hurt. She was a scientist. She trusted what she could hold in her hands, what she could see and touch and measure.

But now...

"Okay," she said at last. "Okay. I trust you."

But first, there was one thing she needed to clarify.

"You turned into – into a –"

"Into a griffin, yes," Hector said. "It's… a long story. And I'm going to tell you it. But right now, let's go."

Myrtle let Hector take her hand and lead her outside. His

palm was warm against hers, and her skin tingled at the contact. Myrtle shivered.

Once they were outside again, Hector busied himself with the laptop, resting it on the inside of his left forearm while he rapidly typed with his right hand.

"Okay, that's that done. Self-destruct initiated. There won't be anything left for anyone to find now, if they happen to stumble on this place. Clean up team'll be here in a day or so to remove any last trace that this was ever here to begin with."

Despite what he'd told her earlier, Myrtle still found herself waiting for something dramatic to happen, though of course, nothing did.

"And I've sent the beacon," Hector explained as he snapped the laptop shut and then slipped it into the sports bag. "Someone'll come to pick us up from the shelter ASA-F-P."

Myrtle supposed she didn't need to ask what the 'F' stood for.

"We'll be safe there," Hector explained. "It's only accessible by air."

Myrtle frowned. "But if it's only accessible by air, how are we going to –"

She cut herself off as she realized she already knew the answer to her own question.

Oh my God. No. Really?!

Hector must have realized it too, because he took a deep breath, and held out his hand.

"You *do* trust me, right?"

Myrtle's subconscious must still have been ahead of her waking mind, because she had already nodded before she knew what she was doing, and the words *Of course I do* were on the tip of her tongue.

By her side, Ruby whinnied softly as if to back her up, squirming a little. A feeling of impatience suddenly shot though her, and Myrtle glanced down at Ruby, confused, and found her looking up at her as if asking *Well, what are you waiting for?*

Did that come from her?

"Here." Hector reached into the sports bag, pulling out a huge sweater that could only have been one of his. "Put this on. You'll get cold otherwise."

She passed him Ruby to hold as she took the sweater from him, slipping it over her head. She had to roll the sleeves up over her wrists and the waist dropped down past her hips, but it was warm and comfortable.

And it smells like him, Myrtle thought, shivering.

Which was a strange thought to have, considering that if she'd been asked, she wasn't sure she could have described how Hector smelled. But the lingering scent of him on his sweater was warm and familiar somehow, like a scent she knew well, rather than something she couldn't possibly have smelled until a few hours ago.

Like comfort, Myrtle thought, as she closed her eyes, breathing it in. *Like home.*

"Here – tuck Rubes in here," Hector said, his voice soft. "Make sure she stays put. I don't think she's that good at flying yet."

Myrtle nodded. She took Ruby back from him, tucking her up under her sweater.

"*Meeh!*" Ruby wiggled around, shifting against her, until she popped her head up out of the neck. She shook her head, mane flicking against Myrtle's throat.

"Hey, that tickles!" Myrtle said. "You better behave yourself in there."

"Me-eeh."

Myrtle took a deep breath and looked up at Hector.

"All right," she said. "All right. How're we doing this?"

"Like this."

Hector took a few steps away from her, and then, his eyes on hers, he began to – *change*.

It didn't seem like anything at first. Just a shimmer running over his body, like a small wave on the surface of the ocean. But then, he broadened out, massive, feathery wings sprouting from his back, and his body…

Myrtle shook her head. Looking at her now wasn't a man. It was –

A griffin.

Just like he'd said. Myrtle didn't know much about mythological creatures, but she knew a griffin when she saw one.

Or she did now that her brain wasn't frozen in fear, anyway.

She swallowed.

"Hector?"

The griffin crooned, preening a little, lifting its massive eagle's head and spreading its wings as if showing itself off. Its lion's tail swished, muscles rippling over its shoulders and hindquarters as it posed.

The message was clear: *Like what you see?*

Myrtle felt a small smile pulling at the corners of her lips. "Very impressive," she said. "But I think your human form might suit me a little –"

She cut herself off as the sound of motorcycle engines roaring drifted to them from the distance.

They're back. Oh, shit.

Myrtle turned back to Hector, who'd clearly heard them too.

He made a low, urgent sound, gesturing with his head.

"So," Myrtle said as she hurried over to him, "just to make sure I'm not *completely* misreading the situation, you want me to ride you, right?"

He made another low sound that, to her ears at least, was a definite *Yes! Now hurry up and climb aboard!*

Hector lowered his head and scooped up the straps of the sports bag in his beak. He made another urgent sound, the bag dangling.

"Just so you know," she informed him, "that looks really silly."

She reached out, touching his side.

How do I – um –

She'd never so much as ridden a *horse* before. This was going to be a steep learning curve.

Hector crouched slightly, lowering his shoulder. He made an encouraging noise, slightly muffled by the bag.

Myrtle gritted her teeth.

Clutching Ruby with one hand, she took a handful of feathers on Hector's shoulders and hauled herself up onto his back, sitting just in front of his wings. She clutched his neck between her thighs, leaning forward over him, and tried not to close her eyes.

"Okay. Okay, I'm –"

She didn't get to finish the sentence before she heard an almighty *whoosh!* as Hector beat his wings. Myrtle gasped at the feeling of his powerful body lifting up into the air, coiled muscles springing to life, and carrying them up, up, *up* –

Myrtle didn't even have time to be frightened. If anything, she felt the opposite. A mad kind of elation spun through her, and she had to fight down the urge to laugh.

The air whipped past her face, and adrenaline surged in her veins. She couldn't *quite* bring herself to look down, but she didn't need to. She knew where she was.

High in the sky over the Australian outback, riding on a griffin's back with a baby pegasus tucked into my sweater.

The last half an hour or so had been a rollercoaster ride of emotions, and Myrtle knew that at some point all of this was going to catch up with her. She was coasting on adrenaline now, but when it wore off she knew she was in for one hell of a come down. But right now, she supposed she didn't really have any choice but to sit back and enjoy the ride.

And later, Hector, she thought, as she snuggled her chin into his sweater, pressed her cheek against his feathers, and took a deep, *deep* breath, *you're going to have some explaining to do.*

CHAPTER 7

AS MUCH AS SHE WANTED TO SIMPLY SIT BACK AND ENJOY THE ride, Myrtle knew her brain wouldn't let her relax for long.

It was in her nature to analyze things, categorize them and classify them – it was part of what had made science her favorite subject at school, and why she'd eventually chosen it as a career. It had combined everything she loved in one: her need to sort things through and look into *why* they were the way they were, and her appreciation of the beauty of nature and desire to protect it. And how could humanity protect what it didn't understand? That was the whole reason she'd come here in the first place: to understand *why* moth numbers were dropping, and what could be done to protect them, and to protect the animals that relied on them for food.

Myrtle had always thought that humanity had made great strides in the past fifty years in terms of understanding what it was up against when it came to looking after vulnerable species of animals. Sitting here on the back of a griffin, however, she was now wondering if, in fact, they hadn't even begun to scratch the surface.

Hell, I don't even understand the last half an hour.

Ever since she was a child, when confronted with something she didn't understand, Myrtle had made lists. It had soothed her and made things seem a little more explicable. She had to admit, however, that the list she'd been making in her head wasn't doing much to make things less overwhelming:

1. *You confronted bikers smuggling a rare animal.*
2. *The rare animal just happened to be an extinct pegasus, which shouldn't exist outside of storybooks.*
3. *You were rescued by an extremely hot Australian cop.*
4. *The extremely hot Australian cop turns into a griffin. And you're riding on his back right now.*
5. *You definitely kissed him.*
6. *He didn't seem to mind it, or at least, he didn't visibly freak out.*
7. *When talking to the pegasus, you thought of the extremely hot Australian cop as her dad.*
8. *Does that make me her mom?*
9. *What does that make any of this?!*
10. *No really, what the fuck??!!*

It was not, she had to conclude, the world's most helpful list.

As if sensing her rising panic, the griffin – *no, Hector,* she reminded herself – turned his head slightly, making a soft, questioning noise around the gym bag dangling from his beak.

"I'm... fine," Myrtle said. "I'm just... well, this is a lot to take in, you know?"

Hector made another soft, soothing noise. Maybe she was beginning to understand the griffin language, because somehow, his meaning was clear to her: *Not long to go now.*

Sure enough, after a minute or two, she felt Hector's wings behind her dip slightly, guiding them in a wide circle. She held on tightly as they circled lower and lower.

She thought the landing might be bumpy, but instead, it was remarkably soft – a couple of small jolts as his legs hit the ground and he ran a few paces with his own momentum, and then he folded his wings, looking over his shoulder at her.

"I guess this is my stop," Myrtle said, blinking.

Hector made an encouraging noise, before lowering his head and setting the sports bag gently down on the ground.

Holding Ruby close to her chest, Myrtle slid down from Hector's back, looking around. There shouldn't have been any light, but somehow, she could see everything around her quite clearly. The land around her was bathed in a soft, blue light, like she'd wandered into a dream.

Starlight, she realized suddenly. *I'm seeing by starlight.*

Looking up, she gasped. She'd never seen such a star-studded sky before. They glittered like diamonds against the black velvet of the night sky, utterly clear and unclouded. The misty white streak of the Milky Way arched through the sky to the horizon, its untold billions of stars twinkling gently.

"Oh," Myrtle said. "Wow."

"Beautiful, isn't it."

She jumped a little at the sound of Hector's voice. She turned to find he'd shifted back into his human form while she'd been enraptured by the stars.

She wasn't sure why, given that she'd already seen him change from one form to another, but she'd almost expected him to be naked – certainly, his griffin form hadn't been wearing any clothes.

Or maybe that was just wishful thinking on my part.

She supposed keeping his clothes was the least weird thing about it all – and pretty convenient too.

Myrtle swallowed as she looked at him. In the half-light of the stars, his features looked even more ruggedly beautiful than before, cut to absolute perfection.

"I used to look at them when I was a kid, and wonder if I'd ever be able to fly that high," Hector said, coming to stand by her side, looking up. "But I think this is as close as I'm going to get."

Swallowing, Myrtle looked around, taking in their surroundings properly for the first time, and realized how high up they were, nestled on the side of a large, rocky mountain. The crag they were standing on jutted out from its side, a large flat surface with a few scrubby bushes growing on it.

"Where are we?" she asked.

"Somewhere safe," Hector replied. "This is the emergency pickup point for when an agent needs somewhere to hide out. I wouldn't normally bring civilians here, but in a situation like this…"

Myrtle nodded. He didn't need to finish the sentence. She understood that under these circumstances, it was better to be safe than sorry.

"I hope you know I have a lot of questions for you," she said.

Hector nodded. "And I want to answer them. But first…"

He gestured toward her chest. Myrtle glanced down to see Ruby, her eyes closed, sleeping soundly against her shoulder.

"Oh, right."

Despite the warm sweater Hector had given her, Myrtle could feel the chill of the night air against her skin.

"Do we have a way of keeping her warm?"

"Absolutely," Hector said, picking up the sports bag. "This way."

She followed him across the outcropping, her eyes adjusting more and more to the half-light as they went. Eventually, she was able to make out a small shed, mostly concealed in the scrub growing out of the side of the mountain.

"It's not much, but it has enough to keep someone alive for a few days," Hector said as he opened the door, rusty hinges scraping loudly. "A battery generator, a store of water collected during the rainy season, food rations. I don't think we'll be here long enough to worry too much, though."

Putting the sports bag on the ground, Hector rifled through it a moment before pulling out the heat lamp. Clearly, he'd thought of everything.

He spent a few moments setting things up with cables and switches, before turning the generator on. It let out a low hum, and then the heat lamp flickered to life.

"Pop her down here," Hector said softly as he reached into the bag again. "We can make a nest for her out of this blanket."

Together, they molded the small, thin blanket into something vaguely nest-shaped, folding it over itself to create high sides before curling it into a circle.

"There you go, little one," Myrtle murmured as she gently extracted Ruby from her sweater, cradling her tiny sleeping form in her hands and placing her with care in the center of the nest. Ruby didn't stir even once. But then again, Myrtle thought, the first day of her life had been an exciting one. She didn't blame her for being completely tired out.

They crouched together, side by side, looking down at Ruby's sleeping form.

"She's really beautiful," Myrtle said after a long moment. "Perfect."

And she's the only one left in the world.

The thought made her breath catch in her throat. Anger suddenly surged through her.

And someone was trying to smuggle her as if she was just an object, instead of a living, breathing creature!

She had no idea what the person who'd been planning to buy Ruby might have wanted with her, but she had no illusions about the kinds of lives most exotic animals kept as pets led: sad, lonely, and usually locked up in cages that were far too small for them. Unlike with zoos or ordinary pet owners, most exotic animal collectors didn't care about the animals themselves: they only wanted a prize, a status symbol to show what their money could buy.

But all of this reminded her just how many unanswered questions she still had.

"Hector –"

"I know. Let's go outside." He jerked his head toward the door. "We should leave her to sleep, and we should keep the door closed. The light from the lamp will be visible for miles up here."

Myrtle nodded. Hector grabbed a couple more blankets from the bag, and then, together, they went back out into the clear, beautiful night. Hector spread out the blankets on the rocky ground, before gesturing for her to sit.

"All right," he said, sitting next to her. "You ask. I'll answer."

A million questions flooded Myrtle's mind. She had to struggle to pin a single one of them down. Pulling in a deep breath, she forced herself to be calm.

Be logical. Be rational. What's the first thing you need to know?

"What are you?" she blurted out, realizing even as she said it that this was hardly the most tactful way of asking. "I mean – what I mean is –"

"Nah, it's fine," Hector said, shaking his head. "I get it.

And to be honest, in a lot of ways, your guess is as good as mine. This is just how I've always been. How *all* of us have always been."

"So... you were born this way?" Myrtle asked. "You didn't, like... get bitten by a were-griffin during a full moon or something?"

Hector laughed, the sound deep and rich. It sent a warm shiver straight up Myrtle's spine.

"Nope, nothing like that. It runs in the family. My parents were shifters, and so were my grandparents, all the way back as far as anyone can remember. Which is pretty far back." He cocked his head slightly. "My great-great-great-great-great-great-great grandfather was one of the first convicts to be transported to Australia. Seems like he couldn't stay out of trouble, though, and he went on the lam after getting his ticket of leave and did some pretty minor bushranging with some other escaped convicts. He eventually settled down with the local Indigenous people, had a wife and kids, and learned how to live off the land – that if you take care of it, it'll take care of you. He never went back to the colony. So that's where I came from. Well, eventually."

"And you don't know which side of the family it came from? His or his wife's?" Myrtle asked.

Hector shook his head. "No. There's shifters all over the world, so it could have been either. Or maybe both. If anyone knew, that's been lost now."

Myrtle swallowed. Hector's tone was open and candid. It seemed that he really *did* want to tell her everything, or as much as he knew, anyway. She still couldn't quite believe what she was hearing, but then, hadn't she seen it with her own eyes?

She'd just been telling herself she was a scientist. Hector's story might have been unbelievable if it had just been words, but she'd seen the proof with her own eyes.

You rode around on the proof of it, she reminded herself. *You flew across the sky on the proof of it. It's a bit late to start doubting the evidence now.*

"I assume there have to be other people like you," Myrtle said. "Are they all griffins, or do some of you turn into other things?"

"No, there's all sorts. Koala shifters, possum shifters, Tasmanian devil shifters, crocodile shifters. And a lot more. I'm a bit unusual, even for us, but there's plenty of others who shift into creatures I guess you'd say were mythical. There's others, too – I've got a mate who turns into a diprotodon. You know, the giant prehistoric wombat. He's the size of a rhino when he's shifted."

Myrtle decided she'd deal with that information later. "And you're really a cop? A... a griffin cop?"

"Not strictly speaking," Hector said. "But I *am* in law enforcement. That's what I'm doing out here. One of our deep undercover agents passed us word about what those bikies were claiming to be selling, but we didn't really think it was genuine. Like I said, no one's seen a pegasus in centuries. But what made us interested was that the bikies seemed to have a pretty serious buyer lined up. *That* was who I was after."

"Oh. Huh." Myrtle looked down, biting her lip. "I guess I messed that up pretty good."

"It wasn't your fault," Hector said quickly. "You had no idea. The bikies heard your accent and jumped to the wrong conclusion. You didn't know what you were getting into the middle of."

"I suppose," Myrtle said reluctantly. She frowned as she thought over what Hector had said. "Well, obviously the buyer would have to be someone who'd have the money to pay for it, which I guess isn't *that* useful information. But they'd *also* have to know what a pegasus was. If everyone thought they were extinct, and shifters are *that* secretive, then it'd have to be someone with a bit of insider knowledge."

Hector nodded. "You can see why we were interested. Animal smuggling in Australia's a big problem to start with, but that's an issue for the regular cops. But when there's a shifter involved, then it becomes *my* problem."

Myrtle blinked, about to ask another question, before the full implication of Hector's words dawned on her. "Wait, a *shifter*? You mean... Ruby's like you? She could shift into an actual *baby* at any moment?"

Hector hesitated. "I don't *think* so," he said. "Most shifters don't start shifting until they're in their teens, at least. It's not something that's easy to do – it'd never happen accidentally. It needs concentration and training."

"So did *you* start off as a tiny baby griffin?" Myrtle asked. She tried to picture it, and failed miserably.

"Nah, not me," Hector said. "My mum gave birth the normal way, no eggs, no hatching. I had to learn how to go from human to griffin. I guess for Ruby it'll be the other way around. Maybe that's just what pegasi are like."

Myrtle nodded. It sounded fantastical, but she could accept it. Given everything she'd seen over the past few hours, she didn't really have much choice.

And she supposed what Hector had been telling her about being in law enforcement made sense, too. Shifter cops for shifter crimes. She couldn't imagine how the regular cops might react to a baby pegasus popping out of an egg. *Law and Order: Special Shifters Unit* made sense, even as it raised *a lot* more questions than it answered. If there were shifter law enforcement agencies, did that mean the *government* knew about them?

Maybe it's like aliens, she thought, head spinning. *The presi-*

dent finds out about shifters the same day as they tell him what really happened at Roswell and what Area 51 is all about.

"So… your family… have they always been in this line of work, then?"

Hector shook his head. "Our family've been stockmen for decades – we come from a long line of boss drovers. Me and my brother Rhys are the first ones who aren't working on a farm." He shrugged. "I'm not going to pretend my dad was thrilled when me and Rhys went and told him neither of us would be taking over the family business, but luckily we have a sister who's twice the farmhand either of us ever were. She's running the place now. Most shifters are just like them, just wanting to live their lives in peace. If you passed one on the street, you'd never know it. I mean, provided they weren't a dragon at the time or something."

"Yeah, I hope I'd notice that," Myrtle said, even as her brain shrieked, *A DRAGON?!*

"I'd say so," Hector laughed. "Is there anything else I can answer for you?"

There were lots of things, actually, but Myrtle decided she'd learned enough for now. Her head was already spinning. Anything else and she thought it might fly right off her neck.

"No," she said. "I think… well, I think that's enough for now."

Hector nodded, his eyes intense. Myrtle swallowed as she looked at him.

"If you don't have any more questions, then I think there's something *I* need to get off my chest," he said.

Something about the way he said it made Myrtle need to take a deep, *deep* breath.

He'd been polite enough not to bring up her half-dazed macking on him earlier; perhaps he was about to tell her he was flattered, but he already had a gorgeous Australian girlfriend who was a mermaid shifter and competitive swimmer who supermodeled in her spare time, Myrtle thought, allowing her eyes to drift down over his body. *Or he's gay, and he's going out with a long-lost Hemsworth brother. That's the kind of partner he'd have. Not a nerdy bug scientist who can't even control her frizzy hair.*

Myrtle swallowed, and looked away.

"I think I know what you're going to say," she blurted out. She was the one who'd forced the kiss on him, after all – the least she could do was show a bit of grace and apologize. "And I want to say right away that I'm sorry. I guess I just… had had a bit of a shock. I – I misread things. I really hope I haven't made things awkward between us. I can promise you it won't happen again."

She didn't dare look up. Embarrassment twisted in her stomach. She'd never been good at this kind of thing – or, well, any other kind of social interaction, really. That was why she liked moths. She sincerely doubted she was ever going to accidentally kiss a moth.

Eventually, however, the silence had continued long enough that Myrtle chanced a glance upward at Hector's face, and found him frowning in confusion.

"Sorry, what?"

Myrtle blinked. *God, he's not going to make this easy, is he.*

"I'm sorry," she repeated. "About what happened back there."

Nothing. His face was blank.

"The *kiss!*" she finally said, throwing her hands up. "I wanted to say I was sorry about the kiss!"

Hector looked thunderstruck.

"You wanted to apologize about the kiss?" he asked, enunciating each syllable as if he'd never heard quite those words in quite that order before. "Why?"

Now it was Myrtle's turn to feel completely flummoxed. She could feel her face going red.

"Well, it wasn't very professional of me, was it?" she said. "You were trying to get us out of a dangerous situation, and all I was doing was… well, *that*, and besides which, you can't just go around kissing people. Especially not when I'm this… and you're… *that*…"

She gestured helplessly to all Hector's *that*, hoping he would understand and drop the subject. She'd humiliated herself enough for one evening, hadn't she?

Hector stared at her a moment longer, before shaking his head.

"No, no, no. I think we're getting our wires crossed here, Myrtle. I don't have a problem with the kiss. The opposite, even." He glanced at her, before looking away again. "Look, there's no easy way to say this. So I'm just gonna come right out and say it."

Myrtle was too confused even to anticipate what he might say next. He leaned toward her, taking her hand. Myrtle gasped at the contact, a warm jolt shooting up her arm.

"Myrtle," he said, his voice husky. "You're my mate."

Myrtle blinked at him. *His… his* what?

Then it came to her.

"Oh – right," she stuttered. "That's some Australian thing, isn't it? Like we're friends now. We're mates. Okay, well, I guess that's cool."

She was glad he was willing to put this whole thing behind them and move on. Though she didn't quite understand why Hector was staring at her now with an intensity that bordered on desperation.

"That's not what I mean," he said. "I mean you're my *mate*, in the shifter sense of the word."

The shifter sense of the word?

Myrtle was about to ask what on earth he was talking about, when he continued.

"We shifters... the fact we can change forms isn't the only way we're different from humans. We also have a mate – a person that's meant for us."

Myrtle felt her mouth go dry. Hector's gaze didn't waver, his fingers tight around her own.

"A mate is someone you can give yourself to, and know it's forever." Hector paused, taking a deep breath. *"That's* what I mean when I say you're my mate, Myrtle. I knew it from the first moment our fingers touched. My *griffin* knew it."

Myrtle swallowed heavily. Her mind drifted back to that moment, and she recalled the weird spark of electricity that had seemed to run through her body when Hector's hand had brushed hers, and how her skin had tingled every time since then that she'd touched him.

Oh my God.

"I know this is a lot to spring on you," Hector said. "Especially with everything else that's been going on tonight. I get it if you need some time to think about it."

Myrtle could feel her mouth hanging open, but just now she felt powerless to close it.

I'm... I'm his mate?!

She shook her head. Pegasi she could accept. Griffins, too. But *this?*

Grappling to get some angle on the situation she could handle, Myrtle asked, "So, who you're meant to be with is just like... coded into your DNA?"

"If you're looking for a technical explanation, I'm afraid you've got Buckley's of getting one out of me," Hector said.

"I'm just going to assume that means you don't know," Myrtle said slowly. "Aren't you curious about it though?"

"I suppose." Hector shrugged. "It's just something I've

always known about. Do humans ever wonder why they fall in love?"

"I guess not," Myrtle admitted. "The scientist in me wants to put it all down to brain chemistry, something to motivate reproduction. But maybe that's just because I've always been unlucky in love. It seems easier to accept if you put it down to something impersonal like dopamine."

Hector laughed. "Unlucky in love? That's hard to believe."

Myrtle's breath caught as his eyes unabashedly roamed down her body.

"I would've thought a knockout like you would've had the boys eating out of her hand."

Flushing, Myrtle looked down. *Is he serious?*

She'd never thought of herself as anything special. Why would she? All her siblings were more attractive, more popular, more *everything* than she was. After all, she supposed, *This is Lily and her four adorable daughters,* and *This is our son Thorn, he's on a football scholarship,* and *Here's the catalog spread Poppy did last year, doesn't she look beautiful?* all sounded a little more impressive than, *This is Myrtle, she's a Moth Lady.*

So to hear a man like Hector say she should've had the boys eating out of her hand... well.

Excuse her if she found it just a *little* hard to swallow.

"No," she said. "I'm not – really, I'm just –"

"You're perfect, Myrtle." Hector's voice was a low rumble. "Before I even knew you were my mate I couldn't stop myself from checking you out. You're smart, you're dedicated, you're brave. And you're beautiful. That's all I need to know, never mind what my griffin or my DNA has to say about it."

As if compelled by some inexorable force, Myrtle lifted her eyes to his. She could see the truth of what he said, reflected back to her in them – they were like dark pools of desire, looking directly into her soul.

Okay. Wow.

She'd done it before, so it seemed easy to do it again – without another word she leaned forward to kiss him, sweeping her tongue into his mouth. His lips were hot against hers as he opened them, his hand coming up to hold her jaw, his thumb running gently over her cheek.

Myrtle swallowed when she pulled back, stunned by her own boldness, but the look on Hector's face quickly put paid to any fears she had that she'd overstepped any boundaries. He was looking at her like he wanted to eat her all up – and maybe he did.

His lips were on hers again before she could think, hot and insistent. His palm against her face was warm and slightly rough, callused, she imagined, from years of farm work and then hunting down criminals. It sent a shiver down her spine, warmth pooling in the pit of her stomach, winding down between her legs.

She could already feel her desire building within her – hell, it had been building since the first moment she'd laid eyes on him. She still didn't know what to make of this whole *mates* thing, but she *did* know she wanted him. She wanted him more desperately than she'd ever wanted anything before in her life.

Hector's hand was on the small of her back, pulling her forward against him as their kisses grew hungrier, more insistent. Myrtle threw her head back, letting her desire overtake her and carry her away as Hector kissed her jaw, before pulling aside the collar of the oversized sweater and making his way down her neck, his lips gentle on her sunburned skin. But even *that* just made her shiver, her blood surging in her veins. She pulled at the sweater, lifting it over her head, and regretting even the moment's pause it caused in his kisses. Her heart hammered in her chest as his lips dropped lower and lower, skimming the tops of her breasts above the neckline of her tank top.

"Oh, God," she breathed, closing her eyes.

She wanted to feel his bare skin against hers, wanted to feel him against her. Desperation welled up inside her, and, forgetting herself, she tugged at the bottom of her tank top, trying to get it up over her head.

She was stopped by Hector's low, husky laugh, and then, a second later, by his hand on hers, so huge it covered hers completely.

"That's my job," he said, a smile in his voice – and, when Myrtle opened her eyes to look at him, on his lips, too.

She almost groaned out loud at the sight of him, his features bathed in starlight, a dimple creasing his stubbled cheek, his lightly curled hair falling over his forehead and into his dark eyes.

His hands were confident and sure as he lifted her tank top up over her head, exposing her breasts in their white cotton bra. Myrtle at least was aware that Mother Nature had blessed her in this area, even if, unlike her sisters, she also had a belly to go along with her breasts. In the past, she'd always felt a little embarrassed by how she looked naked – she'd never wanted the lights on when she slept with her ex-boyfriends, on the very few occasions it'd actually happened – but the way Hector was looking at her now put any thought of embarrassment completely out of her mind.

He was staring at her as if completely transfixed, his Adam's apple bobbing as he swallowed heavily.

"You're beautiful," he said slowly. "Absolutely beautiful."

Myrtle couldn't help the smile that twitched at the corners of her lips.

"Really?" she couldn't stop herself from asking, and Hector looked up at her, eyes wide.

"Of course," he said, as if the question surprised him. "You're gorgeous – you're everything a woman should be. Everything I've always dreamed my mate *would* be."

She supposed she could see the evidence of that pressing against the front of his jeans. Her mouth watered a little as she took in the sizable bulge, desire mounting within her.

They were both wearing too many clothes, she decided, at apparently the exact same moment Hector came to the same conclusion; the next few minutes were spent fumbling with each other's buckles and buttons, yanking up shirts and pulling down pants, exposing skin.

Myrtle gasped as Hector's body was revealed to her: his smooth, tanned skin, the broad, flat plane of his pecs, his sculpted abs, the hair that dusted his chest and stomach.

She couldn't stop herself from staring, as wetness gathered between her thighs. Hector clearly had no intention of making her wait, however – he lowered his head to her breasts, teasing a nipple between his teeth, making her cry out. Myrtle threw her head back, looking up at the perfect blanket of stars above them as Hector pressed her down onto her back, his body covering hers.

Arching her back, she pressed herself against him, feeling the hardness of his erection pressing against her thigh. She wanted him so badly, and she couldn't restrain the gasps and moans that left her mouth as he moved against her, teasing her with his lips and teeth. Tingling electricity thrilled over the surface of her skin.

She slid her hand down his body, wanting to feel him. He was hot and desperately hard against her palm, and his groan as she ran her hand over his length sounded like it had come from the very depths of his soul.

"Please," she whispered, knowing they were going fast but unable to wait any longer. "Please, I want you so badly…"

She didn't know what had gotten into her – she only knew she had never felt this way about a man before. She'd never *responded* to a man like this before. Hector's every touch seemed to drive her wild; every movement sent her head spinning with desire. She had never thought of herself as a particularly sexual person before, but it was clear that she was going to have to reassess that opinion. It was as if something had opened inside her, something that had previously been locked away, even from herself.

And right now, the only thing she wanted to do was discover more.

She could feel Hector's thigh muscles twitching with every movement of her hand, his mouth on hers hot and demanding. His hand slid down her side, over her hip and between her thighs. She cried out into his mouth as his fingers pressed against her, finding her core, and sending a wave of pleasure through her so intense that she couldn't hold back her cry.

Myrtle dug her fingers into the small of his back, urging him onwards as his thumb slowly circled her clit, sparks dancing along her veins. His fingers were good, but right now, the only thing she wanted was *him*. She squirmed, bucking up against him as he teased her, gasping into the kiss he pressed against her mouth.

"God, please, *Hector...*"

His low laugh told her that her message had been clearly understood. She missed his hand immediately as soon as he withdrew it, but then she felt the hot, hard head of his cock pressing against her, and she forgot everything but that – everything but the feeling of him slowly, carefully, pressing inside her.

Myrtle's toes curled as he moved inside her, her back arching, fingers clutching at his sides. She had never felt so perfectly, completely full before – he felt perfect inside her, like they were made to fit together.

Perhaps we are, Myrtle thought, dazed, as he made his first thrust inside her. *Maybe this is part of being mates. We're made for each other, right down to our DNA...*

Myrtle cried out, thighs cinching around his hips as he moved, sending desperate waves of pleasure through her body, taking her higher and higher with every move he made. His mouth found hers once more, his tongue sweeping between her lips, bringing them even closer together.

Myrtle could feel her climax building inside her, ecstasy surging along her every nerve. Shocks of electricity danced through her, blooming over her skin. She closed her eyes and threw her head back, crying out every time he thrust into her, seeming to go deeper and deeper every time.

Oh, God...

She couldn't tell if the stars that swam across her vision as her climax finally exploded within her were real or just her imagination, but in the end she decided it didn't matter. Wave after wave of pleasure coursed through her, making her muscles clench and her back arch, her head rising and falling on the blanket beneath her. A moment later, she heard Hector cry out too, deep and throaty, and he shuddered, his cock pulsing inside her as he came.

Myrtle wasn't sure how long she lay still, her breath panting in her throat, limbs feeling heavy and boneless. She had *never* experienced anything like that before. Nothing had ever felt so perfect, so *right,* in all her life. Hector was heavy above her, but for now, she couldn't bring herself to care. She played her fingers down his spine, savouring the feel of his skin beneath her touch.

Eventually Hector sat up a little, and Myrtle couldn't hold back her slight protestation at the lack of contact as he slipped from her body. But then he settled by her side, wrapping his arms around her and holding her against his chest.

Closing her eyes, Myrtle listened to the sound of his heartbeat, and wondered how she had ever lived without it.

"That was... Myrtle, that was..."

His voice was a low rumble in his chest. Myrtle smiled.

"Yeah, it really was," she said. "Wow."

Hector laughed softly, before pressing his lips against her sweaty forehead. "Too bad we won't be here for long. Right now, I feel like I could stay here forever."

Myrtle let his words wash over her. Today had been one of the most frightening, bizarre and *amazing* days of her entire life. Trying to put all of the pieces of it together in her brain seemed totally impossible now. How could so many things happen in the space of just a few hours?

There was one thing she *did* know with complete certainty, however: that right now, there was nowhere else she'd rather be but here.

Yawning, she snuggled sleepily against Hector's chest, feeling exhaustion welling up to claim her. She still had about a million questions she needed to ask, and she still wasn't sure what to make of the strange new world that had just been opened up to her.

But for now, she decided, all of those questions could wait until later.

CHAPTER 8

Hector drifted slowly back into consciousness with the kind of languorousness he hadn't let himself enjoy in *years*.

Sure, there were tiny sticks and rocks poking into his back, and his arm had gone numb overnight, but all of that paled into insignificance when compared with the feel of the warm body sleeping beside him, the gentle rise and fall of her chest against his with every breath she took.

My mate. Mine. Ours.

Inside him, his griffin stretched, arching its back and spreading its talons, its tail flicking from side to side.

She is ours. We have claimed her. Finally.

Hector suppressed the urge to roll his eyes at it. The griffin had very black and white views on these things. When you met your mate, you told her who she was to you, you courted her, and then you claimed her. It was all very straightforward, as far as it was concerned. It didn't want to hear it when he tried to explain the human world was often a little more complex than that.

She's not *ours*, he explained to it. *She's hers. She's human. She could still reject the bond.*

The thought sent a chill through him. Myrtle had seemed to accept everything he said last night, but he knew there were still a lot of obstacles in their way. A lifelong commitment might seem daunting to a human, especially since, Hector supposed, they hadn't actually known each other all that long.

Plus, she probably has a life and a career back in the States.

He'd heard how committed she was to her work in her voice. Hector wasn't about to ask her to give up something she cared so deeply about to stay here with him.

Then we will go to her, his griffin said, shaking its head. *It is a simple answer, is it not?*

Hector supposed it was, in the end. He loved his work – it gave him purpose, and there was no feeling like tracking down a criminal and finally putting an end to whatever it was they were up to, satisfying his griffin's need for the thrill of the chase – but in a choice between his work and his mate, there really was no choice to be made at all.

I might miss Rhys, Eve, and Dad, though, he thought. He'd always been close to his brother and sister, and while his relationship with his father was a little more contentious, Hector knew they loved each other. His father had been against him and Rhys leaving the farm, but in the end, he hadn't forbidden them from going, the way an alpha griffin could if he wanted to.

He's probably happy about it now, Hector thought. *Eve's got the place in hand. Better than me or Rhys could've done it.*

Well, as long as the farm was in good hands, he was pretty sure he could live with only seeing his family once or twice a year. It wasn't like they saw each other so often these days – Rhys was assigned elsewhere in the agency and Hector never knew where he was half the time, and it wasn't like running a farm gave you many days off, so his contact with Eve and his father was mostly over the phone.

There you have it, his griffin purred. *You can go with your mate, and she need not give anything up.*

It was hard to argue with it. When confronted with your mate, things tended to seem a lot simpler. Maybe it was the griffin in him, but he'd never really thought of himself as a particularly complicated person, anyway. He liked his work, he liked eating, he liked being outdoors. He liked taking care of things. He liked knowing that what was his was well looked after. And that was about it.

Beside him, Myrtle murmured in her sleep, turning over slightly. Hector waited until she had settled again, before dropping a soft kiss on her forehead and easing his arm out from beneath her.

She will be hungry. We should provide food for her. His griffin was insistent, and at once Hector felt an urge to shift and to fly out over the flat plains below in search of something to hunt. Frowning, he had a sudden image of himself returning, landing on the outcropping in front of Myrtle and dropping a dead snake at her feet, with the air that he expected her to eat it.

He quickly squashed the urge.

She's not going to want that, he told the griffin. *I'll just make her something normal, all right?*

The griffin huffed a little, but it seemed to accept it.

In any case, he needed to check on Ruby, too. It was still very early in the morning – the sun wasn't quite fully up yet – but he wasn't sure how long baby pegasi slept for. But if they were anything like baby griffins, when they did wake up, they were *hungry.*

Standing, Hector found his jeans and put them on, before heading over to the small shed.

Ruby was *very* much awake when he opened the door – in fact, she was perched on a small shelf up by the ceiling, looking down at him with a kind of imperious indignance Hector was sure he hadn't done anything to deserve.

"You learned to fly better overnight, huh?" he asked, looking up at her. Clearly, Ruby was a fast learner. She'd been walking within a few minutes of hatching, and now it was clear she already had the fundamentals of flying down.

"You going to come down for breakfast, or are you just going to sulk?"

Hector wasn't sure if Ruby could understand him, but she certainly cocked her head a little at the word *breakfast*.

"Mee-eeeh?"

The small, soft sound she made was *definitely* a question.

"That's right – baby pegasi who hide up by the ceiling don't get apples," Hector informed her. "If they want to get fed, they come down and be social, like polite little shifters."

Ruby didn't move an inch. She tossed her head and folded her wings.

Is she already in her teenaged phase? Hector wondered as he looked up at her. *That's all we need – a pegasus with teen angst.*

"Fine, fine," Hector said, crouching down to where he'd left his sports bag yesterday. He'd filled a cooler bag with all the bottles of apple puree he'd had in the fridge back at the now-abandoned base, and he pulled one out now, uncapping it.

Ruby's nostrils twitched.

"Yeah, too bad no one's here to help me eat all this delicious apple puree," Hector said, opening a drawer and finding the one single spoon that lived in it. "I'll just have to eat it all by myself."

He hovered the spoon over the open bottle, looking at Ruby out of the corner of his eye.

"*Mee-eeeh!*"

In a flurry of silver and white, Ruby launched herself off the shelf, wings fluttering and struggling to keep her airborne for a moment, before she evened out, finding the right rhythm, and came in to land smoothly on the counter.

She raised a dainty hoof, looking at Hector expectantly.

"That's what I thought," he said, placing the bottle down in front of her. She immediately stuck her head inside, slurping up the puree with gusto.

"All right, now I just gotta find something for us."

Opening the cupboards, Hector found a bag of flour, a sealed jar of honey, an opened jar of Vegemite, a small packet of salt, a chipped bowl with a teaspoon in it, and a large drinking glass. Clearly, this place was not stocked for luxury – but then again, he supposed it wasn't meant to be lived in for very long.

All right. We have flour, we have water, we have salt. We can make damper.

It wouldn't be a fancy meal, but it would definitely take the edge off their hunger.

"C'mon," he said, turning to Ruby and jerking his head toward the door. "Let's go wake your – uh, Myrtle."

Hector frowned as he stepped outside into the new sunshine of the day. He'd almost said *your mum* just then. He and Myrtle might have been Ruby's temporary guardians and caretakers, but they weren't her parents. It wouldn't do any of them any good to start thinking like that.

Especially not Ruby, Hector thought. He hoped she'd understand when it came time to part with each other. The thought sent an unexpected pain through his chest, and he took a deep breath, trying to ignore it.

He turned in time to see Ruby fluttering lightly down from the countertop, landing on the floor before trotting after him, her movements strong and confident. She still wasn't any bigger than a small puppy, but it was clear she was growing up fast – and she'd managed not to get *quite* so much apple puree all over herself this morning.

"Enjoyed your breakfast?" he asked Ruby as he crouched down to place the damper ingredients on the ground.

"Mee-ehh!"

At the sound of Ruby's whinny, Myrtle stirred and then sat up, blinking in the light, and looking around her as if she had absolutely no memory of where she was or how she'd gotten there.

"Morning, sleepyhead," Hector said. "Sleep well?"

Myrtle looked at him, her eyes going wide as she took him in, before they darted to Ruby.

"Oh," Myrtle said softly. "Oh, right. That all happened yesterday." She closed her eyes, shaking her head, before scrubbing her fingers over her face. "Sorry, I was half-expecting to wake up and find out I'd dreamed the whole thing."

"'Fraid not," Hector said, opening the flour. Warmth flooded his chest as he looked at Myrtle, who was wrapping the blanket around her breasts as she searched for her clothes. "I hope you don't mind."

Myrtle glanced at him, eyes wide.

"Oh God, no! I didn't mean it like that! I just meant that – God, how could anything so – so –"

Hector watched, entranced, as Myrtle flushed, lowering her beautiful blue eyes.

"It just all seemed too amazing to be real," she finally finished. Her eyes darted up, and Hector saw her tongue move over her lips, leaving them shining. "*All* of it," she said, and the expression on her face left him in no doubt what particular part of the evening she was referring to now.

Our mate is pleased with us!

His griffin preened, all but prancing in its joy at having made its mate happy.

We should have brought her the snake. It would have been good manners. She would have liked it.

No, Hector told it firmly, *she wouldn't have.*

"Are you hungry?" Hector asked her, as much to silence his griffin as anything else.

"Starving," Myrtle said as she pulled on her singlet. "Has Ruby eaten?"

"Yep. She just about demolished her breakfast. I'm glad we brought plenty with us."

He glanced down at Ruby, who seemed to have sensed she was being talked about and was listening intently.

"Though I suppose we should be careful she's not over-eating."

"Meeh!"

It was clear from the small, dismissive sound she made what Ruby thought of that idea.

Myrtle slid on her shorts under the blanket, and then stood, coming over to where he had opened the flour and was tipping it into the chipped bowl.

"What're you making?"

"Damper – bush bread," he said, as he sprinkled some salt into the flour. "It's not fancy, I'm afraid, but it'll fill you up for a bit."

Myrtle shook her head. "I don't need fancy – I'm used to eating crappy instant meals while I'm out in the field. Can I do anything to help?"

"You could mix this together while I run 'round the side and get us some water from the tank," Hector said, passing her the teaspoon. "Doesn't need much. Just for the salt and flour to be mixed up."

There was plenty of water in the tank when Hector checked it, and he scooped some into the drinking glass before heading back around to where Myrtle was mixing the flour and salt.

Smoke from a fire might give away their location, but Hector figured they could risk it – a quick hunt around the shack revealed some matches, and in no time they had a small fire going.

"So, show me what this damper is," Myrtle said.

"It's not too exciting, I'm afraid," Hector told her as he began adding the water to the salt and flour, mixing it in before kneading the paste slowly into dough. "It's something my father taught me, my brother and my sister to make during overnight trips to move the cattle to new grazing areas. It was the most fun I had as a kid, to be honest – sitting around the fire with my family, cooking bush bread on sticks." He glanced at her. "I feel like I've told you a lot about me, but I haven't asked you much about you or your family." He remembered her implying she had a large family back in the car, when she'd said that her mum was determined to name all her kids after plants and flowers, and that at some point she'd started to run out. "I take it you have a lot of brothers and sisters?"

Myrtle frowned a little, her eyes clouding. "I do – and I love them all like crazy. But they can be a little… much, at times. I suppose when there's eight of them that's probably normal."

Hector looked at her, amazed. "Eight, including you?"

Myrtle shook her head. "Nine, including me. Six older sisters and two younger brothers. And my siblings are all… well, they're all…" She gestured helplessly. "Let's just say I'm kind of the ugly duckling."

"I can't imagine that," Hector said, meaning it. He let his eyes roam over her body, appreciating every inch of it. Her strong, muscled legs, the luscious curve of her hips, her wide shoulders and soft, rounded breasts. Her character shone through in her face, from her strong, determined jaw and the intelligence that flashed in her blue-gray eyes, to her habit of biting her full lower lip when she was thinking.

Like she was doing now as she looked at him, a mildly skeptical expression on her face.

"I really mean it," Hector assured her. "Everything I told you last night – it's really true, Myrtle. I realize it probably all sounded like a corny line, but –"

"No, it didn't," Myrtle said quickly, cutting him off. "I mean I… I believe you. I really do. I think I felt it too, the first time our hands touched. And… last night… well…"

She blushed, looking down. As the color spread adorably over her face, Hector found he had to busy himself with kneading the damper in order to avoid a really unfortunate situation in his pants.

"But I feel like it's going to take a bit of time to get used to hearing that," she finally finished. She took a deep breath. "I guess I'm just kind of used to being overlooked. There were even a couple of times in high school when boys would pretend to be interested in me, so they'd have an excuse to hang around at my place and get closer to my sisters. Not," she went on quickly, "that any of my sisters went out with them once they realized what'd happened. But it still stung, you know?"

"Fucking arseholes." Hector shook his head as he broke the dough into halves, lifting one half up and winding it around a dry stick. He had to do something to distract himself from the fact his griffin had just reared up in his chest, demanding the blood of anyone who had ever made Myrtle feel lesser than what she was – which was perfect.

Absolutely perfect.

"It seems to me like you should've been hearing how special you are every day of your life," he said. "Smart, beautiful, brave – you're everything I've ever wanted. You're my *mate*. And to me, that means you'll never be anything less than perfect."

He heard Myrtle's surprised exhalation. But the only

answer to that was to just keep telling her until she believed it.

He finished winding the damper dough around the sticks before handing one to Myrtle. He held the dough over the fire, and Myrtle followed his example.

"You're not so bad yourself," she said after a moment or two of silence, in which they watched the dough slowly begin to brown over the fire. "Believe me, if anyone had told me this trip would be turning out the way it has, I'd have… well, I don't know what I would have done. Laughed myself stupid, I suppose. I thought I'd be scrabbling around in a cave, counting moths right now."

"You can still do it," Hector told her. "I can do my best to have you back in Good Fortune as soon as possible. I'm sorry this has interrupted all your plans."

Myrtle shook her head. "I hope so. But I –" She bit her lip. "I hope this doesn't sound selfish, but I can't feel too sad about the lost time. Not if it meant that all of this has happened. That I got to meet you and Ruby. And… well. Everything else, too."

She was speaking slowly and hesitantly, and Hector didn't feel the need to reply right away. He was sure she knew how he felt. Griffins might not have telepathy, but it seemed their bond *did* make their emotions clear to each other. Right now, Hector could feel the warmth flowing from Myrtle's heart into his.

My mate.

"I know," he said. "And believe me, this is the last thing I expected to have happen, too. But I couldn't be happier, now that it has."

They sat quietly together for a while. Hector knew they had a lot of things between them that they needed to talk about, but for now, he was happy to sit in contented silence.

"This should be ready now," Hector said, pulling his

damper off the fire. He tested it with a finger. "Yep – cooked the whole way through, just a little black on the edges."

He rested his damper stick against his knees, then reached to his side, grabbing the jars of honey and Vegemite.

"Which one do you want?"

Myrtle made a face. "Like you have to ask!"

"Fine, fine, I'll just be over here, enjoying my salty black yeast byproduct by myself, then," Hector laughed, passing her the honey. "But I feel like you ought to know that I don't make fun of America's national obsession with peanut butter, do I?"

"That's because peanut butter is actually good!" Myrtle protested as she broke off a piece of damper, dipping it in the honey. "Oh my God, I can't believe you'd even compare the two. What the hell?"

"Lie to yourself all you like, you know it's weird for any country to be *that* invested in squashed-up nuts," Hector said, sticking his finger in the jar of Vegemite before smearing it over his damper and taking a big bite.

Hector chewed happily, letting the salty taste of the Vegemite settle on his tongue. The plain damper and the tang of the Vegemite was the perfect combination – delicious and hearty, the perfect way to start the day. People who didn't like it just didn't know what they were missing, and he'd never understand it.

"Ohhhh, yeah," he said, swallowing and sighing with contentment. "That's the stuff."

"Stop," Myrtle muttered, rolling her eyes. "I hope you know I'm *really* reconsidering this whole thing right now."

Hector grinned at her, and didn't stop until he saw an irresistible grin pulling at her own lips.

"Lucky you're hot," she said, shaking her head before dipping more of her damper into the honey. "And that this is so good."

We have provided for our mate!

His griffin stood up proudly, as if it had just produced a three-course gourmet meal.

We are finally showing her some manners! We are showing her how a griffin takes care of its mate!

Hector tried not to grimace. If this was how much his griffin overreacted to him making Myrtle some damper, it was going to be downright insufferable if he ever took her on a date to anywhere even a little fancier than the Engadine McDonald's.

Hector felt a nudge at his side, and looked down to see Ruby nosing at him, nostrils sniffing curiously.

"You want some?" he asked her, holding out a finger. "At least someone in this family has good taste."

He caught Myrtle's surprised blink, and realized once again that he'd referred to them all as a *family*. He'd have to watch that, he thought. In the end, Ruby rejected the Vegemite, screwing up her little nose and turning away with a disgusted *meeh!*

Instead, she trotted over to Myrtle, nosing at her arm and trying to climb up her leg while attempting to snaffle up some honey and damper.

"Hey, hey, table manners, please!" Myrtle laughed, lifting her food up and away from Ruby's nibbling mouth.

"You've had your breakfast anyway, missy," Hector told Ruby. "No more for you."

Ruby looked between them, eyes narrowing, before flapping her wings and taking off, still trying to grab some of Myrtle's breakfast.

"Okay, okay, if you want some that bad," Myrtle said, breaking a little off and offering it to Ruby. It was gone in an instant, Ruby licking honey off her lips in satisfaction.

"That's all though," Myrtle told her sternly when Ruby tried to grab some more. Ruby looked between them for a moment, and then, as if sensing she was beaten, landed on the ground and trotted off to sulk, her back turned to them, tail swishing huffily.

"I suppose we still don't know who was trying to buy Ruby's egg," Myrtle said slowly as she dusted off her hands, before resting them on her knees, gazing at where Ruby was sniffing dejectedly around the dwindling campfire.

"There's a lot about this situation I don't know that I'd like to," Hector said. "How the bikies got the egg in the first place. Who they were trying to sell it to. Where it came from." He shook his head. "The most important thing for now, though, is that we get Ruby to safety – to someone who can look after her properly and protect her. If she really *is* the only pegasus left, she's not going to have an easy life."

Myrtle nodded, her face pensive. "I suppose that's true. If people were trying to smuggle her before she was even born..." She stopped, swallowing. "I hate the idea that she'll never really be free. That she'll always have to be looking over her shoulder. That there'll be no one else like her in the whole world."

As if sensing she was being talked about, Ruby looked up from where she was nosing around in the dirt, ears twitching, eyes bright. "Meee-eeh?"

"Don't worry, sweetheart," Myrtle said soothingly. "Everything will be all right. I promise. I don't know how, but... I promise."

Ruby cocked her head, tail swishing. She blinked.

And the next thing Hector knew, he was standing by the shed door, his hand extended toward the handle, with no thought in his head but *Gotta get some apple puree.*

He blinked.

"What the – what the hell?"

He turned, looking back to where Myrtle was still sitting by the fire.

"Don't ask me," she said, sounding surprised. "You just suddenly stood up and raced over to the door without saying anything. Did you forget why you stood up?"

"No," Hector said, shaking his head slowly. "In fact, I don't even *remember* standing up. I was over there, and then the next thing I knew I was here, thinking I had to get some..."

Apple puree.

There was only one person here who was *that* obsessed with apple puree.

He looked at Ruby, who was watching him intently, tail swishing gently.

"Meee-eeh?"

She sounded prompting, and, as Hector watched her, she blinked again – and all at once he was seized with the urge to open the door and grab the puree. He had to force his hand back down to his side, and shake his head to clear it.

What the hell?

"Is this you?" he asked Ruby, not sure whether to really believe it or not. "Are you –?"

"What?" Myrtle asked. "What's she doing?"

"I... don't know," Hector said slowly. "But I think she just –"

How can I explain this without sounding crazy?

"She just what?" Myrtle asked, confused.

"I think *she's* the one who wants something," Hector said, approaching Ruby slowly. "I think she's trying to *make* me get her some more breakfast."

She shied away from him slightly, as if knowing she'd been caught out, but then gave him a defiant, *"Mee-eeh!"*

"What are you?" Hector asked her softly, dropping to his knees. "How did you do that?"

"Wait, wait, wait," Myrtle said. "Are you saying that Ruby just, what, *mind-whammied* you into going over there and getting her some extra food?"

"I think so," Hector said, eyes still on Ruby. "I mean, I didn't have any intention of going over there. And *I'm* not the one who wants apple puree so damn much."

"Can... can she do that? Control people's actions? Control their *minds?*" Myrtle's eyes were wide, her voice soft and awed.

"I have no idea," Hector said. "There's nothing about pegasi being able to mind control people in the shifter history books. I've definitely never heard of them having a power like that."

Myrtle leaned down, reaching out to Ruby, who gazed at her warily.

"It's okay, you're not in trouble," Myrtle whispered soothingly. "But no more mind whammies, okay? That's not fair."

Hector glanced at her. "You believe me, then?"

In response, Myrtle let out a low laugh. "C'mon, after everything you've told me in the past twenty-four hours, *that's* the thing you think I won't believe?" She shook her head. "Anyway, it was really weird, the way you just stood up suddenly. Your movements were really awkward and jerky. You don't usually move like that. You startled me – I thought something was wrong. But now I know it was just a badly-behaved little miss taking advantage of you."

They both looked at Ruby, who was looking down moodily, clearly upset that her ploy hadn't worked.

"Don't sulk now," Myrtle told her. "Like I said, you're not in trouble. But you can't do that again. All right?"

Ruby made a small, contrite sound, and nuzzled Myrtle's outstretched fingers. She certainly *seemed* like she was sorry for what she'd done, though Hector had no doubt that if he hadn't come back to himself when he did, she'd be happily eating all the apple puree he could put in front of her.

Ruby pranced a little, her pure white coat sparkling in the early morning sunshine. Now assured that she was forgiven, her spirits seemed to rise again, and she trotted about, nosing at the ground, tail switching.

"So, she's the last pegasus on earth, *and* she has mind control powers," Myrtle muttered as she watched her. "Okay. This is fine. Is it fine?"

"It certainly does complicate things a little," Hector said. "I guess we just have to –"

Before he could get any further, the sound of whirling helicopter blades drifted to his ears.

Is it the emergency pickup team? It took them long enough.

Hector honestly hadn't thought about the amount of time that had passed since he sent the beacon signal. He'd been too caught up with Myrtle, all his focus and attention on her.

Reckless, yet again, he told himself. He'd have to watch that. It was fine when he just had himself to look after, but it couldn't happen now that he had Myrtle and Ruby. His mate and her safety always had to be foremost on his mind. His job never really called for him to use his brains – he was told where to go and what to do. Who his target was. It was the others in intelligence gathering, the deep undercover agents, who did most of the brain work. He had always relied on his griffin's instincts and strength.

"The pickup'll be here soon," he explained to Myrtle, realizing that her ears wouldn't be able to detect the sound of it approaching yet. "Then we can get cleaned up, debrief. Have a proper feed. Then we can talk."

Myrtle nodded. Then her eyes drifted down.

"And Ruby?"

Hector hesitated. "It'll be out of my hands, Myrtle. But I trust that she'll be looked after, by people who know more about how to care for a baby pegasus than I do."

"I hope so," Myrtle said, eyes still downcast. "I couldn't bear it if – if –"

She didn't need to finish the sentence.

As if sensing her unease, Ruby trotted forward, nuzzling her arm, her huge, liquid eyes looking up into Myrtle's face.

A warm feeling immediately washed over Hector, and he recognized it at once as *comfort*. He stared down at Ruby, who merely blinked back at him, face innocent.

You really do have some powers no one else knows about, don't you, he thought, wondering if she could read his mind. *Might be best if you keep those to yourself for a little while, okay?*

The sound of the chopper blades got louder, and when Hector looked up, he could see the helicopter approaching, a black dot in the clear blue expanse of the sky.

"We'd better get cleaned up here, put everything back how we found it," Hector said, standing. "They'll be here in a few minutes."

"Well, I for one am looking forward to a shower," Myrtle said, stretching, and then sniffing her armpit and making a face. "Phew."

Hector had to stop his griffin from rearing up inside him, growling with lust.

Our mate's scent is the most desirable smell in the world, it said, eyes narrowing to slits. *We should revel in it.*

I think that's a third date conversation, Hector told it, trying to swallow down the seething heat that had suddenly risen within him. *And in any case, let's get ourselves presentable, yeah?*

His griffin grumblingly acquiesced, and Hector leaned down, picking up his shirt from the ground.

"What a shame," Myrtle said, her eyes darting over him one last time, a smile tugging at her lips. "But I suppose it has to be done."

"Plenty of time for that later," Hector said, shooting her a grin. "I promise."

CHAPTER 9

Myrtle scooped Ruby up in her arms as the sound of the helicopter drew closer. Ruby, unsurprisingly, didn't seem to like the sound at all, wiggling uneasily in Myrtle's arms and looking up at her with wide, frightened eyes.

"It's okay, sweetheart," Myrtle said soothingly, running her hand down Ruby's neck in what she hoped was a comforting gesture. "Everything's fine. These people are here to help."

Even as she said it, she hoped it was true.

What will happen to Ruby once we have to hand her over?

She couldn't believe anyone would try to harm her – if what Hector had told her last night was true and Ruby had a human form, then surely there would be laws that would protect her in ways that they might not had she been just an animal, albeit a very rare and special one.

I wonder what other powers she has, Myrtle thought as she looked down at the little creature in her arms. *What other things she might learn to do as she grows up.*

The sound of the helicopter's whirring blades grew almost deafening as it finally came to hover overhead. Myrtle had to cover her eyes to protect them from the dust that blew up around them, shielding Ruby with her body as she did so.

Hector had finished putting the blankets and food away, and stood a short way off, waiting to greet the man who was now rappelling down from the helicopter. He looked exactly how Myrtle would have expected someone in this situation to look: dressed all in black tactical gear, his face obscured by a helmet and dark goggles.

She approached as he landed on the ground.

Just over the sound of the helicopter, she heard Hector say the words, "Did you call Mario?"

She was confused, until the man in black responded, "Yeah, extra pineapple, no onion, right?"

Oh, it's codewords, she realized. Random phrases that would verify someone's identity. Evidently the man had given Hector the correct response, because Hector gestured her over.

"Time to go," he said in her ear. "You want me to take Ruby while you go up?"

"Probably for the best," Myrtle said. She swallowed. The helicopter obviously wasn't going to land, so she guessed she knew what Hector meant when he said *go up.*

She passed Ruby over to Hector, and, sure enough, in the next moment, she felt the man in black's arm wind around her waist.

"Hold on tight, miss," he said, but before she could move, she felt herself lifting up into the air, her feet leaving the ground with a frightening swiftness.

The strange feeling only lasted a moment, however, and then she was being lifted into the helicopter, another man placing a helmet on her head before helping her into a seat, strapping her in. She'd been in a helicopter before – sometimes it had been the only way to get out to a remote location she'd be doing fieldwork in – but the whole 'men in military gear' thing was new, and kind of intimidating. Aside from the man who'd rappelled her aboard, two more men sat across from her, dressed the same way: black from head to toe, their faces obscured beneath their gear. She gave them a small smile. They didn't respond.

Hector appeared a moment later, holding Ruby in one arm and the sports bag containing the things he'd brought from the base in the other. Ruby was still wide-eyed with fear. Myrtle imagined for a moment that she could feel it, pressing against her own mind: a wild, fluttering feeling, like a bird trapped in a cage.

Maybe I really can *feel Ruby's fear.*

It would make sense, given what they'd already learned about her psychic abilities.

"We should put that thing in a cage," one of the men in black said, his voice crackling over the headset in the helmet. "We can't have it getting loose in here."

Hector frowned slightly. "A cage?"

"It'll be for its own safety," the man said. "It could get hurt if it's not secure."

Hector hesitated a moment longer, before nodding. "Okay. But she stays where she can see us."

"Wait –" Myrtle started to say, but the man in tactical black had already turned away, sliding a large cage out from beneath the bench seat. He opened it up, and Hector reached forward, Ruby in his hands –

A sudden, tearing burst of fear ripped through Myrtle's mind, so strong she initially thought someone had blared an air horn directly into her eardrum. She lifted her hands to cover her ears, only to find the helmet was in the way, and she struggled with the chinstrap, fingers fumbling.

No, no, no no nonononono!

The word repeated itself over and over again in her head as Myrtle gasped, her heart thumping, her vision blurry.

What on earth was that?!

It took her a moment to realize that the blast of fear had come from Ruby, who was now struggling desperately in Hector's arms, crying out in terror.

Hector had pulled her back against his chest and was trying to soothe her, while the man in the tactical suit had dropped the cage and was shaking his head, clearly affected by the same explosion of psychic terror that Myrtle had felt.

"It's okay, sweetheart, you don't have to go in there. C'mon, it's okay. Don't worry. No cage, I promise."

Hector's voice was soothing, but Myrtle could hear the way it shook. Clearly, Ruby's dread of the cage had ripped through them all.

"What the fuck was that?!"

A man's voice sounded in her headset, loud and panicky.

"Was the fucking – *what is that thing?!*"

Myrtle blinked, trying to organize her thoughts. Clearly, no one was going to be able to do anything if Ruby was broadcasting her fear to everyone – Myrtle didn't want to think about what another blast like that could do to the pilot's concentration. She didn't blame Ruby for being frightened – suddenly being thrust into a world of loud noises and strangers and cages would freak *anyone* out, let alone someone who was literally born yesterday – but the men were right when they said she needed to be secured.

"I can hold her," Myrtle said, her own voice sounding weak and shaky. "I think I can – I can keep her calm, without the cage."

One of the men glanced at her, his lips below his dark goggles frowning. "I don't think –"

Hector interrupted him, his voice low and clear. "She's *not* going in the cage. Clear?"

The man hesitated again, looking like he was about to argue.

HECTOR

"Just do it," barked a voice over the headset. "We need to go, and if it does *that* when we try to put it in the cage then we don't exactly have much choice."

The man nodded, and Hector brought Ruby over to where Myrtle sat. Ruby's eyes were wide, the whites showing around them. When Myrtle placed her hand on Ruby's chest, she could feel her heart beating wildly.

"C'mon, baby, it's okay," Myrtle said, as she took Ruby from Hector's arms. "I'd never hurt you – you know that. When we get to where we're going, we'll give you all the apple puree you like. Deal?"

Ruby looked up at her, her sides shivering.

Frightened. Frightened.

"I know, honey, I know." Myrtle felt tears springing to her eyes. She wished she could do more to convince Ruby she was in no danger, but for now, all she could do was stroke her neck, and hope she could pick up the waves of calm Myrtle was trying to project to her. "But we'll be out of here soon. Right?"

She looked up at Hector for confirmation, who nodded.

"Not too long. A couple of hours."

That seemed like quite a long time to be stuck on a helicopter to Myrtle, but she supposed there wasn't any way around it.

"Okay. I can keep her calm for that long. As long as we follow up on that apple puree promise, or she'll never trust us again."

"Deal," Hector said. He looked up at the men in tactical gear. "We're fine now. We can go."

"Don't let it do that again," one of the men said gruffly.

Myrtle didn't like the way they kept referring to Ruby as *it*, but she supposed perhaps they didn't know what she was – to them, maybe she was just an animal, though she assumed they had to know what shifters were if they worked with Hector. Nonetheless, she nodded.

"She's calm now, so it'll be okay. I'll make sure she stays that way."

"You better," the man grunted.

Myrtle ignored his tone. Maybe this was just how macho military men talked. She didn't have much experience of them to know.

In her arms, Ruby seemed at least a little more settled than before. Myrtle glanced across at Hector as he settled on the bench next to her, strapping himself in before giving her a small, tight smile.

Myrtle wished she could take his hand to reassure herself – to feel how large and solid it was – but with all the men in black around she wasn't sure it was a good idea. For the moment, she contented herself with closing her eyes, feeling Hector's shoulder bump against hers as the helicopter flew them out of the desert.

Myrtle awoke with a jolt. She wasn't sure how much later it was – and to be honest, she wasn't sure how she'd even managed to fall asleep in the first place, given the noise and the bumpiness of the flight... but she supposed she'd had an exhausting day yesterday, and she was used to sleeping in some pretty uncomfortable places.

Ruby seemed to have taken a cue from her and was curled up in her arms, head resting on her hooves, her sides rising and falling in sleep.

Thank goodness, Myrtle thought. Maybe Ruby had exhausted herself sending out the blast of fear earlier. Or perhaps growing pegasi just needed their sleep. Either way, it was better for everyone that she slept through the remainder of the journey.

Myrtle looked around for Hector. He hadn't moved from her side, but he wasn't looking at her. Instead, he had his head slightly cocked to the side, a stony expression on his face.

Myrtle raised an eyebrow and lifted her hand slightly to get his attention, gesturing *Everything okay?* when he looked across at her.

In response, Hector's frown only deepened, his eyes narrowing. He shook his head slightly.

Myrtle felt a chill run up her spine.

That was *not* the universal signal for *everything's fine, go back to sleep, honey.*

Swallowing hard, Myrtle glanced uneasily at the men sitting across from them. They didn't *seem* to be paying much attention to them, but who would know where their eyes were? They were hidden behind the black goggles of their helmets.

Hector's hand pressed against her thigh, and she looked down to see him holding the phone he'd brought with him from the abandoned base. He had the notes application open, and there was text on the screen.

The way their bodies were angled shielded it from the view of the two men sitting across from them, and intuitively, Myrtle knew better than to make a big deal out of what she was seeing. She lowered her eyes, turning her head slightly, reading the text from beneath her lashes.

Problem
helicopt fling in rong direct
we need to get out
wait

Myrtle swallowed. She hoped the men across from them couldn't see the way the blood had just drained completely out of her face. Despite the fact that it was obviously a quick, typo-riddled note, she understood it loud and clear. Something was wrong.

She glanced up at Hector, but he wasn't looking at her. Instead, he was studiously staring at the wall. She felt his hand move, and when she glanced down again, there was more text for her to read.

checking
be ready

Myrtle barely had time to read what he'd written before he'd covered it with his hand again, and then, barely moving, he slipped the phone away.

The next thing she knew, Hector had cleared his throat, his voice crackling on her headset.

"So, where exactly are we going?"

The man closest to them swung his head around to look at them.

"We're taking you back to HQ."

Hector was silent a moment. "No, you're not. HQ is in Sydney. We're heading too far north for that."

The man paused. It was only a beat, but to Myrtle, it seemed a damning, endless silence.

"There was a change of plan," the man said. "We decided Brisbane would be –"

"I don't think so," Hector said, his voice low and calm. "We just flew east over Lamington National Park. Too far north for Sydney, and it's the wrong direction for Brisbane. So how about you tell me where we're *really* going."

There was complete silence over the comms.

Myrtle saw the uneasy way one of the men sitting across from them glanced at the other. His eyes were shielded, but she thought she knew exactly what kind of look she'd see in them if they weren't.

"Bit of a smartarse, aren't we?" A hard, low voice

crackled over the headset. "But there's not a lot you can do about it now. My advice is to sit there and belt up. You don't wanna try anything stupid right now." There was a harsh chuckle. "And next time, don't accept rides from strangers."

Myrtle felt cold panic ripple through her.

What the hell is going on?!

She'd heard Hector check that these men were from the agency, and she knew he'd never have let her and Ruby get into the helicopter if he'd sensed any danger whatsoever, or had even the slightest idea that these men were people they shouldn't trust. So why was this happening?

She glanced at Hector, her eyes wide with growing fear, and found him sitting stock-still, mouth set in a thin line, expression hard.

"Who are you working for?" he asked.

The man simply chuckled again. "You'll find out soon enough. We're almost there."

"Where are we going?" Myrtle blurted out, instinctively tightening her arms around Ruby.

Wildly, she wondered if Ruby might be able to sense the tension in the air and let fly with yet another of her psychic blasts – one that was just long enough to let Hector take control of the situation – but Ruby simply snuggled against her, seeming to know something was wrong, but otherwise doing nothing.

Myrtle recalled back at the camp, how Ruby's first attempt to mind-whammy Hector into getting her some more apple puree had been irresistible, but her second had barely made an impression.

Maybe the psychic blasts are the same, she thought. *Maybe she can only manage it once before she needs to recharge.*

The blast of fear Ruby had broadcast before had been so overwhelming that Myrtle could well believe it had left her depleted for a while. They wouldn't be able to count on it happening again.

Then I'll keep you safe myself, Myrtle promised Ruby in her head. *No matter what it takes. No matter who these men are. I'll protect you.*

And somehow, she could tell that Hector was thinking exactly the same thing.

Whatever happened next, she knew she'd have to wait for Hector's cue. She had no experience of this kind of thing – there was no academic short course she could have taken that would have prepared her for this. *Hijacked Helicopter 101* was simply not something that her college offered.

But it was, she assumed, exactly the kind of thing Hector was trained for. Questions about who or what these men were could come later – right now, the only thing that mattered was getting out of this helicopter.

Beside her, she felt Hector tense.

Whatever he did, she would trust him. There was no question of it.

Thank God he transforms into something that can fly.

"I'm warning you again – don't do anything stupid," the man's voice came again, just as, in a blur of movement, Hector shot forward toward them.

The first man was taken out before Myrtle had any notion of what was going on. But the second one had time to call for help, his voice loud in her ear, before he dodged Hector's attack, ducking his head to the side as Hector's fist shot past it.

In the close confines of the helicopter there wasn't much room to maneuver, and Hector had to pull back quickly. Myrtle hunched over, lifting her legs onto the bench seat, curling her body around Ruby. She was sure the little creature could hear her heart hammering, but there wasn't anything she could do about it for now – she could only do what she could to try to reassure Ruby that no matter what, she and Hector would look after her.

Hector grabbed the man who rushed at him by the shoulder, slamming him into the wall with a *BANG* that seemed to ricochet around the hold. Myrtle caught her breath, hyperaware of how fragile the thing they were flying in was; what it could mean if it were to lose control.

And are there buildings below us?! What would happen if we crashed?!

"Myrtle! Here!"

Hector held out a hand to her, the other poised on the handle of the helicopter's hatch. Curling her arm around Ruby, she smashed at the buckle of her strap, releasing it. She grabbed his hand.

"When I say jump, *jump*. I won't let you fall, I promise."

Myrtle sucked in a breath, terrified, but she trusted him. She knew that once they were out in the open air, he would shift and catch her on his back, flying her and Ruby to safety.

She trusted him totally, but it didn't do much to counter the queasiness in her stomach when she thought about the fact she was about to leap out of an airborne helicopter.

Gritting her teeth, Myrtle nodded, hoping Hector could read her trust in her eyes. He started to yank the handle of the hatch down –

– And at that moment, another man burst out of the helicopter's forward section, brandishing something in his hand.

Myrtle didn't get a good look at it before he leapt forward, slamming into Hector's side with a terrifying speed and ferocity.

"Hector!"

Myrtle stumbled back, her legs hitting the bench so she sat down hard, still protecting Ruby with her body. She could feel Ruby squirming in her arms, but she couldn't do anything to comfort her just now.

Hector and his attacker were moving too fast for her to see, but she knew they were struggling against each other, grappling and trying to get the upper hand – and then the man's arm flashed down, smashing into Hector's shoulder, before he tore himself out of Hector's grip, backing away.

Hector stumbled back, bracing himself against the back wall of the helicopter's hold. He was panting hard, clutching his shoulder.

Myrtle gasped as she saw what was embedded in it: a large, silver syringe. It was what the man must have been holding when he'd dashed out of the forward compartment.

A chill ran through Myrtle.

Oh, God. What –

With a rattling snarl, Hector snatched the syringe out of his shoulder and threw it to the floor, where it fell with a soft rattling sound.

"What the fuck did you do?" Hector's voice was low and rasping. It made Myrtle shudder to hear it.

The man laughed. "Just a little something to slow you down. Don't worry – there's no side effects. Except for the fact that you won't be shifting for a while."

Hector frowned, staring at him.

"What do you –"

"Try it if you like – go on, jump. See what happens. I'm sure you'd be willing to bank your own life on it, but are you willing to bank *theirs?*"

He jerked his head in Myrtle and Ruby's direction, a cruel smirk on his lips.

Hector stared at him. Myrtle saw his eyes flicker, before a look of confusion crossed his face.

"My griffin –"

"Slow on the uptake, aren't you?" The man shook his head. "Your griffin's gone – at least for now. So you can either sit there quietly and accept it, or throw yourself out of the helicopter and see for yourself. Your choice."

"We're coming in to land any moment now, anyway."

The voice of a man who Myrtle assumed was the pilot crackled over her headset.

Myrtle was still having trouble processing what she was hearing. She looked down at the empty syringe lying on the floor.

He gave Hector something that suppresses his ability to shift? Is that even possible?!

One thing was for certain, however: Hector wasn't about to tell her to jump out of the helicopter to find out.

"I'm sorry, Myrtle."

Hector's voice was strained. She stared at him wildly, to find him grimacing in pain. Her stomach clenched. She wanted to run to him, but at the same time she felt frozen in fear – and knew that making any move would probably just make things worse.

"Sorry that I – I –"

Myrtle cried out as Hector pitched forward, collapsing face-first onto the floor of the helicopter's hold. Finally, she felt terror release its hold on her limbs, and she dropped to her knees by his side, reaching out to cup his cheek with her palm.

"Hector! *Hector!*"

"He can't hear you, so don't bother," the man leaning against the wall sneered. "He'll be fine, though. For now, anyway."

Myrtle looked up at him, her brain refusing to comprehend what he was saying, her eyes wide with fear.

The man's own eyes narrowed cruelly.

"I can't make any promises about what'll happen once we land, though, and *she* gets hold of him."

CHAPTER 10

Hector tried to focus his sluggish mind, but he felt like the world around him was slipping through his fingers – almost as if he were only half awake, and not sure what was real and what was a dream.

Myrtle...

He wasn't sure if he'd spoken her name or just thought it, but the sound sent a surge of renewed strength through his body.

I have to protect Myrtle...

He struggled against the feeling that he had leaden weights tied to his limbs, and that they were dragging him down to the bottom of a deep, dark body of water. Every movement felt slow and difficult, as if his muscles weren't listening to him.

And even worse than that, when he called to his griffin – the source of his strength and power – he got no response whatsoever. It was as if it had retreated within him, hiding itself away in some corner of his mind he could no longer access.

The thought should have terrified him, but his mind was

so lethargic he could barely comprehend the idea.

I've got to... got to...

It felt like reality was slipping further and further away from him with every breath he took. He felt hands gripping his upper arms and hauling him to his feet. He struggled, but he could barely move, and he knew he wasn't making any impression on the people who were restraining him.

"... Hector... Hector please, are you..."

The words washed over him, hazy and indistinct, like an echo. He tried to answer, but found he couldn't, his tongue heavy in his mouth.

Myrtle. It's Myrtle. I've got to save her.

He could feel rage tearing through him, but once again it was as if it wasn't a part of him – as if he was observing his own emotions taking place from somewhere else far distant.

It would have been an odd feeling anyway, but for Hector, who had had to learn to be in control of his body at all times, it was an utterly foreign sensation. Shifters needed iron control to live with the other halves of themselves, and those who couldn't deal with it sometimes ended up being stuck in either their human form or their animal form, unable to shift back. Either the animal completely took over their minds, or they had to suppress it so thoroughly they could never risk letting it out, even for a moment.

For Hector, such disconnection from himself was a strange and horrible feeling.

If I get out of this, he thought vaguely to himself, as he felt himself being dragged across rough concrete, *I swear I'll never snap at my griffin or tell it to shut up ever again.*

He felt his knees being banged against a series of steps and heard Myrtle's voice again, before there was the sound of a door being slammed shut and it cut off abruptly.

The urge to fight rose up within him once more, and this

time he managed to yank his arm out of the iron grip of one man, swinging his fist toward his face.

"Hold him – for fuck's sake!"

"I'm trying – I told you to give him the full dose! Fuck!"

"I *did*."

The men continued to argue as Hector struggled against them, which told him all he needed to know about what a pathetic job he was doing. It was like one of the awful dreams he sometimes had, where, no matter how hard he tried to lay a punch on someone, nothing would land, and they just continued to laugh in his face as he flailed against them.

He growled. Whatever they had jabbed him with was strong, and clearly, it wasn't about to wear off anytime soon.

He felt himself thrown backward, the wind knocked out of his lungs as his back hit a hard surface. He thought it was the floor for a moment, until his swimming head registered that he was still upright, his hands resting on armrests. No – not resting. *Strapped in.*

There had never been a good situation that started with someone strapped to a chair, Hector thought – well, maybe *some*, but they were a world away from what he guessed was about to happen now.

"Wake up, arsehole."

Vaguely, he felt a slap to his face.

"You gave us a lot of trouble, shithead. Good fight. You put up more resistance than we thought you would. So sit back and relax now, all right?"

As sluggish as Hector's brain was, he could still detect the sharp edge of malice in the man's voice.

"Is he secure?"

The next voice he heard belonged to a woman. There was something different about it, though, and it took Hector several moments to realize that it was because she had an American accent.

Before he had time to think – though *think* was probably a generous description of what his mind was doing right now – he felt another jab in his shoulder.

He rose back into full consciousness as if he was rising to the surface of a murky lake, filled with weeds and stagnant water. He heaved in a gasping breath the same way as if he'd been submerged under water for too long as well, his head clearing, almost painful in its sudden clarity.

Instantly, he snarled, straining against his bonds, reaching for his griffin.

But it wasn't there.

"What the fuck have you –"

"Oh, shush."

The woman spoke up again, and Hector twisted his head, trying to see her while taking in his surroundings. He was in some kind of sterile, completely white room – like a dentist's examination room, or something along those lines. A counter ran along one wall, with a stainless steel set of drawers resting on it. There was no carpet on the floor, only white linoleum, and the smell of antiseptic filled the air.

Again, nothing about this boded well at all, but it wasn't as if Hector was *expecting* anything pleasant at this stage.

He heard the tap of high heels on the floor as the woman who'd spoken earlier walked around in front of him. Hector took her in as she stood before him. She had an air of complete self-possession, cool and calm. Her arms were crossed over her chest, and she wore what was obviously an expensive pinstriped suit and silk blouse. Her pale blonde hair was pulled back into a tight bun, and her eyes were an unusual silver color.

Hector clenched his fists as he stared at her, but he could feel that without his griffin's strength, he wouldn't be able to break the bonds that were restraining him.

The woman looked him over, her gaze appraising.

"Well. They said you gave them a bit of trouble, and I can see why."

Hector felt his lip curl in disgust. *What the fuck?!*

"Oh, don't look like that," the woman said breezily. "We're going to be friends, all right?"

She paused, her extremely white teeth flashing between her extremely red lips as she smiled.

"Or at least, things will be *much* easier for you if we're friends. So keep that in mind, won't you?"

Hector stared at her.

"Who are you?" His voice was like sandpaper against his throat, and his tongue still needed to be forced into co-operating with his brain.

"Cecelia Marsden," the woman said. She held out her hand as if to shake his, before withdrawing it, laughing to herself. "Oh, wait. No. That's not going to work, is it? Never mind."

"What have you done with Myrtle?" Hector asked, snapping the words out before he could stop himself. "If you've hurt her or Ruby –"

"Oh, are those their names? I'll make a note of that," Cecelia said. "Ruby's especially. We're going to need to know what to call her, after all."

Cold fingers of dread clutched at Hector's stomach, and he jerked against the bonds on his wrists once more, calling desperately to his griffin.

Where the hell are you?! C'mon...

"There's no need for that," Cecelia said smoothly. "Remember what I said about us being friends. And if that's not sufficient incentive for you, then I can tell you it'll also be easier for – what did you call her? Myrtle?"

Rage pulsed in Hector's throat.

"Don't you even dare fucking say her name," he growled out.

"No need to get snippy." Cecelia's voice was crisp. "It was just a piece of information for you. Something to consider. We're not in the habit of involving civilians in what we do if we can help it, but if we find there's no alternative then naturally, we do what we have to."

Civilians?

Hector frowned.

"Who are you? Who're you working for?"

"Business interests," Cecelia said. "I'm not going to tell you the name of the company, but you probably know us. In fact, your agency – well, your international affiliates, anyway – have been causing us quite a few headaches lately. It's hard to expand your interests if you're constantly being thwarted by silly things like 'international law' and 'Geneva Conventions' – those things really make it hard to turn a profit, you know."

Hector stared at her. At first, he couldn't think what she might be talking about, before sudden realization dawned. "Hargreaves."

A twitch of a smile crossed Cecelia's lips. "Got it in one. Good to see the agency recruits for brains as well as brawn, I suppose."

Hector couldn't keep the snarl off his face. He should have known – and in fact, he wondered if his superiors at the agency had already had *some* idea of who they were dealing with.

Hargreaves Incorporated definitely had deep enough pockets to pay any price for the egg of a creature thought to be extinct – even if it was likely to be fake, they'd probably still have no problems paying for it on the off-chance it turned out to be real. That was how it was when you made your money in the highly profitable business of arms trading and supplying private armies to international trouble spots.

"You're a mercenary," he growled. "War for profit."

Cecelia flicked a hand in a dismissive gesture. "Absolutely not," she said. "I'm a lawyer."

"For Hargreaves," Hector spat out. "Who are mercenaries."

"We prefer 'private security'." Cecelia cocked her head. "And you're making it very difficult for us to provide any security to anyone lately. Everywhere we go, there's the agency, poking its nose into our business. Not very market-oriented of you, I have to say."

Hector didn't even try to keep the disgusted expression off his face.

'Security' was the last thing Hargreaves Incorporated was interested in providing. In fact, it was strongly suspected they were involved in the exact opposite: stirring up conflicts in parts of the world that were teetering on the brink, and then selling arms and hiring their soldiers out to both sides – with sky-high profits, of course.

And then there was the other part of their business: mining and drilling. Whichever side won the conflict had a funny way of cutting a *very* lucrative deal with Hargreaves Inc. to extract their country's resources – again, with sky-high profits.

But no one could *prove* anything.

Hargreaves were notoriously careful about covering their tracks, and while there were plenty of eyewitness accounts and intelligence reports that *suggested* what they were doing, solid proof was hard to come by.

But what the hell do they want with Ruby?

"I won't let you harm her," he spat out, staring at Cecelia levelly. "Either one of them."

"Yes, yes, heroic speeches, blah blah blah, get it out of your system then," Cecelia said, sighing heavily. "I've heard it all before. Usually right before they accept a massive cash deposit into a Swiss bank account, but occasionally we get the nut that's a little harder to crack." She looked at him, her silvery eyes flickering oddly. "You're not going to be one of those, are you? It'd be a pity to waste all that… talent."

"I'm not interested in your money," Hector said, and he wasn't. He didn't give a flying fuck about money, and never had.

If he'd wanted money, he would have become a mercenary himself: shifters could command high prices as soldiers for hire, assassins, and freelance intelligence gatherers. They were hard to trace and difficult to counter, they healed fast, and were far stronger than ordinary humans. Hector knew of shifters who'd worked as soldiers of fortune or something similar for a few years before retiring in luxury. But it wasn't the kind of life he'd ever wanted – money was nothing if you couldn't look yourself in the mirror at the end of the day, and know you'd lived your life the right way.

Cecelia stared hard at him for a moment or two, before shaking her head. "No, I don't believe you are. That's irritating. I thought we could be better friends." She sighed. "Well, no matter. The offer's there if you change your mind. We could even throw in a bit more, since you've saved us quite a significant sum of money by bringing that fascinating little creature right to us."

Ruby. She means Ruby.

"If you touch a hair on her head –"

"Oh, relax. We have no intention of harming her – she's *much* too valuable for that. No, your little – Ruby, was it? – is going to be brought up in the lap of luxury, like a little princess. We can't have her turning against us, after all. We'll be needing her."

Needing her.

What Cecelia meant, Hector realized, was that they'd be needing Ruby's powers.

They know what she can do.

Somehow, they knew about the extra powers she had already begun to display.

Hector could only imagine what an organization like Hargreaves could do with a shifter who could control people's minds.

Despite the fact he'd never heard of pegasi having the kind of powers Ruby had already displayed, he couldn't deny what had happened to him back at the emergency evac point. Ruby's innocent desire to overstuff herself at breakfast had totally overtaken his mind for a moment.

But what could she do if the bigwigs at Hargreaves were the ones controlling her?

Hector shuddered to think about it.

After what Cecelia had said about Ruby being brought up in the lap of luxury, things began to slot into place in his mind.

It was a terrifyingly simple plan, and terrifyingly effective. Raise Ruby as one of their own, indulge her every whim, bring her up to believe that they were the good guys – or at least, that they were the ones taking care of her, who had her best interests at heart. Make her believe she was even doing good, if they had to. Ruby was such a sweet and trusting thing that Hector had no doubt she'd want to believe the best of these kind people, who'd only ever been good to her.

Later, once she'd learned how to shift into her human form, she would be able to pass unnoticed almost anywhere. No one would know she was a pegasus – and no one would know about her powers.

With her mind control powers, she could influence anyone to do anything, Hector thought, a chill running down his spine. *Lawmakers, prime ministers, presidents...*

"I see from your face you've figured out our little plan," Cecelia said. "Good, isn't it? It'd save us having to get around laws, if they're tailor-made to suit us. Not to mention how much time we'd save on trying to stir up trouble, if all we have to do is *suggest* to someone that a war might be something fun for them to try."

Hector shook his head. Hatred welled up inside him, both for Cecelia personally and for everything she represented. He stared at her, teeth bared, fury pulsing in his heart. "I should've known."

"You probably should have, yes," Cecelia said calmly. "Though I have to say, you *almost* threw a real wrench in the works when you reported that the egg was fake. I had to argue my boss to death to convince him I was onto the genuine article."

Hector stared at her. How had she known what he'd said about the egg? Had Hargreaves managed to crack their encryption codes? He'd been mistaken about the egg being fake, of course, but he'd never had the chance to correct his initial report. Cecelia must have been totally convinced the egg was real to ignore that and send her own men to infiltrate the pickup anyway.

She chuckled, crossing her arms over her chest.

"So, this has worked out very well for me," she said. "I see a bonus *and* a promotion in my future. I'll be able to get that beach house in Majorca. Good news, right?" She cocked her head, raising a pale eyebrow. "What do you see in your future, I wonder? I see two possible roads. Either you can get on board with this, line your pockets, and help us out, or you can be difficult. It's really up to you."

Hector swallowed. Naturally, he was going to be difficult. But he couldn't forget what Cecelia had said about Myrtle – nor the fact that right now he was strapped to a chair and couldn't get free, and Cecelia's men were holding Myrtle prisoner.

Myrtle. Please. If you can hear me somehow, I'm coming for you. I promise.

He wasn't sure how, but he'd find her and get her away from here, even if it took every last breath in his body.

For now, however, there was only one thing he could do: play for time.

"I couldn't give you any useful information anyway," Hector said, shaking his head. "Do you even know how the agency works? I only know the details of my mission. I have no idea who's deployed where, who's in contact with who and what they might be talking about. Hell, I can probably only give you the names of about four other agents, and I couldn't tell you what their assignments are. As an asset, I'm not much good to you."

He kept the speech going as long as he could. He had no idea how long the crap he'd been injected with would take to wear off – but at the moment, every second counted.

Cecelia sighed. "That's a very defeatist attitude." She turned away, going to the set of stainless steel drawers over in the corner of the room. "I'm not asking you for your opinion on how useful you think you'd be to us," she continued as she opened the top drawer. "You'd be amazed how even the most desk-bound paper-pusher can come in handy. How do you think we got our own men onto that chopper today? It wasn't because we got some macho hero-type to hijack it, that's for sure."

She smiled coldly over her shoulder at him as she withdrew her hands from the drawer. She turned back to him, and Hector could see she was holding a syringe and a bottle in her hands.

Hector gritted his teeth. Was it more of the shit they'd given him on the helicopter, or was it something different? He knew all about the kinds of poisons and venoms that were on the black market these days. Most of them were totally untraceable. Wyvern venom was the most effective and painful, but there were plenty of others out there too, some of which left the victim's system without a trace, leaving no clue at all as to how they'd died.

As a method of torture, he supposed it suited Hargraves to a T – if whatever was in the bottle killed him, there'd be no gunshot to analyze, no wounds to examine. His agency could *suspect* all they liked, but without evidence they could never be sure. Hargraves was careful not to leave their fingerprints on anything they touched, and Hector knew he would be no exception.

"So, Agent Richardson – what'll it be? It's entirely your choice." Cecelia held the bottle in front of his face, raising an eyebrow expectantly. "Come on, tick tock. I haven't got all day."

"Go to hell," he snarled.

Cecelia sighed again, shaking her head. Lifting the syringe, she flipped off its plastic cap before plunging the needle into the seal of the bottle, filling it with a brilliant green liquid.

"You don't seem to be getting this. We've *won*. We have what we came here for – Ruby. We have that woman you were with. And as for you –" she gestured to his bonds, the filled syringe in her hand "– well. Not much use to anyone, are you, and you're about to be even less so. I'll ask you one last time. You can either be helpful, or you can be tiresome."

Hector glared at her.

C'mon, griffin. C'mon. Where are you.

It was clear, however, that Cecelia was out of patience, and he was out of time. She lifted the syringe.

"What will it be, Agent Richardson – the money or the box?"

Hector snarled. There wasn't much he could do now. He had to hope that whatever she had in store, he could withstand it. He'd been trained for this, after all.

And once I find my griffin again, this will be all over for her.

He had to hope so, anyway. For Myrtle's sake, and for Ruby's.

"You know the answer to that," he snarled.

Cecelia pursed her lips, rolling her eyes.

"Not the answer I was hoping for. But I've taken a liking to you, so I'll give you another chance to answer in half an hour and see what you say then. But for now, sure, let's do it your way. The box it is."

CHAPTER 11

"Where did they take him??"

Myrtle could hear that her voice was shrill with fear, but right now, she simply couldn't bring herself to care. She was no good at the silent and stoic act – there was literally no one in the world who wouldn't be scared out of their mind in this situation, and she wasn't about to try to pretend otherwise.

She looked around, but the corridor they were in was totally featureless. It could have been a corridor in any corporate office, anywhere in the world. They were all the same: white walls, gray carpet. The occasional white door leading into, she imagined, an equally white-walled, gray-carpeted room. It didn't *look* like the kind of place where evil-doers would lurk, but then, she supposed, that was probably the point. It was just an everyday office, with nothing outwardly sinister about it.

The only reason she had any even slight idea of where they were was because she'd caught a glimpse of the brilliant blue ocean extending to the horizon after she'd first been dragged off the helicopter. They were in a beachside city, in one of the skyscrapers that lined the white-sanded beaches she'd seen countless times in Australian travel brochures. Cities and beaches had never been her thing, but she had to admit that it *had* looked a little tempting in photos. Obviously, she would have preferred to visit in somewhat different circumstances, however.

Of course, the two men standing on either side of her said nothing. She'd madly yelled out Hector's name as the other two men from the helicopter had dragged him down a side corridor, but he hadn't seemed to hear her. She'd struggled, but that had only made the men escorting her tighten their grips on her upper arms, until their fingers were digging into her skin painfully, hard enough to bruise.

She couldn't break free.

Ruby was quiet in her arms, as if sensing that making a fuss wouldn't help – but it was the one time when Myrtle wished she *would*. Ruby was small enough and mobile enough that she might have had a chance to escape if she really tried.

Unless these men turn into flying animals, Myrtle thought, looking uneasily at first one and then the other. They still had their flight helmets and goggles on, so she could only see a sliver of their faces – just their cheeks, noses and mouths, which were set in hard, impassive lines.

Not friendly types at all.

"Where are we going?" she asked. Not that she was expecting an answer. But at the very least, she thought she might be able to goad them into talking a little – perhaps they'd let something slip. "I'm an American citizen, and I have rights –"

"It doesn't matter," one of the men said gruffly. He glanced down at her. "So don't try that."

Well, at least she'd gotten a response. Now all she had to do was keep picking.

"What do you mean, it doesn't matter? Of course it

matters! Unless you tell me who you are and where you're taking me –"

"We're not even interested in you," the second man spoke up. "Only in that... thing. But if having you around keeps it calm, then you're coming too. Satisfied?"

A little more than before, Myrtle thought, but they hadn't told her anything she hadn't been able to work out for herself. In the moments between her whirling, terrified thoughts about Hector and Ruby, she'd been able to figure out that much, at least. Whoever these people were, they were clearly the ones who'd been out to buy Ruby's egg. Somehow they'd managed to infiltrate the organization Hector worked for and send their own people to pick them up, rather than anyone more friendly.

But how? How had they known? How did they know where we were?

She recalled that Hector had reported in to his HQ a few minutes after they'd arrived at the shipping container base.

Could that have been it? Myrtle wondered, swallowing. *Could they have... tapped the call somehow? Or is there something else going on? Was this an inside job?*

A cold shudder ran through her.

How they knew is a problem for later, Myrtle told herself firmly. Right now, she had more immediate issues. Like *How the hell am I going to escape from these goons, find Hector, and get out of here?!*

She looked down at Ruby, who was watching her with wide, frightened eyes.

It's okay, sweetheart... all right, it's not, but I promise you I'll do everything I can to make *it okay.*

Thinking back to the psychic blast of fear in the helicopter, Myrtle swallowed.

I suppose it's too much to hope for that you've got another one of those in you, isn't it, Rubes.

She ignored the way she'd switched over to Hector's nickname for Ruby. It was a forlorn hope, anyway – Ruby needed time to recharge her powers. Myrtle would just have to save both of them.

"Mee-eeh?"

Ruby let out a soft whinny that sounded almost questioning. Myrtle would have held her closer if she could, but the goons' grip on her arms prevented her.

Until, suddenly, they weren't holding her arms anymore.

Myrtle stumbled a little as they suddenly let her go. They'd been dragging her along so forcefully that she almost hadn't been moving by her own power at all, and once their grip was gone, Myrtle had to steady herself.

What the...

"Mee-*eeh!*" Ruby said again, as Myrtle regained her balance, and this time, her whinny sounded urgent.

Catching her breath, Myrtle turned, just in time to see the goons staggering, their hands covering their helmeted heads, their mouths pulled into pained grimaces.

"What the *fuck* –" one of them muttered, his voice strained. "Fucking – *what is this* –"

But Myrtle knew *exactly* what was going on. Ruby had gathered all the strength she had left and was using it to psychically attack the two men.

If what she was doing here was even half as disorienting as the attack she'd broadcast on the helicopter, then Myrtle knew they'd be in no fit state to pursue her, though her own head felt completely clear. Ruby was a fast learner, after all – she was managing to direct her powers now, and use them only against certain targets.

And Myrtle was using the opening that Ruby was putting all her strength into giving her to stand here and stare stupidly.

"Meee-*eeeh!*"

That was *definitely* a *'Come on, hurry up!'* sound, Myrtle decided.

One of the men was already shaking his head to clear it, seemingly beginning to recover from Ruby's efforts to cloud his mind.

Wildly, Myrtle looked around. She was looking for an escape route – not easy in a long, featureless corridor.

Myrtle caught her breath.

Featureless, except for one thing.

There was a medium-sized fire extinguisher hanging on the wall a couple of feet ahead of her.

Very safety conscious for an evil organization, Myrtle thought as she made a lunge for it. She'd never done a single violent thing in her entire life – she'd only just barely passed the self-defense course she'd taken because she'd been so worried about hurting the instructor during her test – but right now, with her adrenaline surging and with the safety of Hector and Ruby on the line, she knew what she had to do.

She didn't like the thought of hurting anyone, but to protect Ruby and Hector – well, it wasn't really a choice, was it?

"Ruby!"

She called out her name to warn her before she threw her arms up, sending the tiny pegasus up into the air. Ruby, understanding, took off, her wings fluttering to keep her airborne.

As soon as she was gone, Myrtle grabbed the fire extinguisher, yanking it from the wall before using her whole body to swing it around in a wide arc, catching the first of the staggering goons in the side of the neck. He crashed against the wall of the corridor before collapsing onto the gray carpet, and didn't move.

"What the *fuck* –"

The second man had clearly begun to recover. He stood

upright, but his knees were still buckled, his movements shaky and uncertain. Myrtle didn't intend to let him get any further.

Letting out an inelegant grunt of effort, Myrtle heaved the fire extinguisher up, using every single muscle she'd built up during hundreds of hours of fieldwork carrying all her equipment across treacherous terrain. The extinguisher caught him in the jaw, sending him over backward, spinning around before he landed face-down on the ground.

Myrtle paused, breathing heavily. The men groaned, but didn't move. It was clear she'd only incapacitated them on a very temporary basis, but she supposed that was to be expected.

She looked up at Ruby, who was hovering in the air by her shoulder.

"Ruby, come on!"

She turned away, racing down the corridor. She didn't care how white and featureless an office building was – unless it was designed by Kafka, it still had to have an exit.

Not that I can leave yet, she thought, as Ruby zipped through the air beside her. *I still have to find Hector.*

It seemed bizarre to her that someone as strong and massive as Hector might be in need of rescue by *her*, but she'd seen what that stuff they'd injected him with on the helicopter had done. She didn't know what it was, but it was clear what effect it had had on him. There was *no way* Hector would have allowed them to drag him away like that if he'd been in any fit state to prevent it.

So he needs me.

Myrtle paused when she reached the end of the corridor. After this, it branched off into two separate sections, heading left and right. She bit her lip as she looked first down one way and then the other. They were both identical, with nothing to tell her which one might lead anywhere useful.

In the end, she went right, with Ruby following after her.

There was no reason for her decision, other than the fact she couldn't simply stand there staring.

Perhaps it had been the wrong choice, because there was nothing at the end of the corridor except a white door that, when she opened it, simply led into a large meeting room, with a wide conference table and some cheap plastic chairs inside.

Fuck. Fuck damn fuck.

Myrtle realized profanity wasn't going to get her anywhere just now, but she allowed herself a few moments to curse anyway, as cold dread filled her stomach. She'd trapped herself, and Ruby with her. She knew she'd had no way of knowing where the corridor would lead and she'd had to take a chance, but Myrtle couldn't help but feel horribly responsible. She had promised Ruby she'd keep her safe, and now, she'd failed her.

"Sorry, Ruby," Myrtle said, her heart sinking. "I took us the wrong way. I'm sorry."

Ruby just cocked her head as if she didn't understand, her beautiful eyes wide and still filled with trust. Myrtle closed her eyes, not able to look at her, as pain filled her heart.

I'm so sorry, Ruby.

Somewhere behind her, she could hear the shouts of the men she'd hit – and they didn't sound happy. She didn't have time to run back down the corridor and try the other direction. They'd see her as she ran past.

Wanting to put off the moment they found her as long as possible, Myrtle slipped inside the meeting room, closing the door as silently as possible behind her. The best she could hope for was a few more seconds, but right now, she'd take it.

Ruby alighted on her shoulder, hooves slipping a little on her skin.

"You're already a little too big for that," Myrtle murmured

as she crossed the room. There was a window in here, at least – it looked out over the city, and beyond that, to the ocean. From here, it was beautiful – glittering and brilliantly turquoise blue. Myrtle kind of wished she'd had the chance to dip her feet into it, now.

And suddenly, she decided she was going to. New resolve filled her. They hadn't caught her yet. And she wouldn't give up – not while there was still even the smallest chance that she, Ruby and Hector could walk out of here together.

Think. Think.

She was under no illusions that she could use her trusty fire extinguisher to break the glass of the window. Up this high, it was sure to be heat tempered and virtually impossible to smash.

If it weren't, Ruby might have had a chance, she thought. Could Ruby fly well enough yet to make it safely to the ground from this height? Myrtle didn't know, and she wasn't certain it was worth the risk.

Looking around the room, Myrtle tried to find something – anything – she could use to her advantage.

"Mee-eeh?"

Ruby's wings brushed her cheek as she took off again, fluttering up close to the ceiling.

The ceiling.

Myrtle stared at it. It looked like the same kind of ceiling they'd had back in the cheap, crappy office she'd shared with four other adjuncts back home.

A memory fired off in her brain of the time there'd been a leak, and they'd had to call an electrician out to fix the wiring. He'd climbed up on a desk and taken one of the ceiling panels off in order to get up and crawl around in it to find the problem…

Without waiting another second, Myrtle set down her fire extinguisher and hauled herself up onto the conference table. Reaching up, she pressed her fingertips to the center of one of the large, white squares that made up the ceiling.

It lifted easily, shifting aside to create a space she'd fit through with room to spare.

"Meeh!"

Ruby was clearly urging her along, but Myrtle was already going as fast as she could. She wasn't tall enough to push the ceiling square away fully, nor pull herself up into the space above. Her heart in her throat, she looked around the room. Stacking chairs on top of the table would be a dead giveaway as to where she'd gone, but – but –

There.

Over in the corner of the room there was a large plastic box full of computer cables and other junk. Surely, that was the kind of thing that might not look completely out of place in the middle of a conference table?

Jumping down onto the floor, she heaved the box up, pushing it along the table. It was only at the last second that she realized she really ought to take the fire extinguisher too – leaving it in the room would be extremely incriminating evidence. Lifting it, she slid it up into the ceiling cavity, before, using the last of her strength, she pulled herself up after it, wiggling onto the solid paneling next to the soft ceiling tiles. Ruby fluttered in after her a moment later, and Myrtle slid the ceiling panel back into place.

She held her breath, not daring to move an inch.

It was just as well, because a moment later she heard the door to the conference room open, and then the sound of a man swearing.

"She's not in there," he called to the other man. "Must've gone the other way."

Still, she didn't hear the door close yet. Looking at Ruby, Myrtle lifted her finger to her lips.

Ruby blinked at her – and almost seemed to nod.

I guess you can understand a lot more than I give you credit for, Myrtle thought as she held her breath, frozen in place.

After a long, silent moment, Myrtle heard an exaggerated sigh, and then the door slammed shut again.

She waited, but she didn't hear anything more. The man *must* have left to search for her elsewhere.

C'mon, she told herself. *Move. Move.*

But now that the adrenaline had worn off, paralyzing fear had begun to creep in.

What if it's a bluff? What if he's down there, just waiting for me to make a sound...

In the end, Myrtle had to force her limbs into action. It took more effort than anything else she'd done before in her life, fighting against every single instinct that was screaming at her to just stay where she was, curled in a nice, safe ball in the darkness.

Hector needs you, she reminded herself. *Ruby needs you. You have to move.*

Pulling in a deep, shuddering breath, Myrtle rolled over onto her hands and knees. It was slow going at first, but she forced herself up.

Okay. Now walk.

Moving as quietly as she could, she got to her feet, taking her fire extinguisher with her. There wasn't enough room for her to stand upright, so she moved forward in a crouch, Ruby by her side.

It was eerie up here – dusty and dark, with ducts and wires running through it. Shafts of light rose up from vents and the occasional misplaced ceiling tile, but that was the only reason she could see more than a foot in front of her face.

"Where do you think we're going?" Myrtle whispered to Ruby as they went along. She knew she was talking to keep her fear at bay and to stop her limbs from seizing, but still, it was working. "It's a little hard to navigate up here, but at least we can move from room to room freely. Do you think we –"

She stopped suddenly as a sound made its way to her ears. It had only been faint, but she'd definitely heard *something*.

Myrtle held her breath, trying to listen.

There it was again: the sound of a woman's voice.

Swallowing, Myrtle wondered if she ought to head away from it – the woman could have nothing to do with the goons and might even be a source of safety, but she didn't want to risk it.

Motioning with her head to Ruby, Myrtle was about to turn back the way she'd come when another noise pulled her up short yet again.

Hector?

Myrtle felt a panicked lump rising in her throat. It had only been brief, but there was no mistaking it. That voice had been Hector's.

She hadn't heard what he'd said, but his voice had been harsh and ragged.

Like he's in pain. Like he's...

Myrtle didn't stop to think again. Cold fear clawed at her throat, but she ignored it, moving swiftly and silently, as if guided by instinct.

The voices grew louder.

"... really not making this easy for yourself, are you?"

The woman's voice was low, with a strange, gravelly quality to it.

"This could all be going so much better for you, not to mention your little girlfriend. I could bring her in here, if you like. Would that help you make up your mind? She's only human, after all – quite disposable. And *very* delicate."

"Fuck. You."

Hector's voice sounded raw, and it tore at Myrtle's heart to hear it. Whatever was going on in the room below, it was obvious what the woman was talking about, and what she was doing.

"Language," the woman with the gravelly voice chided, her voice dropping even lower. She was clearly in control, but Myrtle could hear the note of frustration that belied her seeming ease. "You're really getting on my nerves now, you know. Don't you think it's time to drop the heroic act?"

Getting down on her hands and knees, Myrtle peered through the slats of a vent in the ceiling, and down into the room below.

She couldn't make out much, but she *could* see the woman who'd been speaking. Tall, blonde, and power-suited – the kind of person she usually had to go be interviewed by twice a year to justify why the college should continue spending money to keep her employed. The woman was standing with her arms crossed over her chest, her red lips pulled down into an angry frown.

But where's Hector?

Myrtle crawled around to the other side of the vent, trying not to let her steadily rising panic take her over.

Oh my God...

Myrtle's breath caught when she finally saw him, seated in a chair, his face distorted by a grimace of pain. Whatever the woman had done to him, he was clearly in agony.

Myrtle's heart thundered in her ears.

I have to stop her. I have to do something...

She had no idea whether the woman was a shifter or not, but right now she couldn't bring herself to care. It didn't matter. Either way, she was going to save Hector.

If I can just figure out how.

It took her several moments to realize that her fingers were clutched in a death grip around the handle of the fire extinguisher she'd dragged all this way with her – somehow, she'd forgotten she was holding it like a safety object. Taking a deep breath, she loosened her grip, easing it out of her hands.

It wasn't much, but it was what she had. That, and the element of surprise.

Shifter or not, you won't be expecting this, Myrtle thought, and she stood up as tall as she could, before bringing her foot, clad in its solid hiking boot, down with force on one of the flimsy ceiling tiles.

It crumbled beneath her foot, falling down into the room below in a cascade of dust and jagged fragments.

Myrtle had time to see the woman's shocked expression before she pulled the pin on the extinguisher, aimed the nozzle, and then sent a blast of white foam directly into her face.

"What the *fu–*" the woman started to yell, foam coating her face and head, before Myrtle threw the empty can at her with as much force as she could muster. It hit her in the shoulder – clearly, she had too much foam in her eyes to see to duck – and Myrtle scrambled down, dropping through the hole she'd made in the ceiling and onto a table in the middle of the room.

"Myrtle!"

Hector sounded shocked, his voice still ragged, breath panting.

"You've got to run," he grunted, as Myrtle jumped off the table and ran to him.

Shit, he's strapped into the chair.

Without a moment's pause, Myrtle tore at the restraints, yanking the buckles open. Behind her, she could hear the woman muttering and cursing, flailing around as she tried to wipe the extinguisher foam from her eyes.

"Not without you," Myrtle told him, getting one restraint

open and then tearing at the other one. "There's no way we're going anywhere without you."

Her fingers fumbled and she cursed her own clumsiness, but then finally the strap came free, and Hector yanked his hand away.

"Ruby –" he started to say, a moment before she fluttered down to sit on Myrtle's shoulder. She tossed her head, as if resenting the implication that she might not have played a very important part in his rescue.

"Meee-eh!"

"You have to get her out of here," Hector muttered, as Myrtle slung his arm over her shoulder, pulling him upright. "They want to use her powers to – to control everything. They'll take her if we don't –"

"Quiet now," Myrtle murmured.

She turned toward the door, and as she did so, a small bottle sitting on the counter next to it caught her eye.

It must have been whatever poison this woman had given Hector, Myrtle realized. Instinctively, she grabbed it, shoving it into the pocket of her cargo shorts. It was poison treatment 101 to know what kind of poison you were dealing with, and once they got out of here she wanted Hector to be able to receive the right antidote. Treating poisons incorrectly could have deadly results.

"C'mon, let's go," she muttered. Together they limped toward the door.

Myrtle had no illusions that a bit of foam would hold the woman back for long, but right now, she was only thinking a few seconds ahead. Every moment, every step, counted as a win right now as far as she was concerned.

"Oh, for fuck's *sake*."

Myrtle heard the woman's exasperated voice as she and Hector made their slow way along the corridor.

"What is it with you people? Always trying to play the hero. Why can you never make life easy for yourselves?"

Myrtle frowned. *An American accent?*

She didn't have time to think about it further, however, as in the next moment, Myrtle heard a shaking sound from behind her, as if something large and heavy had hit the table she'd jumped down onto.

"Fine. I didn't want to do this, but I guess you've forced my hand." The woman's voice sounded more powerful now, almost as if she'd grown in size somehow.

Myrtle ignored her. She didn't dare turn around – at, least, not until she heard a thunderous crashing sound. Surprise made her turn her head... and then, she kind of wished she hadn't.

She turned just in time to see the final stage of the woman's transformation: her human body seemed almost to evaporate, disappearing into thin air as a massive, black, scaled form erupted into existence in its place, taking out the walls to either side of it as it filled the entire space of the corridor.

Myrtle couldn't hold back her gasp as terror seized her.

Is she a dragon??

But no. Now that her form had settled, Myrtle could see she had no wings, no legs. A long tail settled on the floor behind her, the front half of her body rearing upwards.

Not a dragon at all, Myrtle realized. What the woman was, was a monstrous black snake, staring at them with malevolent silver eyes.

Myrtle had seen some enormous snakes in her time, but *nothing* like this. This woman was clearly no ordinary snake. She was *massive*, her head reaching the ceiling, her body filling the corridor, blocking any way past her. She flickered a tongue that was easily as long as Myrtle's arm, and just as black as her scales.

For a moment, Myrtle couldn't breathe. Terror seared through her, but Myrtle wasn't about to give up without a fight.

"C'mon, Hector," she muttered, pulling him along the corridor, her fear making her shake.

If we can just find a way out of here... surely she wouldn't go out onto the street looking like that...

Their path had been determined for them, since the other way was completely blocked by the giant snake. Myrtle paused as the corridor turned sharply, leading to a closed door. Hector pointed to it.

"There – over there."

Myrtle trusted his judgment – but it also wasn't as if they had a lot of choices about where to go. At the moment, she was happy to take *anywhere that wasn't here.*

"I can hear the wind outside that door," Hector muttered. "It'll get us to a stairwell that'll take us outside, but I don't know how helpful that'll be. It might –"

"Right now, we don't have any other way out of here," Myrtle said. "It's a risk we'll have to take."

Gritting her teeth, Myrtle made for the door. Behind them, Myrtle could hear the snake hissing, the rough sound its scales made as they pressed against the walls as it moved.

She's toying with us, Myrtle realized as they reached the door. *She's enjoying the chase.*

The door was opened with a long bar that ran across its width, like an emergency exit. Myrtle pushed down with all her strength, and the door sprang open. Musty air gushed out to greet them – and sure enough, beyond the door was a small stairwell, leading upward.

Going out onto the roof didn't seem like the best option right now, but they had nowhere else to go. She started to pull Hector into the stairwell.

"Myrtle. You go." Hector pushed himself away from her, standing on his own two feet. "I'll hold her off."

"What?" Myrtle stared up at him. "Hector, no. You can barely walk. I'm not letting you –"

"I need you to get Ruby to safety," Hector said, putting his hands on her shoulders. "She needs you – that's the only thing that matters. She knows you. She *trusts* you. And she's going to need someone to protect her."

Why is he talking like that? Myrtle thought wildly.

"We're *both* going to protect her," she said, hearing the tremor in her own voice. "Hector, I – *please* don't –"

She didn't get out any more words as Hector leaned forward, pressing his lips to hers. Myrtle closed her eyes, digging her fingers into his arms, trying to keep him with her just one more second –

But then he broke away, his hand cupping her cheek for a moment, as he looked into her eyes.

"Go," he whispered, before pushing her into the stairwell.

"Hector!" Myrtle turned just in time to see him grip the bar attached to the door in both hands, before he ripped it clean off, leaving the door sagging on its hinges.

It had clearly taken all of his strength – depleted by whatever the woman had done to him – but the way he wielded the pole was full of confidence as he faced down the snake slithering up the corridor toward them.

"C'mon, Cecelia," he yelled. "Try it."

Myrtle didn't want to leave him, but she knew he was right about needing to get Ruby away from danger.

Her chest felt like it was filled with molten lead, but she didn't have any choice. She could feel a hopeless sob rising in her chest. She ignored it, forcing her legs to move. She couldn't allow herself to give in to her fear before she got Ruby to safety.

"Come on, sweetheart," she said, forcing the words out past the tightness in her throat. "We need to –"

It seemed Ruby had other ideas. With a defiant *meeh!* she leapt off Myrtle's shoulder, flying back through the destroyed door.

"Ruby!"

Myrtle dashed back down the stairs.

"Ruby! Please!"

She shoved the remains of the door aside – and gasped.

Cecilia was still in her snake form, but she had reared back, fury clear in every line of her body. Hector was standing in front of her, wielding the bar like a club as Cecelia's head wove and bobbed.

Oh my God.

As Myrtle watched, Cecilia darted her head forward, striking at Hector again. This time, he dodged aside, bringing the bar down on the side of her head with a loud *thwack*. It wasn't enough to stop her, though – although her bite didn't land, her head still smacked into Hector's side, slamming him into the wall.

"Hector!"

He grunted in pain, clutching his side as Cecelia hissed in outrage, rearing back, her tongue flickering, eyes crazed.

Myrtle glanced around wildly, looking for Ruby.

"Myrtle! I told you to get out of here!"

Hector's voice sounded strained, and though he was speaking to her, his eyes never left Cecelia's darting, weaving head.

"It's Ruby – I don't think she'll go without you," Myrtle answered. Ruby fluttered into her line of sight at last, and she reached out for her. "C'mon, Ruby, please –"

But Ruby was intent on not co-operating. She slipped out of Myrtle's fingers, rising higher in the air.

She looked back at Myrtle, and for a moment, Myrtle

could have *sworn* she heard the words *Let me help!* echo inside her head.

Whatever the case, Ruby zoomed forward, her wings beating, weaving her way toward Cecelia.

"Ruby, n–"

But it was clear that Ruby wasn't listening. She darted forward, flying at Cecelia's face, front legs kicking out at her left eye. Distracted, Cecelia snaked away from Ruby to avoid her hooves. She let out an infuriated hissing sound, followed by something that Myrtle was *sure* were the words *Why you little –*

But before she could process anything else, she saw a form moving so fast it was little more than a blur leaping up toward Cecelia's face.

Hector.

She barely had time to realize what she was seeing, before Cecelia let out an infuriated half-hiss, half-scream, and began shaking her head madly, entire body writhing and shuddering.

Staring, Myrtle realized what Hector had done – he'd jammed her mouth open with the bar from the door. Cecelia was shaking herself furiously in an attempt to dislodge it – which Myrtle supposed was a handicap of turning into something that had no limbs.

"Come on, let's go." Hector was by her side in a moment – and Ruby a moment after that.

Myrtle grabbed her, pulling her close to her chest.

"Don't you ever pull a stunt like that again," Myrtle chided her as the three of them raced up the stairwell.

Ruby, a contrite expression on her face, stayed silent – at least until Myrtle heard a *Do you think I would leave without him?* softly drift through her mind.

No, she answered after a moment. *No, I don't think you would at all.*

They reached the top of the stairwell, only to find a padlocked door barring their way.

"Stand back," Hector said, raising his foot, as the sound of Cecelia's screams filled the corridor behind them.

The door gave way the third time Hector kicked it, splintering apart before flying off its hinges.

They emerged into the outside world. Myrtle could tell right away that this wasn't the roof they'd landed on earlier. It was some kind of large outdoor patio or balcony, half paved, half covered with a rooftop garden.

"I can try to shift and fly us out of here," Hector muttered.

"Aren't you injured?" Myrtle asked, thinking of the way Cecelia had slammed Hector into the wall. That *had* to have done some damage, shifter or not.

Hector grimaced, holding his side. "Just a couple of broken ribs, but I don't have time to worry about that now. We need to –"

He stumbled before he could finish the sentence, his knees giving way beneath him.

"Hector!" Myrtle caught him before he could fall, wrapping an arm around his shoulders, still holding Ruby in her other arm. "Hector, I don't think –"

"It's the only way," Hector said, his teeth gritted. "Can't go back through the building. Can't –" He groaned suddenly, holding his side. "*Fuck* that hurts."

Myrtle tightened her arm around him as they made their slow way across the expansive patio. Wind whipped at her hair, chilling her skin. The sun might have been blazing hot, but this high up, the wind was cruel and cutting.

"Hector, you can't even walk," Myrtle murmured, even as her fear grew frantic within her. "How can you –"

"I'm going to protect you, Myrtle," Hector said, vehement and determined. "You and Ruby both. I have enough strength for that. I can get you to the ground – get you to safety."

"And what about you?" Myrtle asked. "How will you –"

Her words were cut off by a sound behind them. Myrtle didn't need to turn around to know who it was – the sound had been a terrifying, reptilian hiss of fury, followed by the horrific screech of metal scraping and bending as something huge forced its way through the doorframe.

Despite the fact she knew exactly what she'd see, Myrtle turned her head, her heartbeat hammering in her ears.

Cecelia.

The massive snake she had become was slithering out onto the patio, her jet-black scales shining in the sun. Her black tongue flickered in and out of her mouth, beady eyes fixed on them.

"Hector…" Myrtle could hear the shake in her own voice as she backed away, watching the doorframe crumple like paper as Cecelia advanced through it. Her body was a long, deadly column of muscle, designed for just one thing: killing.

Ruby struggled against Myrtle's hold, and Myrtle could feel her tiny heart hammering against her palm.

"It's okay, Ruby, it's okay," she whispered, though Ruby had to know that wasn't even remotely true. They were trapped. Even if they somehow managed to get past Cecelia's uncoiling form and make it back down in the building, Myrtle didn't know how many men were in there still looking for them. They were three-quarters of the way up an eighty-story building, with no way down except to jump.

Ruby can fly.

Myrtle swallowed as the thought ran through her head. That was true, but so far, she'd only flown short distances. She was still learning how to control her wings, and Myrtle wasn't sure if she'd be strong enough to deal with the winds that buffeted them. But just at this moment, she wasn't sure what other choice she had.

"Ruby might make it," Myrtle said, swallowing, her eyes

never leaving Cecelia as she slithered toward them, tongue flickering. "I could – I could –"

She couldn't bring herself to say it. She could set Ruby down on the edge of the building and hope she knew what to do, but the choice seemed impossible. What if she *couldn't* fly well enough yet? What if – what if –

She couldn't even think it.

But if she didn't, then Ruby would be taken away by Cecelia and her men, to be raised as their tool for evil. She'd never have a life of her own – and if she refused to do what they wanted, who knew what they'd do to her?

Impossible. Both choices are impossible.

Cecelia finally finished emerging onto the patio, the full length of her enormous body curved out in front of them. She'd managed to get rid of the bar Hector had shoved in her mouth, but Myrtle could see blood dripping down from her scaly lips. She darted her head, opening her mouth, her cruel fangs slipping forward.

"Did you really think you could get away?" Cecelia hissed, her words long and sibilant. Myrtle had no idea how a snake could *talk*, but she had to admit that it was probably one of the less weird things she'd seen recently.

Actually, no, scratch that. It's definitely *the weirdest thing I've seen over the past two days.*

"Even if you'd managed to escape, we would have hunted you down," Cecelia rasped out. "You would never be safe again. Not from me. Our reach spans the world – there is nowhere you can hide."

Myrtle trembled, her teeth chattering. The malevolence in Cecelia's voice was compelling – not for a second did Myrtle doubt she was telling the truth. Even if she did manage to get Ruby off the roof, and even if Ruby *could* fly her way to safety, how long would that safety last? No matter how quickly she'd developed in the past couple of days, she was still just a baby. How could she defend herself from these people? How could she look after herself, all alone?

Desperately, Myrtle looked around them, looking for something they could use to defend themselves. There was nothing obvious in sight, but there was a small maintenance shed nestled by the wall of the building, almost hidden behind the foliage of the roof garden.

If there's workman's tools in there, something we could use as a weapon...

Myrtle glanced at Hector. He gave her the briefest of nods, which she hoped meant that he'd noticed the same thing. It wasn't much, but it was, at least, a chance.

In the next moment, Myrtle felt herself being pushed and pulled – and realized that Hector had moved her so that his body was between her and Cecelia, shielding her.

"Try it, Cecelia," Hector growled. "If you want them, you'll have to go through me first."

There was a short silence, and then Myrtle heard a long, strange, choking sound that chilled her to her very bones. It was a long moment before she realized what it was: Cecelia was *laughing*.

"You?" she asked, her tongue flicking in amusement. "One lone shifter who can barely stand? What can you possibly hope to do? You can't shift, you can't heal. How exactly do you expect to win this fight?"

Cecelia's voice held a terrifyingly malevolent amusement.

Myrtle's gut churned with anger and fear. How could anyone be this callous?

I will not let this... this thing *have Ruby,* Myrtle vowed. No matter what it took, she wouldn't allow it.

And she knew Hector felt exactly the same way.

"When I push you, run as fast as you can into the garden and keep your head down," Hector said, his voice barely above a whisper. Myrtle swallowed, but didn't otherwise react.

Her eyes darted to the rooftop garden. The shrubbery was fairly dense, and there were a few large, frondy ferns and small, squat palms that lined the edge of the balcony. It didn't offer a lot of cover, but it was better than nothing.

Cecelia had finished laughing, it seemed, and was now staring at them, her eyes flickering back and forth as she apparently made up her mind which one of them to go for first.

Myrtle felt Hector tense, his hand tightening on her arm. And then –

"*Go.*"

Clutching Ruby against her chest, Myrtle ran.

CHAPTER 12

Hector wanted to look behind him to check if Myrtle had made it into the garden, but right now, he couldn't afford to take his eyes off Cecelia even for a moment. He ran in the opposite direction to Myrtle, hoping that even the split second of indecision it would create in Cecelia's mind would be enough for him to use.

Pain seared through him – whatever junk Cecelia had given him back inside had done its job with a terrifying effectiveness. He couldn't feel the usual itch of his swift healing knitting his bones together again, and when he called out to his griffin, he got no response whatsoever.

The thought that his griffin might be gone for good sent a chill through his gut, but he couldn't let himself think like that right now. Without his griffin and without his fast shifter healing, he'd need every ounce of concentration just to keep Cecelia from making mincemeat out of him in five seconds flat.

The only advantage he had right now was that he was fighting for his mate – and for Ruby.

And I will never let anything happen to either of them.

He'd already managed to injure Cecelia when he'd jammed the pole from the door into her mouth, but with her shifter healing that wouldn't slow her down for long.

I have to find something else. Something I can use as a weapon.

He heard Cecelia's frustrated hiss, heard her scales sliding against the tiles of the patio –

Hector ducked over into a roll an instant before her head shot over the space where he'd just been. He knew she was a titanoboa, and therefore not venomous, but boas in their natural habitat were stealth hunters: they dropped on animals from above without warning, wrapping them in their coils and constricting them before they had a chance to fight back.

Since they were *very much aware* of Cecelia's presence here on the roof, Hector supposed she was going to try striking with her fangs instead – boas might not have any venom, but their bites could still be painful, their fangs long and sharp.

And a boa of this size...

Well, her fangs would likely go right through him, dealing him a wound that would be dangerous even *with* his shifter healing – and without it, completely deadly.

Hector gritted his teeth as his injured shoulder slammed painfully into the patio tiles. He was in pain, his muscles slow to obey him, but he knew the only thing he could do was try to keep Cecelia focused on him. All he needed was something he could fight back against her with.

Or, if I can keep her distracted, maybe Myrtle and Ruby would have a chance to escape...

Not that that had gone so well last time he'd tried it, but if things became hopeless, he had to trust that Myrtle would know what to do. Ruby's safety came first, even if she had to be forced to leave him.

Forcing himself up, Hector glanced over his shoulder to

check where Cecelia was, and found her collecting herself, the coils of her body folding over each other as she wound herself up for another strike. She was fast, but she was imprecise, it seemed – and Hector knew he could use that.

Changing directions, he ran toward the maintenance shed, forcing his legs to move. He couldn't reach the speeds he normally would, but right now, he'd settle for *fast enough*.

He chanced a glance over at the rooftop garden. Myrtle and Ruby were nowhere in sight, hidden amongst the green foliage.

Stay that way, he tried to mentally transmit to them, knowing they couldn't hear it... although, with the surprising powers Ruby had displayed, perhaps she could.

In that case, he hoped she'd listen.

He reached the maintenance shed and turned, pressing his back against it. Cecelia, clearly angry, was slithering toward him, silvery eyes narrowed. She'd obviously decided to take him out before she went after Ruby, which was probably a smart move on her part: griffin or human, she knew Hector wouldn't let her leave with the baby pegasus.

Come on, then, Hector thought. *Make your move.*

And then, she did.

Hector used the ounce of shifter speed that remained within him to dive out of the way at the last second, ducking and rolling out of range of Cecelia's striking head.

Behind him, he heard an almighty *CRASH* as she smashed into the side of the maintenance shed. When Hector glanced behind him, he saw that her strike had mostly demolished two of its walls, debris spinning through the air.

Good. Great.

While Hector couldn't say he was thrilled to see the evidence of just how powerful Cecelia's strikes could be – with all the power of her coils of muscle, he'd probably be dead just from the impact, never mind the piercing wounds from her fangs – she'd behaved just as he'd hoped she would, and done the work for him in terms of getting at whatever was inside the maintenance shed.

If there was a garden up here, Hector was willing to bet there were gardening *tools* in the shed – sharp-pronged forks, replacement tiles, shovels – not perfect, but the kinds of things that could definitely be used as makeshift weapons.

Cecelia flopped on the ground, apparently dazed by her high-speed head-first encounter with the shed. Hector didn't waste a second. Turning, he vaulted over her twitching coils, landing by the destroyed shed. Lifting up a couple of larger pieces of debris and tossing them aside, he searched for anything he could use.

Come on, come on, there's gotta be something in here...

His eyes fell on a reel of heavy steel cabling – the kind used to suspend window-washing carts. It was thick and heavy, and designed to stand up to the worst kind of punishment.

That'll do.

Springing forward, Hector reached for it – only for Cecelia's swaying form to block his path.

She'd recovered faster than he'd thought she would, and she hissed at him furiously, eyes glinting in the sun.

"How dare you –"

That was as far as she got before something smashed into the side of her head, making her falter.

What was that?!

As one, Hector and Cecelia turned.

Myrtle stood in the garden, Ruby hovering by her shoulder. One hand was clenched by her side, but her other was winding back, getting ready to throw –

Hector barely had time to register what was happening before Myrtle had heaved her arm forward, sending what she was holding in her hand sailing toward Cecelia's head.

A brick, Hector realized, a moment before it crashed into Cecelia's neck.

Myrtle had deadly aim and an incredible throw, and Hector had to wonder if she hadn't inherited some of her family's athleticism after all. Cecelia writhed, hissing in pain, her tongue flickering. It was clear her animal fury was beginning to take over her mind – though with animal fury came animal instincts, and the inability to hold back in a fight. If Cecelia's shifter mind took over, she might forget all about how Hargreaves had sent her to find Ruby and bring her back to be coddled into a life of destruction, and instead start striking at random.

And besides which, Hector didn't intend to waste a moment of the opening that Myrtle had given him.

Diving forward, he grabbed the reel of cabling, unwinding three thick loops. He held the two ends in his hands as he planted a foot on Cecelia's back, leaping upward, threading her head through the circle of the cable – and then, he pulled tight.

Cecelia, realizing what was happening, began to thrash, trying to throw him off, but Hector gritted his teeth, simply pulling the cable tighter and tighter around her throat. The rough metal rope tore at the skin of his palms, blood running between his fingers, but he held on, determined that Cecelia wouldn't throw him off.

He could feel her grow frantic as more and more of her air was cut off, enraged gasps and hisses escaping her mouth. But the more she thrashed, the tighter he pulled the cable. Hector could feel his muscles straining, his hands slipping in his own blood, but he couldn't afford to let his grip loosen, even for a moment…

"No! *No!!*"

Cecelia's cry was filled with rage, but it was strained and harsh. She heaved her body over, and Hector had to shift his position on her neck to avoid being crushed, his grip slackening for a moment.

At first, Hector thought it was her last convulsion before she slipped into unconsciousness, but as her body continued to writhe, he realized that Cecelia had more life left in her yet.

But he realized it a moment too late.

Hissing in fury, Cecelia flicked her thick tail through the air, toward the garden –

– And caught Myrtle square in the chest.

"MYRTLE!"

Without a second thought, Hector let go of the cable, leaping down from Cecelia's back and sprinting across the patio.

I'm too late. I'm going to be too late –

And he was. Before he could reach her, Myrtle, a look of terror on her face, stumbled back toward the edge of the balcony, and fell.

CHAPTER 13

OH. OH, SHIT.

Myrtle supposed *oh shit* might be something of an understatement, in the moment she had before gravity caught up with her, and she caught up with her stomach, the lurch within her as she began plummeting toward the ground almost painful.

She hadn't realized what was happening until it was too late. Cecelia's final, heaving writhe had caught her across the chest with more force than she'd expected, knocking her off her feet and against the railing of the balcony – but her momentum had been too strong, and she had tumbled over, fingers scrabbling uselessly at the edge of the railing.

Myrtle heard Ruby's distressed cry as she watched the edge of the patio begin to disappear from view. She'd always thought she'd scream if she fell from somewhere so high, but now her throat felt closed tight – shock and terror pounded through her, adrenaline screaming in her veins as she threw one hand uselessly up, knowing it was hopeless –

Only to have a strong hand close suddenly and tightly around her wrist.

For a moment, Myrtle didn't dare believe it had really happened. Her mind, unable to deal with the idea that she was plummeting to her death and leaving Ruby behind to be taken by Cecelia, had substituted reality with something it could deal with.

It – it can't be –

But after a moment, Myrtle realized that *no*, she wasn't falling any longer. She was dangling in mid-air, legs kicking out, heart pounding in her ears, her fall arrested by the hand around her wrist.

The... the hand that's covered in blood, which is making its grip kinda slippery...

"Myrtle!"

Myrtle was jerked out of the last of her terror-induced daze at the sound of Hector's voice. She raised her head, eyes wide, to see him leaning over the edge of the balcony, holding her wrist in one hand, the other gripping tight to the lower portion of the railing, his torso sticking out into the open air. His face looked pained, but his grip was strong and sure. Myrtle's shoulder hurt where it had been wrenched in its socket when he'd caught her, but compared with splattery death she thought that was pretty small potatoes.

"I need you to reach up and grab my arm," Hector grunted. "Come on, you can do it."

As if to emphasize the urgency, Myrtle felt her wrist slip against the blood on his hand.

Oh God, that's his blood, Myrtle realized. It was dripping down her arm now, and if she didn't hurry, Hector would lose his grip.

Setting her jaw, Myrtle forced herself to heave her other arm up, catching his wrist in her hand. Grunting with effort, Hector hauled her up, his biceps straining to lift her and to keep a grip on the edge of the balcony.

Myrtle tried to do what she could to help him, digging

her toes into the side of the building to lift herself up, and grabbing onto the balcony's edge as soon as she could, pulling herself up. Her heart hammered against her sternum, her legs shaking in terror even as Hector pulled her the last of the way through the gap in the railing.

Myrtle felt as if she couldn't breathe, her entire body trembling.

"Myrtle – fuck, Myrtle are you okay?" Hector's voice was frantic, his hands on her face.

Myrtle stared into his eyes, trying to organize her thoughts enough to tell him that she was fine, that she was more worried about him, that he really needed to –

But in the next moment, Hector wasn't there anymore. Myrtle gasped at the rush of wind by her face, unable to understand what had happened for a moment; until she realized that she was staring at the long, black column of Cecelia's body, mere inches in front of her face.

"*Hector!*"

His name left her lips as she realized what had happened. While Hector had been saving her, Cecelia had collected herself, shaken off having been strangled with wire rope, reared back, and made her strike.

Myrtle forced herself to her feet, her knees feeling weak, smashing her fist into Cecelia's side. Of course, Cecelia didn't even react – there was nothing that Myrtle, as a human, could do to her that she'd probably even *feel*.

Forcing down the scream that was threatening to break free from her throat, Myrtle charged forward, running alongside Cecelia's long body.

"Hector?! Hector, *please* –"

Her words cut off as she saw him, a gasp of horror escaping her lips.

Hector lay on his side by the garden, unmoving. Myrtle couldn't see his face, but she could see that his ribs weren't moving. Blood pooled beneath him where Cecelia's teeth had torn through his chest.

Oh God, he's not breathing.

Or if he was, it was too shallowly for her to see it.

All thought of Cecelia leaving her mind, Myrtle ran toward him, terror ripping through her chest.

"Hector!"

Somehow, she could feel Hector's life ebbing away inside her own heart, pain slicing through her with every slowing beat.

She dropped to her knees by his side.

No, no, no.

Helplessness filled her heart. She wanted to reach out and touch his shoulder, almost didn't dare in case it felt cold. It was then that she noticed that the strange, painful feeling of life sluicing away had all but left her chest. Myrtle felt panic clawing at her gut.

"Hector?! Hector, are you –"

"I have had just about enough of you," Cecelia hissed, her tongue flickering. Her voice sounded strained, and when Myrtle turned to look up at her once again, she could see the soft scales on her throat were damaged, blood trickling down her body.

"If you'd just come quietly, there wouldn't have been any need for any of this," Cecelia continued. "So unnecessary. And now, I've had to kill someone who might have been a fine asset to our company."

Myrtle stared at Cecelia, fury filling her. Myrtle had never felt such a pure rage in all her life – the idea that she had only just found Hector, found *Ruby*, only for Cecelia to take them both away from her was an idea she couldn't stand.

I won't. I won't let her.

Myrtle looked around, trying to find something she could

use as a weapon. The remains of the shed were too far away, and there was nothing else in reach.

No. There has to be something. *I won't let her get away with this...*

As Myrtle let her rage fill her, she suddenly remembered the bottle she'd taken from the room where Cecelia had been torturing Hector.

Without stopping to think, she shoved her hand into her pocket, her fingers closing around the bottle.

The bottle. Filled with poison.

Myrtle stared down at it in her hand.

Doesn't it have to be injected, though? I can't use it.

Or could she?

She looked up, just in time to see Cecelia opening her mouth wide, her long fangs shining in the sunlight, readying herself to strike.

Without another thought, Myrtle raised her arm to throw the bottle with all her might. She might not have had the same kind of athletic prowess as her siblings, but for this, it was enough. The bottle flew upward, sailing through the air – before landing directly in Cecelia's wide open mouth.

For a moment, nothing happened. Cecelia, clearly uncertain as to what Myrtle had done, closed her mouth, blinking.

To be honest, Myrtle wasn't sure what she was expecting herself. But it certainly wasn't what happened next.

Cecelia let out a sudden scream, green ooze dripping from her mouth and tongue.

Myrtle realized after a second what must have happened: the bottle had been crushed when she'd closed her mouth, releasing the poison into Cecelia's system.

The same poison she used on Hector, Myrtle thought, ducking her head as Cecelia thrashed her body wildly, shrieking. *The poison that made him unable to heal – or shift –*

Myrtle knew she ought to run to get out of the way, but

she couldn't bring herself to leave Hector's side. Instead, she leaned forward, covering his body with hers, lowering her head to his side, curling herself around him.

Please, Hector. Please. We're so close. We're a family. It can't end this way...

Cecelia's screams of pain grew lower, her coils collapsing against themselves as the poison worked its way through her body. Finally, she lay still, her head lolling back, tongue dangling on the tiles of the patio.

But despite the fact Cecelia been defeated, Myrtle couldn't bring herself to care.

Not when Hector was still lying on the ground in front of her, his face an ashen gray, eyes closed, blood still pooling on the tiles beneath him.

No, no, no, no!

Myrtle looked around frantically, searching for something she might be able to use to treat his wound. She knew that with an injury as serious as this Hector really needed to get to a hospital, but how could she call an ambulance here? She didn't have a phone – and it wasn't like she could tell them to come to the balcony garden of a building she didn't even know the name of.

But I can't give up – I can't. I've got to do something...

Myrtle screamed in frustration, her throat feeling raw.

There's nothing. There's nothing I can do.

Getting shakily to her feet, Myrtle was about to run to the edge of the balcony on the wild chance she might be able to wave her arms around and attract someone's attention, when Ruby fluttered down to the ground beside her.

"Meee-ehhh?"

Ruby looked up at her, eyes wide, almost as if she didn't understand what was happening.

"I'm sorry, Ruby, I'm so sorry," Myrtle sobbed. She

wanted to gather Ruby up in her arms and cry, but she wasn't ready to completely give up just yet.

Hector had always been so strong – it seemed impossible that he could be lying here now, totally unmoving.

I don't believe it. I refuse to believe it.

As Myrtle watched, Ruby lowered her head, nuzzling gently at Hector's face, as if she was trying to wake him.

The sight broke her heart.

And she knew she couldn't let things end this way.

"Ruby, come on," Myrtle said, gritting her teeth. "I'll – I'll somehow –"

"Mee-eh? *Mee-eeeh?*"

This time, Ruby sounded like she was asking a frantic question, her eyes widening. She lifted one front hoof, her head turning to first look up at Myrtle, and then down at Hector.

Myrtle shook her head, panic wild within her.

How can I explain it to her? she thought. *How can I –*

Before she could finish the thought, Ruby lowered her head once more, this time pushing against Hector's face with more urgency. She let out another frightened, high-pitched whinny, and then –

Myrtle gasped. For a moment, she was certain her eyes were playing tricks on her. It looked as though the light around Ruby was shimmering, a silvery halo emanating from her and radiating in all directions.

I have to, I have to try...

The voice was in her head, but Myrtle knew it wasn't her own. She caught her breath as a sudden bright flash of light made her raise her hand to cover her eyes.

Had that light come from Ruby? Myrtle lowered her hand, confusion clouding her head, while, at the same time, a strange, soothing warmth bloomed in her chest, gently filling her from the inside out.

What the hell is going on?!

Myrtle shook her head, trying to clear it. Her thoughts felt jumbled, as if the flash of light had disordered them, and she almost couldn't remember why she was here or what she was supposed to be doing.

When she looked down, Ruby was staring up at her, eyes wide – before she staggered, her tiny legs collapsing beneath her.

"Ruby!"

Fresh panic swept through Myrtle's heart.

No, I can't lose both of them – oh my God –

She caught Ruby in her arms before she could fall. Ruby snuggled against her, curling her legs up, nuzzling her chest.

"Mee-ehhh."

The sound was soft and small, but at once, Myrtle felt comforted by it – as if Ruby was letting her know that she was all right.

But what was *that – what did she do?!*

She stared down at Ruby. As Ruby looked back at her, the wind lifted the strands of her mane, and Myrtle caught her breath as she saw something shining on her forehead – something that definitely hadn't been there before…

But then, all other thoughts left her mind, as Hector let out a low, deep groan, opened his eyes, and sat up.

"Hector!" Myrtle didn't even think as she cried out his name, before she threw herself forward, unwinding one arm from around Ruby to reach out and touch his face.

It was cold and clammy, but it was *real*. It was *solid*.

He was alive.

Somehow.

Blood still soaked his shirt, but when Myrtle let her hand drift down over his chest she found the terrible wound that Cecelia had inflicted was gone. Hector himself seemed to be looking down at his own chest in surprise, before turning his hands over to look at his palms.

They'd been bloodied too, Myrtle remembered, from the cable he'd used to choke Cecelia. But now, dried blood aside, there wasn't a mark on them. They were completely healed.

Myrtle felt light-headed.

She almost didn't dare speak, in case it shattered the dream she worried she had wandered into.

"Myrtle –" Hector began to say – but that was as far as he got, before she leaned forward and kissed him.

CHAPTER 14

"Hector," Myrtle breathed, when she could finally bring herself to pull back. "Are you all right?"

The words caught in her throat, as if she could barely bring herself to say them.

Hector grimaced a little, before raising a hand to rub his eyes. "I *think* so," he said, and then shook his head. "A few lumps and bumps maybe, but as far as a weekend up the Goldie goes, I suppose it beats being glassed on the Glitter Strip by some roided up wanker with a Bintang singlet and a schnozz full of goey."

Myrtle shook her head, blinking the fresh tears that had sprung up out of her eyes. "I have no idea what you just said, but I'm going to assume it means you're okay." She bit her lip, her words fighting past the sob that rose in her throat. "But I thought you were dying. I thought –"

"I thought I was, too," Hector said, his voice quiet. "I don't – I don't think I can explain it. I couldn't move. I couldn't make my body obey me. I could feel my heartbeat getting slower and slower, and then –"

"Meee-eeeh!"

Myrtle heard Ruby's whinny a moment before she felt her hooves against her shoulder as she perched there. She really was getting a little too big for it already though, and she couldn't keep her balance for long before, with a flutter of her pure white wings, she took off again to land on Hector's much broader shoulder.

Myrtle blinked.

Ruby? Did she –

Her mind flashed back suddenly to the memory of the warmth in her chest, the strange glow she had seen. It had looked as though the air around Ruby's bowed head had been shimmering with light and energy.

No. No. Really?

Myrtle stared at Ruby in wonder. "Did you... do that? Did you really *heal* Hector?"

Hector looked at her, frowning. "What are you talking about?"

"It was Ruby," Myrtle said. "I – I don't know how, but she – she healed you. One moment I thought you were dead, and the next –"

She cut herself off, not quite able to bring herself to say it. Hector swallowed, his Adam's apple bobbing.

"No, I know," he said. "And I think you're right. Without Ruby, I would have –"

Myrtle shook her head, not wanting him to say the words. She felt tears springing into her eyes as she stroked her fingers through Hector's hair. "Do you really feel all right?"

Hector paused, as if assessing himself. "Yeah. In fact, better than I've felt in years." He rolled his neck. "The twinge in my shoulder – that's gone. I think she fixed up a few other things she found while she was there."

Myrtle laughed. She couldn't help it. All of this seemed like a dream. To have thought she was about to watch Hector die, only to have him in front of her now, making jokes, checking his joints and making small, appreciative noises as if he was surprised when they worked – it seemed impossible.

Before she could stop herself, she leaped forward, capturing his lips in a kiss. She had to reassure herself that this was *real*.

And if it's not, I'm not sure it's a dream I want to wake up from.

But Hector's lips were sure when they opened against hers, his hands on the back of her head solid, holding her close. Myrtle closed her eyes, sinking into the kiss, allowing herself to lose herself in the moment. Hector's fingers curled through her hair, and he inhaled as if he couldn't get enough of her, and needed to breathe her essence into his lungs.

Myrtle felt breathless when they finally broke apart, but her eyes were at last dry. She knew she wasn't dreaming. Hector really was here, warm and solid and *alive*.

"Meee-eeh?"

Myrtle looked down at the sound of the soft whinny by her side. Ruby stood there, one tiny hoof raised, eyes wide.

"Did you do that?" Hector asked her, reaching out to run a hand gently over her neck, fingers ruffling her mane. "I didn't know pegasi could heal wounds."

"But Hector, I don't know if she *is* a pegasus after all," Myrtle said slowly. "Look."

She brushed back the silvery strands of Ruby's mane where they fell over her face, revealing the tiny golden horn that now sat in the center of her forehead.

Hector sucked in a quick breath, his eyes going wide.

"Was that there before?"

"No!" Myrtle said, rolling her eyes. "Don't you think we would have noticed that?"

"All right, I suppose so," Hector said good-naturedly. "So... it's new, then. As in, new in the last few minutes."

Myrtle nodded. "Maybe it grew there when she healed you. Perhaps... perhaps calling on her power to heal made it come up. I don't know. It's the only thing I can think of, though."

"It'd be a pretty big coincidence otherwise, I suppose," Hector agreed.

"I've never heard of a pegasus with a horn," Myrtle said. "Though I guess I'm not really an expert. It's not impossible, though, is it?"

"Obviously not." Hector gave Ruby's head an affectionate pat, and she pranced a little, her limpid eyes pools of joy as she looked at him. "How do you keep getting more and more powers?" he asked her, frowning a little. "What's next? Finding a carparking space at Sydney Olympic Park?"

"Be serious," Myrtle said. "If Ruby's not really a pegasus, then what is she?" A second thought occurred to her, and she looked over at where Cecelia lay, unconscious. "And what is *she?*"

"A titanoboa," Hector said, voice grim. "They're extinct now, except in their shifter forms."

"I suppose that's something to be grateful for." Myrtle shuddered as she looked at Cecelia's long, thick body, glistening in the sun. She usually liked snakes – or at least, they didn't bother her – but the memory of Cecelia's fetid breath on her face gave her the creeps. Not to mention how close she'd come to killing Hector.

"Will she recover? I threw that poison she gave you into her mouth – I wasn't sure it'd do anything, but –"

Hector glanced at her, an impressed, appreciative look on his face. "I figured from the green goo all over the place, but gee whiz, Myrtle. That's some throwing arm you have."

Myrtle felt herself flush with pleasure. No one *ever* complimented her on her athletic prowess.

"But yeah, I guess she'll recover. Eventually. That poison seems to slow down shifter healing and takes away the ability to shift. Once it wears off she'll be able to heal and shift back into her human form, but it won't be for a while yet."

"And your griffin," Myrtle said. "Is it –"

"I can feel it in there," Hector said, raising his hand to his chest. "It's not ready to come out yet. But it's there." Hector took a shaky breath, and got slowly to his feet. "But I can't worry about that now. I need to get this cleared up. I need to –"

"Hector, what you need to do is *rest*," she said, but Hector just shook his head.

"If I don't call in, we'll still be here when Cecelia comes around. And then we'll really have a prob–"

Hector's words were cut off by a sudden flash of brilliant white light. Myrtle gasped, throwing her hands up to protect her eyes.

Oh for the love of God, what now?!

Fear flashed through her at the thought that this was something to do with Cecelia – that somehow she'd woken in a flash of light, and this time, she was *pissed*.

Myrtle's hands shook, and she prepared to clutch Ruby to her chest and run, her adrenal gland kicking into gear – but in the next moment, any thought of Cecelia was wiped utterly from her mind.

Because there, hovering in mid-air above the wrecked stairwell doorway, were two pegasi.

Myrtle stared at them, open-mouthed. There were pure white, just like Ruby, their manes and tails long and silvery. Their wings flapped gently as they guided themselves down to the roof, silver hooves tapping softly on the concrete.

They seemed somehow to be wreathed in an unearthly halo of light.

They were the most beautiful things that Myrtle had ever seen.

Their legs were long, slender, and perfectly proportioned, their necks arching elegantly. Their wings – whiter than the wings of doves – folded neatly by their sides, as they turned their heads, looking around them.

It was then that Myrtle noticed them: the slender golden horns both the pegasi had growing from the middle of their foreheads.

Just like the one Ruby has now, Myrtle thought. *But I'm sure pegasi don't have horns – that's unicorns. What the hell is it that has both wings* and *a horn?*

She realized this was all a little beside the point, but she was too exhausted, too utterly wrung out by fear to even wonder why they had appeared, or what they might want. Beside her, she felt Hector tense.

Fear flashed through Myrtle.

"Who –" she started to ask, before she was cut off.

"Mee-eeeh!"

Ruby let out a sudden whinny, flapping her wings and rising out of Myrtle's arms into the air. Myrtle wanted to hold her back, fear still making her act on reflex, but Ruby was gone in an instant, zooming her way over to where the two were waiting for her.

Almost as if they know her, Myrtle thought, realization suddenly bolting through her brain.

As she watched, Ruby approached them, whinnying joyfully. She landed before them, prancing about their hooves, gazing up into their faces. Myrtle watched as the slightly smaller of the two pegasi lowered its head, nuzzling Ruby softly in a gesture of infinite tenderness.

Are they... her parents?

Myrtle gaped, her mind blank in shock, as the two pegasi suddenly began to change, their bodies moving gently from their winged horse forms to something more human.

Something more human was as close as Myrtle could get right now, because the two people in front of her were *far* more beautiful than any other human she'd seen before in her life. The woman's long blonde hair fell past her shoulders, while the man's skimmed his jawline, and they were both perfectly graceful in the way they moved and held themselves.

Is that what Ruby will look like, when she takes her human form? Myrtle wondered vaguely as she stared at them.

"Who are you?" Hector's voice was suspicious, now that he seemed to have collected himself enough to speak.

The two newcomers stared at him without answering for a long moment, almost as if they were sizing him up before deciding whether to speak. Beside them, Ruby let out a small whinny, and they cocked their heads as if assessing what she'd just said.

"Our names are Tassos and Aleta," the man said finally. "We've come to collect the child."

"The –" Hector said, before apparently realizing who they meant. "Ruby?"

"Is that the name you have given her?" It was Aleta who spoke this time. "Very well. It is not what we would have chosen, but once we alicorns have received our names, we cannot change them."

Oh, like an RPG, Myrtle thought, though she realized what a completely inane thought it was.

"Are you her parents?" Myrtle asked in a shaking voice, watching as Ruby lifted herself on her wings to fly in circles around Aleta's hand, clearly dizzy with joy.

"Yes," Aleta replied, "in the sense that every adult alicorn is the parent of every child. It has always been this way, but in any case, there are too few of us left now to make any distinctions."

An alicorn.

Aleta had called them *alicorns* twice now.

That must be what they are. Winged unicorns.

That would explain the tiny horn that had suddenly grown on Ruby's forehead. Perhaps it also explained the powers she'd displayed that Hector had said he'd never heard of pegasi having. She'd been an alicorn all along, and clearly, they had quite different abilities.

"Few?" Hector's voice was low and surprised. "I thought there were none of you left – pegasi, alicorns, unicorns – you haven't existed in centuries."

Tassos shook his head. "That's not quite true. We've simply decided to keep ourselves as secret as possible from the world. For centuries, humans and shifters alike have tried to use our powers for their own gain – and we decided we had had enough. Our existence is a secret to all but a few. It's easier this way. For us, and for them."

Tassos's voice was soft and didn't contain any anger, but Myrtle felt an indignant lump rising in her throat anyway. But Tassos was clearly telling the truth – Hector had seemed completely convinced that pegasi no longer existed in the world.

What must have happened to convince them that hiding themselves from everyone is the only way they can live? Myrtle wondered, even as she realized that perhaps, they were right.

Cecelia and her men had been trying to do exactly what Tassos said – using Ruby for her powers. They had wanted to raise her to do their bidding, without any free will of her own.

If Ruby doesn't hide herself, will she have to deal with the same thing all her life? Will she ever be safe?

"But – but why was Ruby on her own, then?" Myrtle

blurted out. "If pega– I mean, if alicorns decided they needed to hide in order to be safe, then how come she was left by herself?"

Tassos and Aleta were silent for a moment, before Aleta began to speak. "Our ancestors tried to find all of the unhatched eggs when they decided that they should hide themselves. But some – like Ruby's egg – had powerful magic protecting them. We've always known there might be more of us out there, but we only sensed her presence now because she had hatched and was in enough danger to use powers she shouldn't have developed yet."

Myrtle shifted her gaze to where Ruby stood by Aleta's side – at the tiny golden horn on her head.

"That she shouldn't have used yet?" she asked.

Tassos nodded. "An alicorn's magic is strong, and it can be dangerous. Alicorns need to train before they can successfully wield it. But Ruby here…"

Myrtle sensed Hector tense. "Has she hurt herself?"

Alarm spread through her chest. Ruby didn't *seem* to be in any distress, but oh *God*, what if, in saving them, she had hurt herself somehow?

"Ruby –" she started to say, her voice catching, as Aleta leaned down, and Ruby fluttered into her hands.

"Let's look at you, little one," Aleta said, her long, slender, elegant fingers holding Ruby carefully. She closed her eyes briefly, a look of concentration passing over her face.

Myrtle glanced at Hector, and found her own tense thoughts reflected on his face.

Aleta's eyes opened, and she frowned.

"Is Ruby all right?"

Hector's voice was rough, and Myrtle could hear the concern he was trying to keep at bay in it.

"She is… not hurt," Aleta said. "But I fear that by using her magic now before she really knew how, she may have... changed herself."

"All right, but what does that *mean?*" Hector demanded, his fists clenched by his sides. Myrtle could see the pain in his eyes – feel how responsible he felt for whatever Aleta thought had happened to Ruby. Myrtle reached up, putting a hand on his shoulder.

Calm down, she tried to tell him. *Let them explain.*

"As we said, alicorn magic is powerful," Tassos broke in. "It's true we have healing powers, but the magic we sensed here... it was beyond anything we'd normally have the ability to create."

Myrtle blinked. "Are you saying that Ruby... did something you thought was impossible?"

She stared at the little alicorn. *Was her will to heal Hector so strong that she created a more powerful magic than Tassos and Aleta have seen before?*

"Not impossible," Tassos said. "But... rare, and dangerous. By using it so early and without knowing what she was doing, Ruby may have prevented herself from developing her full powers later in life."

Aleta nodded. "I don't sense much magic in her anymore. In using such powerful magic too soon, she may have permanently lost her abilities."

Myrtle swallowed, feeling something in her stomach curdle. But at the same time, she realized there had been no other choice: without Ruby's intervention, Hector would be dead right now, and she and Ruby would be prisoners.

Don't blame yourself, she thought, looking at Hector. She hoped he wouldn't, but she was pretty sure he would anyway – though she was certain that Ruby would never blame him for what had happened.

"We thank you for keeping her safe before we found her," Aleta said, turning her eyes to Cecelia's massive, unconscious form, her lip twitching. "As you can see, the life of an alicorn can be dangerous. We need to keep ourselves hidden."

"Was this... *person* hoping to use Ruby's powers for herself?" Tassos asked, a note of scorn in his voice as he looked at Cecelia.

Hector nodded. "That's what she wanted – she and her organization. They were trying to get Ruby's powers to control governments, and make laws to suit themselves."

Aleta's eyes flashed angrily. "Then this woman knows about us. That can't be allowed to stand."

She nodded to Tassos, who returned her nod. Walking over to where Cecelia lay, he reached out a hand.

"Wait – what're you doing?" Hector asked.

Tassos looked up. "This woman's memory of us must be erased. The world believes we're extinct. We cannot have anyone who wishes to harm us knowing otherwise."

Myrtle's breath caught. *Can they really do that? Just reach into someone's mind and erase their memories?*

Despite the fact that Tassos and Aleta had done nothing threatening, Myrtle felt a small thrill of fear run down her spine. Clearly, there were more powerful beings in the world than she had ever known about. She couldn't imagine what might happen if an alicorn ever *did* decide to use their powers for evil.

"Wait a minute," Hector called out, raising a hand. "Erase her *memory?* You can't do that."

"I assure you we can," Tassos said smoothly. "It won't take a moment."

"No, I mean, I don't want you to," Hector said. "That woman's a suspect in a major crime – I need the information she has about the organization she works for, what their plans are. What's in her head is *evidence* –"

Aleta held up a hand. "I understand, but we do this for Ruby's sake." Her eyes were hard. "If this woman has knowledge of her and was willing to go to such lengths to try to take her, then can you be sure she will ever stop trying to find her – to find *us*?"

Myrtle glanced at Hector. She didn't necessarily like to agree with Aleta against him, but she *did* have a point.

Hector frowned. "Can you just erase her memories of Ruby, and leave everything else?"

"It's possible," Tassos said. "Maybe. Altering memories isn't an exact science. They are all connected – they run like threads through our minds, and to pull at one can damage others. I will do my best to leave the rest of her mind unaltered. But I can make no promises as to how much she will remember."

Myrtle bit her lip as Hector hesitated, and then nodded. She supposed, in the end, that Tassos and Aleta were right, and this was something that needed to be done to help keep Ruby safe. But still, she couldn't help but feel afraid of the massive power Tassos clearly had at his command as he lowered his hands, pressing them against the side of Cecelia's massive snake's head.

Perhaps she was expecting a flash of light or some other dramatic effect, but there was nothing of the kind – instead, after a moment Tassos simply removed his hands, before turning and nodding to Aleta.

"Done."

"Good." Aleta turned to them, a small smile playing on her lips. Ruby still sat cradled in her arms quietly. "Thank you for what you have done for Ruby, and for us. You have taken good care of her – if you need to take a moment to say your goodbyes –"

"Mee-*eeh!*"

Ruby began struggling in Aleta's arms, her wings fluttering as she took off into the air, zipping away from her.

In the sudden rush of activity, it took Myrtle's brain a

moment or two to catch up with what Aleta had been saying before Ruby had escaped her.

Wait a minute – say our goodbyes?

Ruby shot through the air, barreling into Hector's chest and climbing up onto his shoulder. She steadied herself, her hooves slipping a little, before winding herself around Hector's neck and peering defiantly at Tassos and Aleta.

"Say goodbye?" Hector asked, his voice low. "What do you mean?"

Aleta looked ruffled, her beautiful face set in a frown. "You must know – Ruby cannot stay here with you. She's an alicorn. She needs to be with her own people – people who can teach her how to use her powers, and see that she understands what she is, and how to keep her powers hidden from people who might abuse them."

"But – but didn't you just say she may not even have her powers anymore?" Myrtle asked, feeling cold dread settle in the pit of her stomach. "Will she really be in danger without them?"

"We can't be certain of that," Tassos said. "And besides, we alicorns need secrecy in order to continue to live peacefully. With us, Ruby will be safe, living amongst her own kind. Protected."

"*We* can protect her too," Myrtle insisted. But even as she said it, she knew there was at least a grain of truth in what Tassos was saying. Would they really be able to provide what Ruby needed as she grew up? She was clearly a frighteningly powerful creature. Could she and Hector really raise her?

"Meeeeh!"

Ruby's defiant whinny rang out, and she leapt down from Hector's shoulders, throwing herself at Myrtle. Myrtle only just raised her arms to catch her in time, and Ruby burrowed against her chest, tail swishing.

"Don't be silly, Ruby." Aleta's voice was stern. "This is

what's best for you – for all of us. You'll realize that once you're older. Come on, now."

Ruby didn't move. She curled herself up, her head pushed into Myrtle's armpit.

No. No no no no!

Myrtle heard the words clearly in her head, loud and insistent. She bit her lip. Ruby's desires in the matter were clear, but Myrtle had to wonder if she really did know what was best. Despite how quickly she was growing, she was still only a baby, really. Could she really know how dangerous the world could be?

"Ruby." Hector's voice was low, and Myrtle could hear the pain in it. He turned to her, ducking his head to address the squirming creature in her arms. "Ruby, don't you think –"

Why?! You are mine! Mine!

Myrtle sucked in a quick breath at the same time Hector did, their eyes meeting.

Mine. You are mine.

She knew they'd both heard it.

I will not. I belong here. With you. Mine.

Myrtle swallowed. Hector's eyes on hers didn't waver.

All the times Myrtle had unconsciously begun thinking of them as a family suddenly flooded her mind. The time when she'd called Hector Ruby's dad, and the time he had called them *this family*. When she'd thought of herself as Ruby's mother.

She didn't know if the memories had come on their own or if Ruby was telepathically reminding her of them, but she didn't think it mattered. The memories still meant the same thing: they were a *family*.

That was how Ruby thought of them. Myrtle had wondered if she might have bonded a little with Ruby, but it was clear that Ruby had bonded with *them*, and she obviously knew what she wanted. Alicorn or not, she knew where she belonged.

Here. With us.

"Hector –" she started to say, but she already saw his resolve in his eyes.

He nodded, before turning back to Aleta and Tassos.

"She doesn't want to go. She wants to stay with us."

A frown crossed Tassos's face. "She can't –"

"What we mean is, it will be very difficult for her," Aleta interrupted him, raising a placating hand. "Without understanding what she is, she cannot live amongst you. An alicorn's powers don't come without a price, and the price is total secrecy."

"How about a compromise, then," Hector said, his voice low and level. "I agree, Ruby needs to learn how to control her powers, if she still has them, and Myrtle and I can't teach her that. You can visit her – teach her what she needs to know, make sure she understands what it means to be an alicorn. But we raise her. She lives with us." He paused, glancing over to where Ruby was still burrowing against Myrtle's chest. "It's obvious that that's what she wants. And that's all that matters to me."

Aleta and Tassos hesitated, clearly far from convinced. They glanced at each other, their beautiful faces clouded with dubious expressions.

"It's clear how Ruby feels about it," Myrtle spoke up. She licked her lips, hoping she could stop her voice from shaking. "We can't stop you if you decide to take her with you. But I don't think you'd force her to go when she so obviously doesn't want to."

She looked down at where Ruby was still curled into her chest, flicking her silvery tail over her eyes as if trying to hide herself from Tassos and Aleta. She let out a low, soft sound, and Myrtle found herself hugging her tighter to her chest.

Finally, Aleta's face softened.

"No," she said. "We would not force the child to go if she truly has bonded with you." She paused, pursing her lips slightly. "But we expect you to keep your word. Ruby needs to learn how to use whatever powers she does still have. Without that, she could be dangerous, both to you and herself. Do we have your promise? We will be able to visit her, and teach her how to be an alicorn?"

"Of course," Hector said instantly. "I understand how important it is. I had to learn how to control my own powers myself. The only thing we care about is that Rubes – Ruby – is taken care of."

"Then we have that in common," Tassos said. "We alicorns are so rare that we need to look after each other. And if you are willing to help… then perhaps we should not turn aside your offer."

"But I hope you understand what we need of you in return," Aleta said.

"Anything," Myrtle blurted, before she could think.

She meant it, though. Relief pounded through her – she couldn't quite let go of Ruby just yet. She still needed to reassure herself that Ruby was going to stay right where she was. Here, with them, where she belonged.

"Keep our existence a secret," Aleta said. "Be cautious who you tell about Ruby, and what she truly is. If enough people were to know about us, we would never know another moment's peace in our lives. We would be hunted, just as we were before." Aleta paused, her strange silver eyes boring into Myrtle. "Will you promise me that?"

Myrtle's heart was in her throat. She nodded. She knew there was nothing else she could do.

"Of course," she finally managed to get out. Beside her, she could see Hector nodding.

Aleta nodded. "Thank you."

"Come, Aleta. We need to go." Tassos's voice was soft. His eyes flickered to Hector. "Trust that we will find you soon. And we will discuss what we need to do for Ruby to grow up safe, protected, and loved."

Myrtle opened her mouth to say something – she wasn't quite sure what – but before she could make a sound there was the same brilliant flash of white light as before that made her scrunch up her eyes and turn away. By the time she turned back, Tassos and Aleta had already re-taken on their alicorn forms, and were rising gently into the sky with elegant sweeps of their wings.

Myrtle stared after them as they went, the faint impression of their light still lingering in front of her eyes. She still couldn't quite believe that anything so beautiful truly existed in the world.

But more importantly, it means that Ruby's not alone after all – she's not the last of her kind.

The thought brought her a great deal of comfort as she looked down at the little creature snuggled in her arms.

After all, raising a baby is hard enough. But raising a baby shifter? A baby alicorn? *We're both gonna need some help with that.*

The thought sent a warm shiver through her – both of trepidation and anticipation.

Can we really do this? Can I really do this?

She supposed she – they – had no choice but to try. Ruby was theirs, now – and she was truly the most wondrous thing Myrtle had ever seen. She couldn't wait to watch her grow up.

"Mee-eeh?"

Ruby made a soft noise, as if she was looking for reassurance that she really was staying here with them.

"Of course you are, sweetie," Myrtle crooned at her, stroking her neck. "You'll always be with us."

"Too right," Hector said, his voice a low rumble, as he reached out to ruffle Ruby's mane. "You're stuck with us now."

Ruby spread her wings, whinnying in delight before zipping up into the air, wings fluttering, as if she couldn't stop herself from flying from sheer joy.

As they stood together watching her, a sudden thought struck Myrtle, and she felt an irresistible laugh bubbling up inside her. Or maybe she was just hysterical from fatigue. Either way, she couldn't stop the laugh from bursting out of her mouth at the idea.

I told Mom I didn't have time to find a man or have a baby because I was going to Australia. And now it seems like I have both.

"What's so funny?" Hector asked, cocking his head slightly.

"I – I'll explain later," Myrtle said, not sure Hector would find the thought as amusing as she did right now. He hadn't met her mother – yet – and probably wouldn't appreciate just how deeply ridiculous the situation was.

"Well, all right." Hector let out a long, slow breath, before looking over his shoulder at where Cecelia still lay. "I suppose I better do something about that, before she wakes up and starts chucking a fit. But first –"

Hector raised his hands, cupping her face with them, before pulling her into a kiss.

Myrtle smiled into it, wrapping her arms around Hector's shoulders, letting herself melt into the kiss. But as much as she wanted to stay here forever, Hector probably had a point about Cecelia. She broke away from him, stepping back from him with only the *mildest* amount of regret. Ruby fluttered down a moment later, alighting on her outstretched arm. Myrtle pulled her close against her chest.

"Come on, let's go," Hector said.

"Where to?"

Hector grinned. "Up there." He pointed upward to the roof of the skyscraper, where the helicopter had landed. "Those bastards took my mobile phone and my laptop, and I'm going to need one or the other to call Callan to come pick us up before someone notices the giant snake up here."

Myrtle gazed upward. The skyscraper rose dizzyingly up before her.

"Okay, but how are we – oh. Right."

One day, she thought, as she watched Hector's body shimmer and then begin to change shape, *one day, I'm going to get used to that.*

She grinned as Hector, now in his massive griffin form – the head and massive wings of an eagle, the hindquarters of a lion – lowered his shoulder and invited her to climb up onto his back. She gasped as he took off, leaping into the air with one mighty beat of his wings.

But that day is not today.

Myrtle snuggled forward, burying her face in the soft, warm feathers of his neck, and smiled.

CHAPTER 15

Two days later

Holding the phone between her shoulder and her ear, Myrtle did her best not to roll her eyes.

"Of course, Mom – I'll definitely bring him home to meet you just as soon as I can."

"Does he have a friend? Or a brother? Could you bring him too?" Her mom was laughing as she said it, but Myrtle honestly couldn't tell whether she was joking or not.

"I dunno, Mom, it seems like everyone over there already *has* a husband."

"Oh, Myrtle, you know I'm just joking. Your father thinks it's hilarious. Don't you, Jules?" A pause. "I said, you think it's hilarious!"

Myrtle didn't hear what her father might have said to that, but her mother continued on after a moment anyway.

"But didn't I tell you, Myrtle? I *knew* you'd find a good man one of these days. You just had to keep at it, bat your eyelashes a little and show people there's more to you than that big brain of yours. Now. Naturally you'll be bringing him over for Christmas to meet everyone –"

"Oh gosh, Mom, I think he's here now," Myrtle said hurriedly, feeling bad for lying, but *really* not wanting to get corralled into her mom's Christmas plans right now. "I better go, we have, uh, lunch plans."

"Oh, he's there right now?" Her mother sounded like she was about to pass out. "Hector is? Well, put him on! I need to make sure he understands how to treat my daughter nicely!"

"Another time, Mom," Myrtle said firmly. "We'll miss our booking if we don't go now. So, bye – I'll talk to you soon."

After several protracted goodbyes, Myrtle actually managed to get her mom off the phone within fifteen minutes – a new record for her.

Once she'd finally hung up, she flopped back on the plush coverlet of the bed, exhaling slowly. It wasn't that she didn't love her mother, but she really could be a bit... *much*, sometimes. Myrtle had finally screwed up the courage to call her to tell her about her trip – and about Hector – and it had all gone more or less exactly how she'd thought it would.

Her mother was delighted – of course – and Myrtle was happy she was happy. But it didn't mean dealing with her happiness was any less exhausting.

Myrtle rolled over on the bed, conscience pricking her a little at the way she'd lied to get her mother off the phone.

I'll make it up to her, she thought. *I really will bring Hector over for Christmas, if he can make it. I'll even ask him if he can bring a friend, just for Mom.*

With a twist in her stomach, Myrtle realized she was thinking as if she were definitely going to stay in Australia with Hector. They hadn't talked about that at all – there'd been literally no time to discuss the future, when the last few days of the present had been so hectic. But the thought had come to her so naturally she'd barely even noticed she was having it.

Myrtle swallowed. *Would it be possible for me to stay here? I'm only on a temporary visa, after all...*

Shaking her head, Myrtle sat up, groping for the TV remote. She couldn't get ahead of herself. She didn't even know where her next round of funding was coming from. She'd have to apply for a new grant in the new cycle, and hope for the best.

But that was nothing new. That was just being an adjunct.

Nonetheless, she couldn't help chewing her lip as she channel flipped. Nice though this hotel room was, and grateful as she was that Hector's agency had put them up in it, she was anxious to get back to Good Fortune and re-start her moth search. At least when she'd emailed the proprietress of the motel she'd been assured all her stuff was still in her room where she'd left it, waiting for her to come back.

She and Hector had spent the last couple of days here. He'd explained that they'd need to stay put until the agency had finished cleaning up the mess Cecelia had left behind – and until he could be properly debriefed.

That was where he was right now. Despite the fact he'd assured her it was all completely standard, she couldn't help but feel a little nervous.

It's only reasonable, Myrtle tried to tell herself. *A lot of stuff happened. Ruby happened. Giant snakes happened. Alicorns happened.*

And she'd been all caught up in the middle of it.

Do they cancel people's visas here for that kind of thing?

She supposed she'd know soon enough.

And I miss Ruby, too, Myrtle thought, pain needling at her heart. It didn't seem possible that she'd only known Ruby for such a short amount of time. Having her here with her now while she waited to find out what would become of her might have helped, but Ruby was off getting a general health check. Myrtle knew it was absolutely necessary, but she still couldn't wait to see her again.

Ruby had looked at her, eyes wide, while Myrtle had explained that the nice doctors would be taking care of her for the next couple of days. Ruby had given her a sad *meeh*, but she'd seemed to accept the situation.

Nonetheless, Myrtle was counting the minutes until she could go pick her up.

Seeking distraction, Myrtle stopped channel flipping on something that looked like a soap. Her head still whirled with questions – the world of shifters was something she still had a lot to learn about. Not to mention everything else she'd have to get used to – the strange cloak and dagger world Hector worked in, and how completely she felt her life was about to change.

Speaking to her mother had at least forced *some* semblance of normality back into Myrtle's life, and she was grateful to her for that, she supposed. Talking to her mother had assured Myrtle that some things, at least, would never change.

Frowning, Myrtle tried to focus on the soap opera she'd landed on. An *extremely* blonde woman was flicking her hair over her shoulder, pouting in distress.

"No, Chloe, you don't understand," she was saying. "I know I just married Shane, but it's not him I love – it's his dad! It's always been his dad!"

Ooh, juicy, Myrtle thought, sitting up a little. Maybe she could lose herself in a little mindlessly salacious entertainment for a while.

"Oh my God, Maddy – you *have* to tell him," Maddy's equally blonde friend replied, eyes wide. "You can't go on like this! You just can't! It's *wrong*! Why would you even marry Shane in the first place if that's how you felt?!"

"I knoooooow," wailed Maddy, "but how can I –"

Myrtle had been absorbed in just exactly how Maddy was going to handle this situation, but at the sound of the hotel room door opening, any thought of Maddy's sham marriage and her feelings for Shane's dad left her head. Looking up, she couldn't stop the smile that spread across her face as Hector came into the room.

Myrtle's heart leapt into her throat and she jumped up off the bed, crossing the room at light speed.

"Hector!"

She threw herself forward, feeling his arms envelop her. He buried his face in her neck, hands clutching at her back, lifting her off her feet as he came into the room, kicking the door closed behind him.

Myrtle pressed her lips to his before she could think, feeling how warm and solid they were. Bliss rose within her.

Okay, this might be a little excessive, Myrtle thought to herself. *He's been gone all of –* she checked the clock *– five hours, and you're acting like you haven't seen him in a year.*

Just now, however, she literally couldn't bring herself to care.

"So, what happened?" she asked when she could finally bring herself to stop kissing him, running her fingers through his hair.

Hector shook his head. "Not much. Just the same old bullshit as usually happens at these things."

Licking her lips, Myrtle asked, "What did they say about Ruby?"

"That she's fine," Hector said. "No problems, no nothing. We can go get her this afternoon."

"Oh, thank God," Myrtle breathed. "I hope she hasn't missed us too much."

"I'm sure she'll be in a good sulk for at least a couple of hours," Hector said. "But then again, maybe they had more lenient apple puree rules than us, so perhaps she won't want to come home."

Myrtle laughed. "You may be right." She paused, frowning, trying to sort out which question she wanted to ask next from the hundreds that were buzzing through her mind. "Has Cecelia still lost her memory?"

Hector nodded, pensive. "Yeah, apparently so. Oh –" He looked at her a little sheepishly. "And they asked me if I thought you were a spy."

Myrtle was so surprised she could barely think. "A *what?*"

"That's what they were hinting at. I shut it down pretty quickly, but at first they thought it was suspicious how you *just happened* to be in Good Fortune at the same time as the egg. And I guess they thought Cecelia was your liaison, because they made a big deal about you both being American." His lip twisted in dry humor. "They suggested you honeypotted me into taking you around with me."

Myrtle stared at him a moment, gaping, before she burst out laughing. "Me, a honeypot? Have they *seen* me?! Like it came down to me and some seven-foot Russian model in a slinky black dress, and the honeypot hiring agency said, 'Sure, send the dumpy American with the frizzy hair?' Yeah, *right.*"

Hector pressed his lips to hers again, silencing her before she could get any more words out. When he pulled back she was breathless and panting, heat rising in her belly.

"If that's what'd happened, it would've been a good judgment call on their part," Hector said, his voice hoarse. "Because I don't want anyone else, seven-foot-tall Russian model or not. Just you."

He kissed her again, as if to press home the sincerity of his words. Myrtle closed her eyes and let herself be convinced – not that it took very long.

Hector's desire for her was undeniable as he lifted her in

his arms again. Myrtle felt the bed against the back of her legs before she tumbled back onto it, Hector above her.

"So how did you convince them I wasn't a honeypot?"

Hector laughed a little ruefully. "I had to tell them you were my mate – but I would've had to tell them sooner or later anyway. Anyway, it completely cleared things up. You're off the naughty list."

"Oh, well, as long as they don't think I'm a spy," Myrtle said, laughing. She shook her head. "I still can't believe that."

"You'd be a pretty effective one, I gotta say." Hector flashed her a smile. "You say jump and I'd jump."

"Well, I promise not to ever use that ability for acts of international espionage," Myrtle said. "I can write that down for your boss, if you like."

"Pretty sure it'll be fine," Hector said, laughing.

They kissed again, and Hector's hands ran lightly up her sides.

"One thing I didn't talk to them about was what happens after this," Hector said, his voice suddenly sobering. Myrtle blinked, not sure what he meant, as Hector looked into her eyes, his expression serious.

"Myrtle, I want you to know that I've thought about it, and I'd be perfectly happy to go back with –"

Knowing what he was about to say, Myrtle lifted her hand to cover his lips.

"I know you would, and I appreciate it. But I've been doing my own thinking, and I want to stay here, if they'll let me. I think… it's time I got out from my sisters' shadows. I feel like I've never really been seen for *me*, as opposed to being Bryony's younger sister, or Poppy's younger sister, or Aster's younger sister. In my hometown, everyone knows everyone, and it's hard not to make comparisons. Especially when everyone in your family is a local celebrity."

Hector's low laugh sent a ripple of pleasure through her

stomach. "Well, all right, but if you ask me no one could hold a candle to you. So I understand if you want to let your sisters have the spotlight for a little while."

"Oh, stop it. Flattery will get you... well, it'll get you quite a lot of places, actually," Myrtle said, as his fingers slipped down her throat and over her chest. She leaned up, kissing him again.

Hector grimaced. "God, as much as I want to do this, I need to get out of this fucking suit, and wash the stench of bureaucratic bullshit off me."

Myrtle laughed, kissing him again. "Okay, then. But don't be long."

"By the way," Hector said when he emerged from the shower a few minutes later, a white fluffy towel sitting low on his hips. "What about your younger brothers? Do they worry about the same kinds of things you do?"

Myrtle shook her head. "Thorn and Rowan? Not really. Maybe because they're boys, or maybe it's just because they're talented in the same way my sisters are, all gorgeous and athletic. Thorn's on a football scholarship, and there's already a lot of buzz he's going to be a star. Rowan's still in high school, though – he's still got Taylor Swift posters on his wall."

Hector frowned, sitting down on the bed. "Taylor Swift? Really?"

"Not a fan of TSwift?" Myrtle asked. "I think she has some catchy tunes."

"It's not that," Hector said, shaking his head. "I'm sure she's lovely. It just reminds me of how old I am. All the pop singers these days – I can hardly keep them straight in my head."

Myrtle laughed. "Well, maybe. So who was *your* fantasy girlfriend as a kid, then?"

Hector looked up at the ceiling, a dreamy look crossing his face. "Chrissy Amphlett."

Now it was Myrtle's turn to frown. "Who's that?"

Hector looked aghast. "No – really? You *have* to know. I refuse to believe you don't know. The Divinyls. No, c'mon, you *do* know." Hector stood up, threw a sultry glance over his shoulder, swiveled his hips, and started to sing. *"I don't want aaaaanybody else, when I think a-bout you I touch myyyyself –"*

"Okay, okay, okay! Yeah, I know that song!" Myrtle cried out, laughing and covering her face with her hands to hide how red she'd gone. Who knew she'd find an impromptu rendition of a '90s hit such a turn on? "Oh my God! Really?"

"Hard not to like a woman who knows what she wants," Hector said, flopping back down on the bed beside her. He rolled over, the water from his shower still glistening on his chest. "And speaking of, is there anything *you* want?"

Myrtle swallowed, feeling her throat grow tight. Hector's gaze was intense, his expression suddenly serious. As much as she'd learned to relax around him – and to be bolder than she'd ever imagined she could be – it still made her heart flutter when she thought about actually *telling* him what she wanted when she looked at him.

Go on, she urged herself. *He just* said *he likes it when a woman knows what she wants.*

"A lot of things," she said, her voice soft.

"What things?"

Myrtle felt herself blush anew. Hector's voice was a throaty rumble, and it sent sparks of heat straight through her.

"Things like this," she said, reaching forward, running her hand over his chest, the tips of her fingers brushing lightly through his hair and over his glistening skin.

Hector groaned as her hand delved lower over his abs, brushing against the edge of his towel. Myrtle took a deep breath, licking her lips.

Their first time out on the mountain had seemed so natural – she hadn't had to think about anything. Her body had guided her, showing her what to do. She'd always been self-conscious during sex, which was probably why she'd never really enjoyed it that much. She had never been able to stop herself from thinking that her boyfriend at the time *had* to be thinking about someone else, or imagining that her body looked different, felt different. That *she* was different.

Looking up into Hector's face now, she felt her self-confidence strengthen. Between the way he was looking at her now and the steadily growing bulge beneath his towel, there was no way she could doubt how desirable he found her.

His brown eyes seemed to be lighted from within, his arousal almost making them glow. The golden flecks around his pupils made his irises look almost caramel-colored, and his forehead creased as her hand wandered lower, brushing between his thighs.

"Myrtle..."

The sound of her name slipping out from between his lips made her groan. No one had ever said her name like that before. She'd always hated it – but she thought she could grow to love it, if she heard it said like that a few more times.

"You're really driving me crazy here," Hector said, his voice strained as she continued to tease him, her fingers playing over his skin. "Any more of this and I'm not going to be responsible for my actions."

Myrtle laughed, her hand slipping down his thigh again – before she quickly pulled it away. "Maybe you should just go crazy then."

She heard the low growl in his throat, and saw the gorgeously wicked flash in his eyes before she suddenly found herself on her back on the bed, the long t-shirt she was wearing whipped away, and Hector above her, his hips between her thighs.

He'd moved so fast she'd barely seen him do it, and she gasped now, arousal flooding through her, wetness growing between her thighs.

His lips were on hers before she even had time to think – hard and hot and demanding, his hands on her waist, his erect cock sliding against her stomach. Myrtle writhed beneath him, crying out into his mouth at the feeling of his hardness against her, and knowing that it was all for her.

Never before had she felt so aware of herself – so aware of the tingling of her skin, of her panting breath, of the droplets of sweat that collected between their bodies. Hector's hands slid up her sides, his thumbs brushing gently over the sides of her breasts. Myrtle shivered, her arms winding around his back, her thighs parting around him.

He lowered his head, kissing his way down her jaw, her neck, her throat. Myrtle cried out when his mouth at last dipped to her breasts, teasing her nipples with his lips and tongue, sending ripples of pleasure through her body. She arched up, gasping, her hands caught in his hair as he took his time over her, bringing her again and again to the brink of release.

Never before had she felt this way. Hector seemed to know just what to do to make her curl her toes and cry out. But it wasn't only the physical sensations that were pulsing through her, bringing her such desperate pleasure. It was the sense that he knew her, the way no one else in the world possibly could – that their *souls* knew each other, and that they were growing closer and closer with every single beat of their hearts.

"God, Hector," Myrtle gasped, her breath hitching. After everything they'd been through together, she knew it was natural for them to feel close – but it was more than that. She had believed him when he'd spoken of the mate bond, of the way their fates and souls were intertwined. She'd felt the spark between them when their hands had touched.

But it was only now that Myrtle thought she could truly *feel* their bond as it grew inside her, wreathing her heart with a golden glowing light that seemed to flow from her chest and into his.

Of course, everything Hector's hands and teeth and tongue were doing to her felt *amazing*, but what it *meant* was even more important: the affirmation of their bond, of what they truly meant to each other.

The scent of Hector's sweat was heady and utterly masculine. His arms around her were stronger than anything she'd ever known. Need for him swelled within her.

"Please, Hector. God, *please...*"

His response to her plea was a low rumble of a laugh. Myrtle shivered as the sound vibrated through her. She was wetter than she could remember ever having been before, desire racing through her veins.

She opened her mouth in a silent cry, writhing on the bed as his fingers brushed against her opening, teasing her gently. Her body jerked up, feet slipping on the sheets, her nails digging into his back as his fingers slipped inside, his thumb circling her clit as they did so.

Myrtle closed her eyes, panting as he moved his fingers inside her. It was all too much and not enough at the same time, her desperation for more making her whine out loud, her muscles clenching and shaking every time he moved.

"Please, God, don't stop," she gasped out. *"Please..."*

She whimpered as she felt Hector's hand leave her, and she wondered what he could be thinking. She'd been so close, *so close* to climax, and –

Oh!

Myrtle twisted on the bed, shuddering as his tongue brushed against her. His strong hands pushed her thighs apart, giving him greater access, as his mouth found every part of her, sending wave after wave of pleasure through her body. Myrtle was helpless against them, her body jerking, heat building in her belly. She both wanted to reach her climax and for this to never end – she wanted to go on feeling this way for ever and ever, these sparks of ecstasy racing along every nerve in her body, stars swimming across her vision.

She cried out when she at last tumbled over the edge, her fingers clutching at his hair, thighs shuddering around his head. Heat coursed through her again and again, seeming to lift her off the bed, until she fell back, senseless and sweaty, against the sheets.

Myrtle still felt utterly breathless when Hector's face reappeared above her, his eyes dark with desire, hair sweaty and tousled.

God, he looks good.

She leaned up to kiss him, opening her mouth to let his tongue twine with hers. His hand came up to cup the back of her head, his fingers tangled in her hair, his lust for her undeniable.

"That was – that was –"

She felt too breathless to get the words out.

Amazing. Incredible. The best I've ever felt in my entire life, she thought, but her head was a mess with a weird combination of post-orgasm lassitude and renewed desire. She could feel heat gathering in her belly again already – she already wanted *more*.

"Do you need to go to sleep?" Hector's voice was hoarse, and she could still feel his hardness pressing against her, his towel discarded. The sensation sent a shiver through her, and she knew that *sleep* was something for some indefinable far-off point in the future.

"Not yet," she said, playing her fingers through the damp hair at the nape of his neck. She reached her other hand down between them, curling her fingers around him, filling her palm with his length and hardness. Hector groaned, his eyes fluttering shut, his head flung back, as she worked her fingers over him.

"Come on," she whispered, watching, entranced, as sweat beaded over his throat. "Please. I want it."

Evidently, Hector had been telling the stone cold truth when he said he liked a woman who knew what she wanted, because a soft groan left his lips at her words, and he looked down at her, his face flushed.

"God, I love it when you say things like that."

Myrtle smiled as she lifted her head, her lips next to his ear. "Please. I *want* it. *Now.*"

She didn't have to tell him again. Hector shifted his hips, positioning himself between her thighs. The next moment, she felt him, hot and achingly hard, pressing against her opening.

Heat coursed through her, filling her veins. Myrtle closed her eyes, holding her breath – only to let out a long, breathy moan as he slid into her, filling her to perfection. She tightened around him and heard his desperate gasp in response, his mouth buried against her neck.

"Fuck, *Myrtle...*"

She let out a cry as he thrust into her and reached up, winding her arms around his shoulders. She wanted to hold him as close as she possibly could, to feel every inch of him – and yet, she knew that it would still never be close enough.

Physical closeness was only secondary, though. She knew that even now, it was their souls that touched each other – the deepest parts of themselves mingled together, bound to each other, never to be torn apart. She could feel the golden glow of their bond in her chest, enveloping her heart and drawing them together, forging an unbreakable connection.

Myrtle opened her mouth, teetering on the edge of climax, every movement Hector made pushing her closer and closer to the brink. She could feel that he was close, his body tense, his muscles clenching, his hoarse cries growing louder and louder.

At last, at last, Myrtle felt the white-hot rush of heat over her body as her orgasm took her over, shuddering irresistibly through her body. Sweeping ecstasy whited out her vision and she cried out, unable to stop herself. Her spine arched, and she instinctively clenched her walls around Hector's hard length inside her, as if trying to draw him even deeper into her body.

Hector's own ragged cry came only a moment later, his muscles twitching, his hands buried in her sweaty hair. She felt him pulse within her, heat filling her, as they rode the waves of their climax together.

Mine. Mine. Mine.

Myrtle could *feel* the words as well as hear them in her mind – beating through in time with her heartbeat.

He's mine. And I'm his.

She had never been more sure of anything before in her life.

Hector lowered his head, dropping kisses against her lips, hand cupping her jaw, thumb stroking over her cheek.

The kiss became slow and languorous, and Myrtle let herself fall into it. Every muscle in her body felt deliciously relaxed – and she knew that this time she wouldn't be able to hold off sleep for long.

Hector eventually rolled slightly away from her, though he immediately wound his arm around her shoulders, drawing her into his chest. Myrtle happily snuggled against him, curling into his side, waiting for her breath to slow.

"Mmmm."

She closed her eyes. Happiness coursed through her. Hector's lips pressed against her forehead.

"Sleep?" he asked her.

"Sleep," she agreed – and a moment later, she was there.

Chapter 16

"Thanks for doing this, Callan. I really appreciate it."

Hector watched as Ruby cautiously sniffed her way along Callan's dining room table, nostrils twitching, tail swishing. She clearly wasn't yet sure what to make of this new environment.

"No worries," Callan said, watching as Ruby inspected the fake potted plant in the middle of the table. "I just hope she likes me."

"Well… we're trying to get her used to being around more people." Hector glanced up at him, raising his hands a little helplessly. "Don't mind her if she's a little standoffish at first. Oh, and don't let her bully you. She knows the rules – one bottle of apple puree per day, for dessert. She has to eat some other stuff first."

Callan laughed. "She looks so sweet. I'm sure she won't –"

At that moment, Ruby glanced up, fixing Callan with a steady stare. Hector watched as Callan blinked, his fingers twitching. Then, he shook himself and frowned.

"What the –"

"That's what I'm talking about," Hector said. "She'll try it if she thinks she can get away with it." He turned to Ruby. "You know that's not allowed. We've talked about this – repeatedly. And you also know it doesn't work anymore, so just cut it out. All right?"

Ruby snorted, tossing her head, before spreading her wings and fluttering up to perch on the ceiling fan.

"She'll come down when she's ready," Hector said.

"Oh. Right." Callan looked up. "When you asked me to babysit, this was *not* what I had in mind. What the hell *was* that just now?"

"She tried to, uh, mind-whammy you," Hector said.

Callan turned to him, raising an eyebrow. "She tried to what? *Mind-whammy?*"

"That's what Myrtle called it, and it seemed like a good way to describe it," Hector said. He glanced up to where Ruby was sulking by the ceiling. "She still likes to try it out, every now and then. But it's not as effective as it used to be."

Hector frowned a little as he looked up at Ruby. No one was sure whether her full powers would ever return to her, or if, in putting all her energy into healing him, she had burned them out for good. Aleta and Tassos hadn't seemed to know either, and Hector couldn't help but feel at least partially responsible.

If she hadn't had to heal me, she'd still have them, he thought. *She'd grow up to be the powerful alicorn she was meant to be.*

He'd voiced this thought to Myrtle before, and Myrtle had told him to stop thinking like that – that if Ruby had to make the same choice knowing the consequences, she'd do the same thing again.

And besides which, we can't turn back time. We're together. You, me, Ruby. And that's the only thing that matters, isn't it?

Hector was forced to admit it was true. And aside from a few sulks when her attempts to sway people to her point of view didn't work, Ruby didn't seem terribly fazed about the loss of her powers.

Hopefully, she just knows something we don't, Hector thought, *and she can still feel them inside her, waiting to come out again.*

On second thoughts, he realized, he wasn't sure if that was a comforting idea or not.

"We should be back in three days," Hector said. "If there's any issues, just give us a call."

Callan nodded. "No worries." He paused, cocking his head, and Hector braced himself for what he knew was coming. This was the first time he'd really gotten to talk to Callan since he'd returned from the mission that had been half disaster, half the best thing that had ever happened to him in his life. Callan had been in the debriefings, so he already knew all about the disaster part: how Hector had misread the signs from the egg, had almost allowed Cecelia to take Ruby away from them, and had very nearly lost his own life fighting her in a rooftop garden on the Gold Coast.

Speaking of...

"I don't suppose Cecelia's had anything to say, has she?"

Callan shook his head. "She still doesn't remember anything. It's the most complete case of amnesia the doctors say they've ever seen. She can't remember anything about who she is, or why she came here."

Hector couldn't help but frown. "That's a little convenient."

"If it's a front, it's a good one," Callan said, shrugging. "Either way, she's in custody."

Hector shook his head, but to be honest, he didn't truly believe Cecelia was faking it. Tassos hadn't been lying when he'd said erasing memories wasn't an exact science – or else, he'd just ignored Hector's request and done what he had always intended to do.

"Believe me, I'll tell you if she starts talking," Callan said. He cocked his head. "But don't you have anything else you'd rather talk about?"

Hector swallowed. He might have had a chance to get Callan up to speed with everything that had happened on his mission, but talking about Myrtle – that, they hadn't had the chance to do. Callan had been the first to know that Hector had found her, and had helped him get his head on straight during those first few minutes when Hector hadn't known left from right. But beyond that, they'd had no chance to talk at all.

And now, he found he couldn't stop the goofy grin that spread across his face at the thought of Myrtle.

"So… I take it your mate thinks you're at least a *little* less of an arsehole now?" Callan asked, a small smirk crossing his lips.

"Let's hope so," Hector said. "It's not like I have a lot left I could do to try to make a good impression on her."

Callan laughed gently. "Well, I'm glad, Hec. Seriously. When you called me and told me you'd found your mate, you know I was… well, you know. I had a hard time believing it for a minute. It was just hard to picture you settling down, and now look at you."

Hector couldn't stop the smile that spread across his face.

Yep. Look at me. Look at us.

The last thing he'd been expecting when he went out to Good Fortune on the trail of some bikie smugglers was to find his mate. And if anyone had told him he'd come back with not only his mate, but also a baby alicorn he now thought of as his own… well, chances were he would have laughed them out of town.

But it happened. And I couldn't be happier.

It was true.

His life might have completely changed, but Hector couldn't imagine being happier about it.

Ruby fluttered down from the ceiling fan, landing on the table once more. Sick of sulking apparently, she'd obviously decided she might have a better chance of getting what she wanted by making friends.

"Do you think there's any more eggs out there?" Hector asked Callan.

Callan glanced at him. "It's possible. We managed to find out that the bikies found Ruby's egg in a cave system they were using to stash drugs and weapons. They must have some shifter connection to know what they had and where to find a buyer, but that's not exactly unusual. We had a team go out to check through the caves, but so far, nothing."

Hector nodded. He couldn't really say he was surprised – and, to be honest, he was also relieved. He didn't like the idea of there being more orphaned alicorns like Ruby out there, still waiting to hatch, and vulnerable to people like Cecelia and Hargreaves Inc., who'd use them for their own purposes.

"So. Seems like you've taken on a pretty hefty responsibility, Hec." Callan looked at him, and Hector knew he didn't just mean raising one of the last remaining alicorns in the world. "Sure you're up to it?"

Hector swallowed, looking at Ruby as she sniffed at Callan's fingers when he held them out to her.

"Yeah," he said, nodding. "Yeah, I'm sure."

All three of them turned at the sound of the front door opening. Myrtle bustled through, looking a little frazzled, but otherwise just as beautiful as the first moment he'd met her. She was wearing cleaner clothes now and her hair was a little neater, but nothing about the way she'd looked the first time Hector had laid eyes on her had detracted from her beauty at all.

Of course not, his griffin suddenly spoke up, lifting its head within him. *She is our mate. She is the most beautiful thing we have ever seen, and always will be. We see her with our soul. That is the beauty we see.*

Hector couldn't help but think the beauty he could see with his eyes wasn't too bad either. Her wild hair, her stormy blue-gray eyes, her determined chin and strong jaw all made her irresistible to him. Not to mention the luscious curves of her hips, her strong thighs, broad shoulders and soft, rounded breasts…

Okay, okay, enough, or we're going to have a problem on our hands, Hector told himself quickly, swallowing heavily and dragging his eyes away from Myrtle's gorgeous figure. *Save it for later.*

His griffin rumbled within him, as if asking what the problem was, and Hector only *just* reminded himself that he'd made a promise that if he got his griffin back, he'd never tell it to shut up again.

It was sometimes a close call, though.

"All right. I think that's everything," Myrtle said, as she joined them by Callan's dining table. "I thought we hadn't remembered the tent, but it was just buried under a few other things."

Hector couldn't help but smile – he'd told her he'd made sure they'd packed everything they needed for their trip, but Myrtle's stubborn streak meant she had to go check for herself one last time.

She turned to Callan. "Thanks again for doing this. You're really helping us out. As much as I'd love to take Ruby with us, a moth hunting trip is a little awkward with a baby alicorn."

"Really, it's no problem," Callan said, laughing. "You and Hector have given me all the info I need. I'm sure we'll get along just fine."

Myrtle nodded, still looking a little tense. "No, I know

you will. Ruby's a very well-behaved girl. And I know she won't make a liar out of me, will she?"

"Meee-eh!"

Hector hoped the indignance in Ruby's voice was simply at the idea that she could be anything other than perfectly behaved.

They said their goodbyes and headed out to the car, Ruby even going so far as to land on Callan's shoulder as he stood in the doorway waving to them, as if to prove just how well she could get along with others.

Still, Hector watched as Myrtle glanced over her shoulder as they pulled out of Callan's drive, her face pensive.

"She *will* be all right, won't she?" she asked, as Hector turned the car out onto the dirt road that would – eventually – take them back to Good Fortune.

Myrtle might have been just asking about whether Ruby would miss them too much while they were away, but Hector could sense the deeper meaning to her words. His griffin hadn't been wrong when it had said that they could see Myrtle with their soul – he might not have had telepathy, or telekinesis, or any other fancy powers like alicorns did, but this, he could do.

He could see the beauty that lived in Myrtle's soul, as well as the beauty of her face and body. He could see her strength, her intelligence, her willpower. He could see the way she never gave up, and the way she had protected Ruby with every ounce of strength in her body.

"Of course she will," he said.

EPILOGUE

The golden ball of the sun was just dipping below the horizon when Myrtle emerged from their tent, stretching her back before pulling her hair back into its usual bun.

It was still hot, but the air was showing promise of its nighttime crispness, and Myrtle for one couldn't wait to be out in it.

"Are you coming, Hector?"

She leaned over, pulling aside the flap of the tent. Hector crawled out a moment later, still tucking his shirt into his pants.

"Where the hell do you get all this energy from?" he asked as he stood up, stifling a yawn. "I'm a shifter, and you've managed to wear even *me* out. This doesn't seem fair."

Myrtle laughed. "It's your own fault – you're always determined to outdo yourself."

"Oh, all right," Hector mock-grumbled. "I'll stop the minute you stop enjoying yourself. How about that?"

Myrtle laughed again, before wrapping her arms around him and standing on tip-toes to press a kiss to his lips.

"Be prepared to be tired for a while longer yet."

She felt Hector's smile against her lips before he deepened the kiss, his hands resting on her hips, fingers playing with the hem of her shirt.

"Stop that," she mumbled, pulling back. "Or we won't get any work done, and all the grant money I have left will go completely to waste."

Hector grimaced briefly, shaking his head. "Oh, all right. But I think your grant providers are placing some pretty onerous conditions on their money."

Myrtle laughed. "Much as I agree with you, them's the rules I'm afraid. I actually have to do some work." Myrtle checked her water bottles, before slipping her pocket flashlight into her belt. "Anyway, you work in environmental science long enough and you realize you better take your cash when and while you can."

"Fair enough." Hector shot her a smile. "Speaking of, have you heard back yet?"

Myrtle shook her head. With Hector's encouragement, she'd applied for a fixed-term job with the University of Sydney – she knew a few people there already from conferences she'd attended, as well as research she'd contributed to. But she'd only sent off the application yesterday; Hector apparently had some unrealistic expectations about how fast they'd jump to employ her.

"I'm not concerned about it right now. If it works out, it works out."

Hector finished putting supplies into his backpack, before hoisting it onto his back. "And you're sure it's what you want? You know I would have followed you anywhere, Myrtle."

Myrtle nodded firmly. "I know you would, Hector – and I appreciate it. But right now, there's nowhere I'd rather be but here. And I plan on staying here, at least for a while."

It was true. In some ways, she missed her huge, loud,

overbearing family. But right now, she felt at home – here in the middle of nowhere.

"It's beautiful," she said, gazing out across the plains, lit by the last of the sun. The silhouettes of the mulga and brigalow trees were pitch black against the brilliant red of the sky, the sandy plains at their feet almost purple. She knew that soon they'd be lit only by the pale light of the moon and the diamond trail of the stars snaking across the midnight blue of the night sky.

"I'm glad you think so," Hector said quietly. "A lot of people wouldn't like it out here – it's too harsh, too rough. The scrub isn't for everyone. But I've always loved it."

They stood together in silence, watching the sun as it finally disappeared.

"Well, we should get going," Myrtle said. "There was that cave we found yesterday I want to get a good look at. Now that the sun's gone the moths will be coming out, if they haven't already started on their migration."

Hector nodded. "I suppose that's what I really *should* be sorry about," he said as they began walking. "That getting caught up with me has meant you might have missed your window to witness the migration."

Myrtle bit her lip. "I won't say I'm not worried," she said after a moment, picking her way between the sections of scrub. "But if I've missed it, I've missed it. We can head south after this and meet them when they arrive for their dormancy period. At least I'll still be able to count their numbers then, though it would have been better to have a comparison. But the people I'm liaising with in Canberra will already have some data. It's not a complete loss."

"You're always so optimistic," Hector said. He flashed her a grin. "Just one of the many things to love about you. I've always been such a sourpuss. Let's hope you rub off on me."

Myrtle laughed. "I think I've been doing *plenty* of that recently."

Hector paused a moment, and then joined in on her laughter. Somewhere ahead of them, they heard a manic rustle in the scrub, just as Myrtle saw something dart out in front of them before it bounded away on two legs.

"Was that a kangaroo?"

Hector shook his head. "About a meter and a half too short for that. He'll just be a wallaby."

Myrtle smiled. "Friend of yours, is he?"

Hector laughed, low and rich. "You never know."

Myrtle had to admit she was still finding the whole idea of shifters difficult to get used to. Back when they'd still been on the Gold Coast she'd found herself staring at an ibis as it sifted through the leftovers sitting on a restaurant table, and wondered if it was in fact a patron who'd simply forgotten to change into the appropriate form before sitting down to their meal.

She'd even asked Hector about it, but he'd just shaken his head and muttered something about bin chickens knowing no shame, before shooing the bird away.

It hadn't really answered her question, but she supposed in some ways she was better off not knowing. She didn't want to have to go through a series of mental gymnastics every time she met an animal. For now, she had decided, she was going to assume that a cat was just a cat, a bird was just a bird, and a platypus was just a platypus until someone told her otherwise.

"Almost there," Myrtle said. She glanced up at the sky. The last of the sunlight was slipping away, and the moths would soon emerge. "Most likely we'll only catch the late bloomers – the ones who've left their migrating to the last possible moment – but it doesn't matter." She smiled. "I suppose I was a bit of a late bloomer myself."

She felt Hector's warm hand on her shoulder a moment before he pressed a kiss against the top of her head. "Not really. You knew what you wanted to do and you pursued it. You didn't waste your time trying to be something you weren't. You were smart, Myrtle, and you knew it. There's nothing late blooming about you. You've always been exactly who you were supposed to be." He paused before continuing. "And more than that, you're brave and compassionate. Do you think it's a coincidence that you could sense that Ruby's egg was alive when I couldn't? Or that she chose to hatch just when she did? She knew if she came out then she'd be in good hands. She knew she could trust you – and she was right."

Myrtle felt her cheeks color at Hector's words, and she swallowed heavily. It was still hard for her to take compliments – but she thought she was finally getting used to it.

"Thank you," she said sincerely. "That means a lot, coming from you. You always seem so sure of yourself."

Hector laughed. "Let me show you my high school photographs some time. The haircut I had... well, let's just say it was 'really something' and leave it at that."

Myrtle couldn't quite believe Hector had ever looked anything other than devastatingly handsome, but she didn't argue.

"We're here," she said, as they reached a rugged outcropping of rock. "It was right around here, wasn't it?"

"Yeah. Just... here." Hector steered her a little to the left, then pointed out the nearly-hidden entrance to the cave. "Just where you said."

"That's it. We shouldn't have long to wait."

She hoped not, anyway. The cave's ceiling had been too low for her to get more than a few feet in, but it had been exactly the kind of place she'd expect the nocturnal valeleaf moth to spend its daytime hours.

Maybe they won't appear, she thought. *Maybe they're all gone, or maybe they were never here to begin with.*

The drought had drastically reduced the moths' numbers. Maybe they wouldn't find any in this cave. Maybe every year there'd be fewer and fewer, until there were none left anywhere in the world at all.

Myrtle swallowed, feeling her eyes growing moist. She knew she ought to focus, and that the idea of the valeleaf moth becoming extinct was a sad enough one on its own, but thoughts like this always led her back to one place: Ruby, and how rare alicorns had become.

It didn't seem fair that she'd be forced to live her life in secrecy, all because people were greedy fucks who had pushed alicorns to the brink of extinction once they started refusing to let people use their powers for their own purposes.

Ruby might have burned herself out protecting Hector, but Myrtle still wasn't confident that she'd grow up feeling safe and secure. They could only do their best to look after her, to take care of her and show her that they loved her for who she was, not because of what she could do – and that they'd never, ever let anyone harm her.

"I hope Ruby doesn't miss us too much," she said. "Do you think she's all right?"

"Pretty sure she's got Callan wrapped around her little finger by now," Hector replied. "It doesn't matter if she hasn't got her mind-whammy powers anymore. She won't need them. Callan's always been a notorious softy."

Myrtle laughed. "Great. She's not going to want to come home."

"Probably not."

They were silent for a moment in the still night air.

"Do you think her powers are really gone for good?" Myrtle eventually asked.

"I dunno," Hector said. "Maybe – but maybe not. I'd like to think she'll one day be able to use them again. I feel like I could learn to look on the bright side a bit more with someone like you around. I've been pretty lucky, after all."

Myrtle smiled softly, leaning into his side. "So have I."

They stood together in the soft purple haze of the night, not speaking, just enjoying the feeling of each other's breathing. Myrtle would have been tempted to close her eyes – if not for the fact that in the very next moment, she thought she detected movement by the mouth of the cave.

"Hector, look."

She scarcely dared to believe her eyes. For a moment, she thought she had to be seeing a trick of the light, but no: a moment later, a moth, black against the velvet blue of the sky, emerged from the mouth of the cave, fluttering into the sky.

She held her breath, waiting for the next one. For a moment, Myrtle was scared that there weren't going to be any more.

But then, another moth, and then another, and then another emerged, until a steady stream of them were flying freely into the night air, soft wings beating, carrying them into the sky.

"Oh Hector, there must be *thousands* of them in there," Myrtle said, pulling out her phone to record their flight. "Not as many as there should be, but it's a lot more than I'd hoped for."

Hector laughed. "They're really cute, Myrtle." He paused, and she felt him looking up into the sky, following the moths' flight. "No, they're beautiful. Really beautiful."

Myrtle felt her heart glow. "They are, aren't they? Usually I have to butter people up by telling them about the cute animals that eat them that'll be hurt if they go, but... aren't they beautiful just by themselves?"

"They are, Myrtle. They truly are."

Myrtle could tell that Hector meant it. She snuggled against his side, still holding her phone up.

So maybe I'm like the moths, she thought. *Maybe I'm not a model or an athlete or a track star or a prom queen. But I am what I am, and that's fine by itself.*

She closed her eyes briefly as Hector dropped a kiss on the crown of her head.

I'm fine. I'm good. I'm me.

For the first time in her life, the words didn't sound hollow as she thought them. They beat in her heart, alongside the bond she felt with Hector – along with the hope she had for the start of her new life by his side.

It was a world full of danger and magic; and sure, perhaps it was a little frightening, but Myrtle was certain that together, there was nothing they couldn't face. She knew as long as they had each other, everything would be perfect.

I can't wait to see what happens next.

The story continues with *Callan: Outback Shifters* – grab your copy today!

Have you read the other books in the series? To see how the story continues, you can read them here:

Hector
Callan
Euan
Trent
Rhys
BOOK SIX COMING SOON!

Or you can grab the first three books here in one convenient collection:

Outback Shifters: Collection One

Want to read an extra bonus story about Hector, Myrtle and Ruby and their adventures as a family? Sign up for my mailing list, and I'll send you a FREE bonus epilogue! https://www.zoechant.com/join-my-mailing-list/

A NOTE FROM ZOE CHANT

Thank you for buying my book! I hope you enjoyed it. If you'd like to be emailed when I release my next book, please click here to be added to my mailing list.

Please consider reviewing *Hector: Outback Shifters* even if you only write a line or two. I appreciate all reviews, whether positive or negative.

You are also invited to join my VIP Readers Group on Facebook!

The cover of *Hector: Outback Shifters* was designed by Isabelle Arden.

MORE PARANORMAL ROMANCE FROM ZOE CHANT

Hector
Callan
Euan
Trent
Rhys
Next book coming soon!

The Lost Dragons Series
A Mate for the Dragon
Fated for the Dragon
Destined for the Dragon
A Bride for the Dragon
Bound to the Dragon

See Zoe Chant's complete list of books here!

Printed in Dunstable, United Kingdom